Frances Ferguson ori
gave it up to get married and produce three children
in quick succession. She started writing as a way of
earning without leaving her infants; now that they are
all grown up she is still writing, but for her own
benefit.

Her grandfather was a judge in India who eventually
retired to New Zealand, and most of her paternal
relatives still live there or in Australia. However, she
herself has been settled in East Kent for the last
eighteen years, and says it is a good place to put down
roots. When not hunched over a word-processor she
studies Shiatsu.

Missing Person

Frances Ferguson

HEADLINE

First published in 1993
by HEADLINE BOOK PUBLISHING

First published in paperback in 1994
by HEADLINE BOOK PUBLISHING

10 9 8 7 6 5 4 3 2 1

ISBN 0 7472 4137 6

Printed and bound in Great Britain by
HarperCollins Manufacturing, Glasgow

HEADLINE BOOK PUBLISHING
A division of Hodder Headline PLC
338 Euston Road
London NW1 3BH

To Robert with thanks

Prologue

The outer London street was fitfully lit and quiet, parked cars lining it here and there like batches of sleeping tortoises. An eddying wind sent flat dust-swirls along the pavement; flapped and crackled at the loose edges of a green plastic sack protruding from a litter bin. None of the houses showed a light, only blackness behind the sheen of glass, or a white glimpse of nets, the darker folds of thicker curtains. High up, the mottled silver disc of a full moon came and went behind a scud of torn-edged clouds whose blotched grey centres promised rain.

A girl hurried round the corner. The wind whipped the edges of her skirt, tossed her short blonde hair around her face. The hunch of her shoulders within a pale belted raincoat suggested distraction, the light click of her heels against the pavement irritation, and a touch of weariness behind the haste. Even the sudden sharp crack as the green plastic sack flapped again didn't make her turn her head, though she lifted her face as a light spit of the threatened rain blew suddenly against her before the angry air caught it and swept it away.

She slowed at the corner of the alley and seemed to hesitate. It was a short cut, well-known and commonly used. Its narrow straightness ran between back gardens, with an overhang of trees, some bushes, garages opening on to it further along where it widened, and a cut-through beyond that to the crescent with its new block of flats. The tossing wind made it a place of flickering shadows interspersed with patches of thick blackness – but the girl paused for no more than a second, with a movement which could have been a shrug. The saving of a quarter of a mile; a further brief spit of rain in her face; at one o'clock in the morning, the gesture said impatiently, these things count more than a few creepy shadows.

Besides, she was late, and there hadn't been any taxis, and she'd come this way last night without any problems . . . Her brief dismissive shift of the shoulders said all this, as she stepped into the alley.

She was halfway along when the footfalls sounded behind her. At first they were so muffled they could merely have been her heartbeat. Or the padding feet of a large animal. For some reason – or perhaps from a perfectly rational fear – the latter seemed abruptly far worse . . . The idea of a pursuing creature sent an atavistic chill down the back of her neck, let alone the newspaper reports about pitbulls and Rottweilers. And the sound might simply be her imagination. Should she stop and look round? No. Kick off her shoes and run? The instinct was there, stamped on by the fear of making a fool of herself. Walk steadily, look normal, trust—

There was suddenly no choice. In a rush someone was close behind her. An arm came across her throat like an iron bar. She was being dragged backwards, roughly, the hardness of a body clamping her from behind, her arms and legs flailing. She was chokingly short of air. As she tried instinctively to twist her head, her wide eyes caught the flash of steel as the other hand came round in front of her face.

She brought both hands up to clutch at the arm across her throat, rolled her spine forwards, and threw him.

It was far from her best throw, even with the benefit of surprise. She couldn't see which hand held the knife, to stamp on it; the black blur on the ground was not even winded, and was grabbing for her; she hadn't found the breath to let out a yell. For a moment she thought it was all going wrong, as cold leather-clad fingers caught her ankle to send her tumbling and the other hand snatched for her hair in a painful yank.

2

She was sharply remembering the glitter of the knife—

The blood was pounding so hard in her ears that for a moment she couldn't hear the other sounds – voices, the thud of feet. Reality came with the vivid dazzle of lights. The path was abruptly ablaze with a brightness which sent the shadows receding. Hands pulled her assailant away from her. A lot of busy legs moved around him; a muffled yell suggested a tight armlock. She could relax . . . Arms were helping her up from the ground, steadying her. She could hear a voice flatly reciting arrest and caution.

From a throat which felt bruised and sore in spite of her trained move in tucking in her chin, she wanted to croak at the nearest person, 'Where were you? What took you so long?'

'Good work, Sergeant Perry,' the Inspector's voice said in her direction. The patronage in it was like a pat on the head. 'We've got him this time! All right? No damage?'

'I'm fine, sir.' Her voice came out with a touch of rawness, but a cough brought that under control. 'He had a knife. It must be about somewhere—'

'Nasty,' one of the CID men said casually, collecting something sharp and black-handled from under a bush with careful precision and a folded handkerchief. He turned his head with a grin. 'So that's why you didn't wait for him to drag you off into the bushes!'

'He's not going to be able to claim he was just out for a walk, is he?' There was a black ski-mask dangling from the Inspector's hand and he glanced down at it with satisfied disgust. 'All right, that's a wrap, so let's get our laddie back to the station and charged, and then we can go home. A nice display of athletics, Perry – he's not going to want to play Tarzan to *your* Jane again in a hurry, is he?'

It was a crack intended to raise a chuckle, and the men around duly laughed. Jane Perry murmured a brief, 'Sir,' by way of acknowledgement, and made sure it didn't sound as if she'd delivered it through clenched teeth. Did she really have to be reduced to some archetypal image of Jungle Jane, swinging through the trees and preferably in as few clothes as possible?

Maybe she was just losing her sense of humour. She certainly ought to be used to it by now . . .

They were beginning to move off with their prisoner, the man she had been used as a decoy to catch. She followed the group, without bothering to spare more than a glance for the rapist they'd managed to nail at last. He was, after all, just a routine part of police work.

'I suppose we won't need to borrow you any longer, and you'll be off back to your own patch.' One of the detectives fell back to walk beside her, sounding friendly and hopeful. He was nice enough, so she opted for being pleasantly brisk.

'Yes, you won't be in need of my unfamiliar mush around here any more. Your CID's going to owe our CID one – no doubt the guv'nors will fix it between them. Well, see you sometime!'

'Or maybe not' was implicit in her voice. And if the transfer she'd applied for came through, she'd be somewhere quite else before long. A month to work out her notice – if she got the job – and then off to make her career really count . . .

As they began to pile into the waiting transport, she glanced up to see the moon still sailing above the ragged clouds, silvering an edge here and there, offering the world below the illusion that it was bucketing across the sky at high speed.

A high-flier of a moon.

If she had been superstitious, she might almost have wished on it. For luck. For a change for the better.

In a German city many hundreds of miles to the south-east, another young woman was glancing up at the same moon with a frown.

A bit more darkness would have been preferable; a few clouds to provide a dappling of cover. Still, it wouldn't matter:

4

this wasn't an area for much night-time activity and the street was empty and shuttered.

She was waiting to kill a man.

Her quarry should appear soon. He was a creature of habit, and on this night every week he called on his brother-in-law and kept him up late and yawning over beer and a game of dice.

His murder would make no headlines. It would merely send ripples into suitable places. Word would go round: don't make the mistake of being seen with the wrong people, or have too much cash to flash around; don't risk looking as if you might be a police informer. Not if you've also been asking questions about the Widow.

After Gerhard's death (could a grown man really die of something as childish as measles?) she had begun to use the title deliberately. 'The Widow' held the right connotations . . . as she stepped out of his shadow, to revive something which had grown torpid. It had to be acknowledged that Gerhard had begun to lose his edge over the past few years; to opt for a softer, lazier life. Things would be different now. Now, there was a new kind of group, hers to lead.

She could have sent one of them to carry out tonight's task. But had chosen to do it herself – perhaps as a signal.

The door she was watching opened, spilling yellow light on to the moon-silvered pavement. It briefly lit the face she was expecting to see. No one had come down to see him off the premises – after all, he was family. She could see he was drunk. He staggered as he pulled the door shut behind him, then took a few weaving steps, before pausing to let out an audible belch.

At the tap of her approaching high heels, he swung unsteadily towards her. She saw him register the female shape, the tart's clothes and make-up, the long blonde hair – a disguising wig, even though he had never seen her in person. She saw slack-mouthed surprise change to a welcoming leer.

He was making it almost too easy.

5

A gun was the weapon she preferred, and a bullet between the eyes would make it more obviously an execution, but on this occasion a knife was better. She had it concealed against her thigh as she slunk invitingly towards him. His leer intensified when she finally slid a hand through his arm, murmuring in his ear and letting him draw her against him.

There was one last moment when his eyes widened in fear and disbelief, his ears registering her final mocking whisper as the blade struck home, sliding lethally and accurately between his ribs from behind. Then he was crumpling down, to lie like any fallen drunk in the gutter. She looked down at him, then walked away casually, to any watching eyes (though there were none) merely disgusted at a potential customer too drunk to do anything more than fall unconscious at her feet.

It was done. Now her target was no more than a pile of garbage for the morning's street cleaners to find.

And a warning to anyone who cared to know.

Take care before you offend the Widow.

PART I

Chapter 1

Jane Perry lay propped on her bed, her shoes kicked off, the door wide open. It was an attractive room with its wide second-floor window looking out on the tops of trees, lit by early summer sunlight. Gazing round, she realised with satisfaction that already it felt like home: her own casual, untidy clutter spread all about her. The whole flat now had a pleasant feeling of familiarity – the familiarity of being settled. Since any member of the police force inevitably had to have her place of living officially vetted, it was lucky that her long-time friend Matty had not chosen to settle in an area favoured by known criminals. Jane raised her voice to carry clearly through to her friend.

'Ironic, isn't it? Six months ago I move my career out here to the sticks—'

'Shaking the dust of dizzy London off your feet in favour of the quiet provincial life,' Matty's voice responded from somewhere beyond the door.

'If that's sarcasm, just lay off! Where was I? Oh yes. I apply for a local vacancy because you'd tipped me off that CID here was being run by a woman Detective Chief Inspector who seemed both pleasant and go-ahead. And so she was! But then what happens? I get the job and everything's hunky-dory. Then just three months after I arrive, like all go-ahead types she ups and goes, to higher things! And what turns up as her replacement? A – a dinosaur to make every other male chauvinist I've ever worked with in the force seem like an enlightened angel!'

'Poor soul.' Matty's husky voice had an amused edge to it, though it also contained a patient sympathy.

'Damn right! There I am, getting well settled in, with a decent DI and good backing from the DCI. But then she does a bunk. And Detective Chief Inspector Morland hoves up on the horizon. I swear to you, if that man could contrive to turn the clock back and ban women from the force altogether, he'd do it! A female CID sergeant under his nose? A graduate, furthermore, who expects to work on the same level as the men, or, heaven forbid, even take charge of them? You can practically see disbelief flashing in his eyes! He'd have me restricted to making the tea if he could get away with it!'

'That bad?' Matty appeared and draped herself against the doorway, a vision of long mahogany limbs and short Afro hairstyle. There were grape-dark smudges of tiredness under her eyes, clearly visible even against the warm brown of her skin; for a busy hospital doctor, a perhaps unsurprising weariness. Her place of work lay just beyond the trees outside, and a bleeper lying somewhere about the flat could go off at any time, day or night.

'It gets worse as the days go by, if anything,' Jane grumbled in disgust. 'Dammit, Matty, don't laugh!'

'Sorry,' Matty said, her lingering grin a flash of white teeth. She added sweetly, 'Are you aware you're the only person I know who complains to *me* about prejudice? Just you try being female and black as well. At least no one ever assumes your natural language is Caribbean patois!' Being the mixed-race child of a high-level African diplomat, her remark was heartfelt. 'I can tell you, too, medicine's just as much of a male-chauvinist kingdom – particularly once you set your sights on higher levels. I suppose you could say it was our choice. We should both have known what we were getting into. And if you can't stand the heat, stay out of the kitchen . . .'

'Easy enough to say with hindsight. Anyway, a police career seemed to offer more of a challenge than anything else I could do with my law degree. And the kind of background I could cope with after growing up with the army, too!' In fact, Jane had taken some care to avoid mentioning her family connections when she joined the force; she had even dropped the 'Rees' from her double-barrelled surname, just in case anyone thought she might look for advantage from being the daughter of a high-profile army General. 'What they don't tell you,' she went on with an edge of bitterness, 'when they put out all that recruiting literature about "graduate entry being a fast track" and "the police being an equal opportunities employer" is the underlying scenario! Which is, of course, that most of your actual serving police are still convinced deep down that the force is really *a man's world*, where anything female, fast-track or not, should keep her head down and be satisfied with a subsidiary position!'

And that was particularly true in CID. But CID was what Jane had wanted, despite knowing that staying in uniform might offer a clearer upward line in promotion. Particularly if she agreed to be shunted into administration, or chose one of the other specialisations considered 'suited to women officers'. After attending the Special Course (promised to graduate entrants once basic training was completed) and coming out with good marks and the automatic rank of sergeant, Jane had stubbornly opted for the detective branch. Where she had gritted her teeth against all the conscious and unconscious resistance she ran into . . .

It was only after eighteen months of it that she had come to a restless conclusion: the Met, for all its vaunted sophistication, was clearly not going to fulfil her ambitions. It was time to look for another angle. And an advertisement in the *Police Review* requiring applications for a Detective-Sergeant job down in Matty's area had looked as if it might be the solution.

A smaller CID force covering a wider area; more chances, then. And, more to the point, a female DCI in charge. Jane had liked her at the interview, too: a woman who seemed tough but sympathetic, someone who had got where she was on her own terms without either losing her essential femininity or playing on it. DCI Greene had looked like the ideal boss for someone with Jane's ambitions – both as an example, and as an encouragement.

Remembering that now, Jane let out a gusty sigh. Just three months into the job and with high hopes, she had seen DCI Greene depart in clouds of glory. What was it one of her former Inspectors had called it when everything which had been going well abruptly fell apart? Oh yes, 'the bugger-it factor'. And that described the arrival of DCI Morland as DCI Greene's replacement perfectly . . .

Suddenly aware that Matty was still standing in the doorway in silent sympathy, Jane abruptly pulled herself together and gave her an apologetic grin.

'OK, you can stop looking like patience on a monument! I'll live – I suppose! Have to, won't I? Anyway, considering you've heard it all before, I don't know why you don't just yell "Shut up!"'

'Would you listen?' Matty stretched, her smiling eyes taking on an edge of mischief. 'I suppose I could try reminding you that you could have avoided all this if you'd married Maarten Van Damm when he kept asking you. Just think, you could be living in The Hague with two point four perfect Dutch children, being the perfect parliamentarian's wife.'

'God, that thought makes my present life seem almost bearable!'

'Poor devoted man – dutifully flying over to see you so regularly, and trying so desperately to get you to fancy him!' Matty ducked as Jane picked up her pillow threateningly as if to throw it. 'We were all laying bets on whether you'd eventually weaken—'

'Oh no you weren't, when have you ever seen me as someone who wanted to be bored to death? The only useful thing

Maarten ever did for me was teach me to speak Dutch!' Jane had found that reasonably easy, since a peripatetic army childhood had given her a facility with languages. She added on a chuckle, 'I do well remember his face when I told him I was going to join the police, though – shock horror, thoroughly *infra dig*! I reckon Pa was the only person who wasn't really surprised.' The General, she remembered, had actually been quite approving. As were his letters, still, from New Zealand, to which he had retired from the army now, investing his golden handshake in a stock farm. Where he appeared to be quite happy occupying himself with the finer points of sheep-dip. Jane grinned at the thought, then gave a sudden glance at her watch and swung her legs off the bed. 'It's time I got moving, I've used up my free hours from being on duty late last night. Heigh-ho, back we go!'

'At least you get hours in lieu,' Matty pointed out, though with a cheerful lack of rancour.

'Yeah. Sometimes. When something hasn't come up. Honestly, looking back on our carefree youth, would you ever have thought we'd both end up in careers where we not only spend half our time beating our brains out against the establishment, but also don't have time for any kind of social life? Was there really a time when I used to spend my evenings going to films? Or dancing? Going out to dinner, even—'

'Let alone a sex life, if that's the next item on your list? No, let's not even think of that, it'd take far more energy than I've got left over these days!'

'Heigh-ho for the life of a career woman . . .' It was half surprising, Jane thought as she came to her feet with both of them provoked into laughter, that Matty's calm beauty hadn't drawn her into matrimony by now, or at least into a long-term relationship. Or, it would be surprising to anyone who didn't know Matty well enough to be aware of her dedication to medicine – and her capacity for ignoring the yearning admiration her looks inspired. Jane gave her another grin, and said, 'I'm going to make an early lunch before I go on duty, d'you want anything?'

'No thanks, I'll grab something at the hospital later.'

'And probably on the wing?' Jane enquired, knowing meals were something Matty ate how and when she could. 'Come and talk to me while I eat, anyway – since you're actually here!'

They moved off towards the kitchen together. In appearance they were an interesting contrast, both medium tall and slender, but one Afro-dark and the other English-fair. Jane's most striking feature was the deep blue of her eyes; Matty's, the almost perfect proportions of her face which had taken the best from both sides of her mixed heritage. Warming to each other on sight when they both arrived at the same university, they had then found innumerable things in common, not least the shared experience of coming from an upper-crust but highly mobile background. The initial friendship had lasted ever since.

They chatted idly while Jane ate. Then she set off to drive to work. Though the main police station was only a brisk walk away, she was obliged to keep her car readily available. As she headed down the hill, the city spread itself out in front of her: a compact centre contained within the remains of medieval walls, then a widening sprawl beyond them. Beyond that, though not visible from here, farmlands surrounded the city on all sides.

It *was* pleasant, she reflected absently, to live in a place of such decorative antiquity in the middle of countryside – after the endlessness of metropolitan streets which she had been used to in London. The change might not have turned out to be quite the break she had hoped for, but there were advantages.

And another advantage too, which had entered into her calculations when she applied for the job here. The city might be small and seem provincial, but because of its history and its famous cathedral, it enjoyed more than its fair share of visiting VIPs, foreign as well as national. Then there was its proximity to the coast: the ferry terminals and the gradually encroaching Channel Tunnel gave it an extra international importance. They were very much on the border of Europe here; the Chief Constable had even come out with a decree that all his staff should learn to speak French. So – it had occurred to Jane – this was the kind of place where an ambitious officer speaking several languages might prove useful. And noticeable. Given the chance to make her mark . . .

So much for hope. As of the last three months – and thanks to the bugger-it factor, a.k.a. DCI Morland – Jane was grimly aware that she wasn't being offered anything to do which would remotely make *anyone*'s mark.

That brought the reminder of Morland's latest move. The night-time warehouse operation. Dan Crowe, Jane's Inspector and immediate superior, had automatically put her in charge of one of the shifts. Late last night she had come wearily off duty to find a memo by Morland countermanding that. A woman detective alone with a male colleague in a car for several hours after dark was 'unsuitable'. He didn't quite have the nerve to say why, in writing, but the thinking was obvious: A Danger of Illicit Relationships Forming . . .

Jane had immediately itched to challenge him on it – or fix him with an icy eye and murmur, 'You cannot be serious!' – but it wasn't worth it. He would love an excuse to claim she lacked discipline, so she wouldn't give him one. No way was she going to give him the least chance to do what she could tell he was dying to do: sink her career without trace.

No, no way!

She arrived at the tall concrete-and-glass building with its bright blue sign announcing POLICE, and swung the wheel to pass through the gap leading to the rear, beside the notice marked *Private. No Entrance to the Public.* A squad car on its way out paused to let her by, the driver giving a friendly

15

acknowledging wave. The gesture reminded her, cheeringly, that at least she had had the chance to get established with her colleagues before (she thought drily) the poisoned fang of acute male chauvinism had struck. She had taken the trouble to get on with people, uniform as well as her own bunch; had carefully ignored overheard remarks which unthinkingly relegated any female to the category of bimbo or slag; had shown she would share information, wouldn't stand on rank unnecessarily, and would readily buy her round. Besides, the previous DCI's fairness and efficiency had gained enough respect to produce at least a small trickle-down effect – the beginnings of the notion that women officers were also human beings with normal human capabilities.

Jane had even sensed an occasional subterranean wash of sympathy lately – which perhaps went to show that others didn't like the new DCI an awful lot more than she did. So maybe she wasn't just suffering from paranoia.

She parked the vehicle, and let herself in through the station's electronically-locked rear door. Signing in, she exchanged a cheerful 'Hi, how goes it?' with a duty sergeant, and moments later arrived in the familiar purlieus of the CID room.

'Afternoon, Guv. Anything new?'

'Not a lot,' Dan Crowe said, acknowledging her arrival with the usual brief twitch of his eyebrows. 'I'll be going out on the warehouse surveillance myself later. Doubt if you're going to miss much.'

'I'm taking it all as a compliment to my irresistible sex appeal.' It was better to make a joke out of it. 'I don't suppose we've got any further with the missing credit cards, have we – What?'

'DCI Morland thinks you're the obvious person to do it. Lectures on detection to secondary schools are an important part of community contact,' Dan Crowe said deadpan, but managing to convey several other messages with his eyebrows.

'Bloody hell. I mean, yes, sir!' Jane re-inspected the memo

16

which lay on top of the pile in her in-tray and bit back a scathing comment. 'Tomorrow morning. And another one in the afternoon. Lovely. Gives me a lot of time to decide what I'm going to say, doesn't it?'

'There's a standard spiel somewhere. Should be on your desk with the memo.' He made no further comment as she found it. She had heard him mutter that it would be nice to be able to deploy his staff in his own way but he'd followed it up with a sharp, 'Nobody heard me say that!'

Some of the others were wandering in now – Kenny Barnes, still a DC in his late forties, who might have been jealous of Jane as a twenty-seven-year-old sergeant but wasn't; Vern Harris, a sergeant at thirty-seven, who *was* touchy about being equal-ranked by a newcomer ten years younger, but hid it behind a Jack-the-Lad charm. 'I've sent Gary and Mike straight out from lunch to follow up that tip-off about the shop manager,' he told Dan Crowe, 'they might just catch him with some stolen stuff on the premises if we're lucky. Afternoon, Jane. How's your stunning friend Dr Ingle?'

'Still stunning, and still trying to repair parts of RTAs which other doctors can't reach.' Several people at the station had come across Matty through routine links between the police and the hospital's accident department, which she was in and out of all the time as neurosurgical registrar. It was amusing that all of them without fail showed a tendency to ask after her with varying degrees of lechery or wistfulness when it was discovered that Jane actually lived with her. 'Is your wife having the baby at the hospital this time?' she asked Vern with an innocent sweetness, just to show she knew that any enquiry from him was definitely lechery.

'Yes – another two months to go.' He moved to pick up the phone as it rang. Kenny was talking to Dan Crowe about his expenses and about the warehouse surveillance and Jane turned to the 'standard spiel' she'd been delegated to deliver next day.

Lecturing to bored school-kids. Somebody had to do it, she supposed. Somebody else had been booked to do it, presumably; probably someone from Community Relations. It was another piece of Morland's interference to switch it to her. As if that was all he felt she was fit for.

If he asked her how it went she could tell him sweetly she hoped she'd managed to act as a role-model to attract more girls into thinking of CID as a career. That should annoy him nicely.

The following morning, however, faced with rows of spotty boys and over made up girls, all herded in unwillingly, it was a wild stretch of the imagination to visualise any of them being suited to a police career. In fact she could recognise at least one youthful face as having been down at the station for a quite different reason. And the questions she was asked, when she invited them, were definitely based on the idea of evasion of the law rather than its enforcement.

The second school was better, a much smaller group of much more willing listeners, tidier in their obligatory school uniform. In fact the number she had to address ('It's just fourth-year Careers,' a teacher had told her apologetically, 'the others are starting GCSEs,') was small enough for her to opt for informality and sitting in a circle rather than rows. One or two of the questions she was asked were obviously an attempt to be clever, but on the whole the response was intelligent.

'Do you ever get sent abroad?' someone asked hopefully.

'Mostly, no,' Jane said, and smiled at the boy who had put the question because he was looking disappointed. 'Somebody from CID here could get sent across to pick up a prisoner after arrest, or to identify someone, but it would be very unusual for us to go and work in another country. We don't know yet if the new EEC arrangements will alter things, but as each country has its own legal methods, it's most likely that we'll go on having national police forces each in charge of their own internal affairs.' She looked round at her attentive audience.

18

'We do liaise with the other European forces from time to time, but only really by exchanging information. Yes, I know, it would help if we could all move around a bit more, considering the criminals do! We see that particularly in this part of the country. If your bike gets stolen, for instance, it may be across the Channel before we've even got the theft logged. Unfortunately we can't just follow a thief to the other side – or not without getting in touch with our opposite numbers first, to make sure we don't tread on anyone's toes!'

'But someone could join Interpol, couldn't they?'

'No. Interpol isn't an international police force, as people imagine; it's more like a giant computer. I'm afraid the only foreign trips I'm likely to get are the same ones you might do yourselves – a day trip for shopping and sightseeing! You go over on school trips, don't you? Like the French children do when they come here?' The locals seemed to view those, xenophobically, as ill-disciplined, ill-mannered, and probably only here for an orgy of shoplifting, an attitude of mind probably repaid when the English schoolchildren went over there. It was an example of the traditional dislike between the English and the French which sometimes made Jane wonder wryly how a united Europe was ever supposed to work. She glanced at the teacher. 'Well, it looks as if I'm being given the sign to pack up. I hope you've found all this interesting and useful. Don't forget what I said: you, the public, are our eyes and ears, and any useful information you can give us will make our job a whole lot easier!'

The session had gone well, she decided, as she made her way back to the teachers' car park in receipt of thanks. If she had to do this mundane task, at least this particular occasion hadn't been too bad. A loudly pealing bell brought a sudden rush of children of all sizes making for the school bus, and reminded her drily that she had never, ever, wanted to be a teacher. On the other hand they did have a day which stopped at half past three—

'Miss? Miss, please, could I talk to you?'

The girl who came to a halt breathlessly behind her seemed to be screwing up her courage. She was shifting nervously from foot to foot. 'Sure,' Jane said, recognising her as a quiet one who had sat opposite to her. She might not have been sure it was the same girl because the curly cascade of brown hair falling from a bow high up on one side seemed to be this month's fashion and made several of them look like clones, but this girl had watched her with a silent intensity which made her noticeable. 'Weren't you one of the ones in there—?'

'Yes. Miss, what do you do if someone's missing? You said – Miss, it's Deirdre, I *know* she's missing, but nobody's doing anything!'

'Hang on a minute. First tell me who you are.'

'Shelley Cura. And she's Deirdre MacArthy. She hasn't been at school for more than a week, and she isn't at home either. But they aren't – they won't – they just told me to mind my own business—'

'Try to be a bit clearer. You're worried about Deirdre because you haven't seen her, and someone – your teachers? her parents? – say that's none of your business? Well, maybe there's a reason they know about and you don't. It's not usually a good idea to jump to conclusions. And if everyone you've told—'

'I'm telling *you*,' Shelley almost yelled, desperation breaking out of her. 'You said that's what we ought to do, didn't you? Pass on information? How can I if even you won't listen? Deirdre's missing, and I know she wouldn't go anywhere without telling me – so I know something's happened to her, I just know it!'

Chapter 2

They went back into school in the end, since a teacher on bus duty hurried over to see why a pupil seemed to be shouting at a visitor. Jane and Shelley were led along corridors whose yawning emptiness suggested a lemming-like flight of all concerned the minute the school day ended. A weary-looking young man was finally produced who was Deirdre's class-tutor. At Jane's polite insistence he checked his register, then looked harassed as they all trailed off again to consult someone higher up. The look he gave Shelley boded ill for their future relationship.

'It's true Deirdre MacArthy hasn't been in school for over a week,' Jane told Dan Crowe an hour later, putting the situation to him in the CID room. 'No explanation given, either. Apparently they usually check up, but this one seems to have slipped through the net.'

'If she's one of the MacArthys from the Ribden Road estate, they're a bunch of roughnecks,' Kenny Barnes commented from his desk across the room. 'Missing school wouldn't mean much!'

'No, but Deirdre's supposed to be the bright one. Quiet, but a hard worker. She's missed school occasionally but not often. Shelley – her best friend – always knows where she is and why, even out of school. But not this time. What do you think, Guv, do we check it?'

'The parents haven't reported her missing, you say?'

'No, I looked that up as soon as I came in.'

'Hm. Anything else from the school?'

'Some concern, and quite a bit of background information. Not from the class-tutor, he's new this term and didn't really know the child. That's the main reason why her absence hadn't been picked up on, I gathered. The senior teacher could tell me more. The family's known to be "difficult". Particularly the stepfather – he married the mother four years ago. Deirdre's the youngest of the older family and there are three little ones in the new young family. All the kids took the stepfather's name. But there was surprise that Deirdre hadn't been in school—'

'How old did you say she was?'

'Fifteen next week. Moderately pretty but nothing special. Quiet. No trouble. They describe her as a promising pupil, ahead of her age as far as work's concerned. Less so emotionally. They didn't know if she had a boyfriend but thought it unlikely. Shelley's her only close friend and they're inseparable.' Jane paused, frowning. 'The last time she was at school was the Friday before last. Shelley saw her on the Saturday, at lunch-time, in the break from Deirdre's Saturday job. She does filing and general tidying-up in an estate agent's office, Crayshaw's.'

'I know them. Watt Street,' Kenny put in.

'So I gather.' Jane flipped over the page in her notebook to make sure she'd got everything else exactly. 'Shelley says they agreed to meet again on the Sunday afternoon, but Deirdre didn't turn up. Shelley doesn't usually go round to the MacArthy house apparently, her parents don't like her to, but she phoned and was told Deirdre was busy. By Wednesday after school, worried that Deirdre hadn't been in touch, she did go round there, but she didn't see Deirdre and came away with a flea in her ear. She hasn't seen her or heard anything from her since that Saturday.'

'This best friend – reliable?'

'Truthful, I'd say. And desperate. She swore that she and Deirdre haven't quarrelled, and I believed her. She's sure something's wrong.' Jane paused again. 'I did look up the stepfather to see if we had anything on him. We don't. Unless Kenny . . .?'

'He's known round the pubs, and used to get thrown out of quite a few for being fighting drunk. Not recently,' Kenny added on reflection. 'He's kept his nose clean lately as far as I've heard.'

'Likely to beat up the girl and keep her away from school because of bruises?'

'I thought of that, but the school didn't respond when I made it an open suggestion,' Jane put in to Dan Crowe's question.

'Hm. Doesn't mean it couldn't happen. Other family?'

'Her real father's dead. There are two older brothers who'd been to the same school, both a different kettle of fish from Deirdre. In fact I gathered they were hardly ever there. The truancy officer used to have to go in regularly. The school will probably tip him off about Deirdre's absence now, but . . . Suppose they wait another week, and there's something more in it?'

'Go and check it out,' Dan Crowe said, coming to a decision. 'Make it look like a routine enquiry – you're seeing all the local kids because of a shoplifting complaint. Or a break-in at school and has she seen anyone hanging around? You know the kind of thing, anything which means asking to see the girl face to face. Take Kenny with you. Tomorrow morning, though,' he added, 'and call the school first to see she hasn't turned up! And don't let it get in the way of your other cases, it'll probably turn out to be nothing!'

Morning made the Ribden Road estate look moderately attractive, however much parts of it might be known as a repository for difficult families. One or two of the houses had neat front gardens, showing some care; one even had a For Sale sign on it, showing that someone had thought it worth buying from the Council. Meadowtree Avenue was less appealing when they swung into it from the main circuit which ran through the estate: on the edge, with a piece of rough grass at the end of it and woodlands beyond, it managed to spoil what must have been intended to be a nicely rural view by its row of beige pebble-dash exteriors and a generally scruffy appearance. Number twenty had a rusting bicycle wheel and several broken plastic toys in its small front garden, but surprisingly white net curtains.

'Still trying, Ruth McManus,' Kenny commented, looking at the curtains. 'Or Ruth MacArthy as she is now,' he corrected himself. 'Used to be a pretty girl once, I'd say, and might have made something of herself if she hadn't always chosen the wrong men.'

'Where Deirdre got her brains from?'

'Don't know if you could say that . . . If you marry one man who drinks himself stupid and then breaks his neck falling off a bus, it's not clever to pick another one who makes his social life round the pub, is it? Still, she's always tried her best with the house and the children, you could say that for her.' Kenny climbed out of the car. 'Let's go and see what she's got to say about Deirdre, shall we? With any luck we'll find the little ones have got chickenpox and they've just kept the girl in as a babysitter!'

The boy who answered their knock didn't look as if anyone who tried their best had got very far with him; he was wearing a grimy if neon-decorated singlet above torn jeans and a skull-and-crossbones earring dangled from one distinctly dirty ear. His face looked like an unwashed invitation to acne. That was all Jane saw before he tried to slam the door on them. It bounced back rapidly, however, from the rapid insertion of Kenny's hard-toed shoe. The DC was already speaking cheerfully.

'Hallo, Jimmy, remember me? Detective-Constable Barnes? This is Detective-Sergeant Perry, and we'd like a word with

24

your mother, if you don't mind. No, it's not about you, or why you're not at school!'

'I've left school, haven't I? Shows how much you know—'

'Oh, are you sixteen already? I thought you'd got another month to go. Maybe I can't add. Just call your mother for us, would you?'

The boy gave in with a glower and bawled out, 'Ma!' with an adolescent crack in his voice. 'Someone at the door, for you! It's the pigs, if you want to know!' he added deliberately, and with that he vanished rapidly towards the back of the house.

A second later there was a distinct yelp, and then a man appeared abruptly and soft-footedly from the direction the boy had gone. He was rubbing one hand as if he might have just delivered a blow with it, and there was a sense of dangerous animality about him which suggested the same. He was almost as grubby as the boy and similarly dressed in a singlet and jeans, in his case marked with black stains of oil. But he was much handsomer: heavily-muscled shoulders, a curling crop of black hair, wide cheekbones, a full-lipped mouth. Irish teeth, Jane thought, noting their slight protuberance with a gap between the front two. She felt his eyes raking over her in an immediate knowing inspection, male to female, but as if it was something he did automatically, his mind elsewhere. And guarded.

'Yes? You're wanting something?'

'Mr MacArthy? I'm Detective-Sergeant Perry and this is Detective-Constable Barnes.' She flipped open her police identification and held it out for him to see. 'We're sorry to disturb you, and this is just a routine enquiry, but we wondered if we could have a word with your wife? Well, actually, with your stepdaughter. It's Deirdre we'd like to see.'

'Deirdre?' He said it Irish fashion, so that it came out 'Deedera'. 'She's not here.'

'No? We've already tried her school. I wonder—'

'She's away staying with relatives. I was meaning to let the

25

school know, I've been busy and forgot. She—'

'Michael, who is it?'

The voice which broke in came from the stairs. The woman who came into view had tear-reddened eyes, that was the first thing Jane noticed about her. A sense of shrinking tension was the second. She might once have been pretty, but she was too worn-looking now for that to be visible. A toddler clung to one of her hands, and another of equal size was heavily balanced on her hip; they were both surprisingly cleanly dressed, and the one she was carrying had a pink bow in its hair. An abrupt wail from upstairs suggested an even younger baby.

'Go back up to the babe, woman, I'll deal with this. They're after Deirdre not being at school, is all. I've said she's away.'

'Mrs MacArthy? Could we come in and have a word? And if Deirdre's not here, could you tell us where we can get in touch with her?'

'She's in Ireland.' It was Michael MacArthy who answered, coming in smoothly. 'She was a bit washed out and her mother and me thought she could do with a holiday. Isn't that right, woman?'

'Yes . . .' But Ruth MacArthy glanced at her husband nervously before she said it. She went on in a rush. 'All the little ones haven't been well and Deirdre's been helping me with them. We've none of us had a lot of sleep—' She looked upwards as the baby wailed again, then back to Jane and Kenny standing silently by.

'When did she leave?' Jane asked pleasantly, keeping her eyes on the woman's face and raising her eyebrows enquiringly.

'Oh, it was Wednesday, wasn't it, Michael? Or – or Tuesday . . .'

'Last week sometime, I disremember the day. But if the school's asking, you can tell them we're sorry, I'd have sent in a note if I hadn't forgot. They make too much fuss about it for a girl of her age.'

'And when will Deirdre be back?' Jane asked, still addressing Mrs MacArthy. 'She is only fourteen, and it is term time—'

'And *I'm* her guardian. Are they sending the polis now to interfere in a family matter?' Michael MacArthy's voice was still smooth, but a barely concealed aggression underlay it. 'Woman, will you go up and see to that babe before he gets right into his crying? And take the twins with you – no, give me Shaunie, he likes being with his Da, don't you, boy?' He stepped forward to sweep the standing toddler up into his arms, a picture of fond parenthood. 'The little one wants feeding and my wife was in the middle of it, so if you'll excuse us now?' Ruth MacArthy had set off back upstairs, silently, her receding figure briefly visible and then gone. 'As for when Deirdre will be back, who knows? Her auntie'll keep her until she's looking better, and she'll be at school again then! So if there's nothing else?'

There was no point in saying there were routine questions they wanted to ask Deirdre. Not if she was in Ireland, as he claimed.

'Did you believe a word of that?' Jane asked Kenny once they were back in the car.

'Could be true. The girl might be pregnant, and that's why they've sent her off. That would explain the way Ruth was looking, too.'

'That nervous? And that worried? Did you see the look in her eyes?'

'He wasn't going to let us talk to her if he could help it, I'll admit. All the same . . .'

'Damn. If we could have seen the wife alone – or if we could have taken a quick look round the house, that at least!'

'You think there might be something in the other idea, and the girl might be upstairs covered with bruises? I'd agree I wouldn't put it past him. Nasty piece of work. We can't prove whether she's there or not, though, without a warrant.'

'And we haven't got sufficient grounds to get one.' A man

27

who addressed his wife as 'woman' all the time might make the hairs on Jane's neck curl, but it wasn't enough to take to a magistrate. 'Social services? Any chance of . . .? Or neighbours, anyone we can ask without—'

'Getting a possible complaint of police harassment?'

'I suppose so. But I'd dearly like – All right, drive on. There isn't much we can do here for the moment!' They had taken Kenny's battered car, because he had said no one would find it worth vandalising if they were any length of time about their interview.

'You're steamed up about it, aren't you?' he asked as they moved off.

'Aren't you?'

'Yes. I've got daughters. But we don't know she's there, and the Ruth McManus I used to know wouldn't have let that happen. She always did look after the kids properly. Even the eldest, the one that's left home now, and he was a right tearaway. Mind you, she does seem well under this new husband's thumb.'

'Shelley would have known if Deirdre was pregnant. We haven't even heard there was a boyfriend! As for that story of the children being ill, those twins didn't look as if they'd had much wrong with them lately to me. Ireland. Conveniently impossible for us to follow up!' She was abruptly aware they were taking an unexpected route. 'Are we driving right round the estate for a reason?'

'Just something I've got in mind. Ah, that's what I thought I might see!'

He swerved suddenly to the kerb, pulled to a halt, and was out of the car in one rapid movement. There was a brief scuffle, then the back door of the car was flung open to admit a recognisable grubby form, his arm held tightly in Kenny's grip as the DC climbed in after him.

'You ain't got no right—'

'Now now Jimmy, we just want a word with you! I thought

28

you might have sloped out the back while we were at your house, and here you are!'

'I wasn't doing nothing 'cept walking along. It's bleedin' false arrest! And police brutality—'

'Am I touching you now? Can you prove I ever did? Besides, the sergeant and I could always say we saw you with a brick in your hand and looking at that nice plate-glass window in the house over there. Or we might not,' Kenny Barnes said amiably, ignoring the stiffening he must have been aware of in Jane's shoulders. 'We only want to talk to you about your Deirdre.'

'Oh, is Miss Toffee-nose in trouble then? What happened, did her posh friends chuck her out?'

'Which posh friends are those, Jimmy?' Jane asked, making it cool and casual and turning round as if she was only being conversational instead of closely watching his face.

'That Shelley Cura. Always going off with her, isn't she? So that's where she'll have gone when she ran off. Why should I tell you anything?' he added, his anti-police attitudes suddenly taking over from sibling spite.

'Maybe to help your sister? When did she run off, then?'

'Didn't come home Sat'dy before last, did she? 'Cos she'd got told off Friday night. Serves her right for comin' in late, I get it round the head enough, and for her it was only a couple of belts and—' He broke off, his face showing a sudden wariness. And an edge of panic. 'If that Mrs Cura's made a complaint, I didn't say nothing about Dee getting belted!'

'But you think that's why Deirdre ran away? You did say she ran away, didn't you? Have you seen her at all since she left home?'

'I'm not saying nothing—'

'I think you've said enough. But suppose we just want to know where Deirdre is? To know she's safe? *Have* you seen her since the Saturday before last?'

'No, I ain't, but if she's gone missing I ain't saying why!

She's prob'ly run off to tart it around London if her posh friends wouldn't have her, and I hope she's livin' in cardboard city! Thinks she's better than all of us, doesn't she? Can I go now? You don't have no—'

'Out,' Jane said abruptly, reaching back to press the handle of the rear door. 'It's not locked!'

Jimmy didn't need telling twice. He was out of the car in a flash, skinny legs pumping him round the nearest corner at speed.

'We couldn't have kept him. We shouldn't even have had him in the car at all, as a minor. Let alone under threat.' She had to say it, but they both knew she was in no position to turn it into an official reprimand. As ranking officer she was responsible, and she had gone along with Kenny's action. 'If he brings it up—'

'He won't, not Jimmy. He's all mouth but too much of a coward to push his luck. Gave us the break we were looking for, anyway, didn't it? Jimmy's too thick to lie. The girl's not in the house. And she didn't get sent off to Ireland in the middle of last week either.'

No. She hadn't come home from work on the Saturday.

Ten days ago.

After being belted by her stepfather on the Friday night.

'We'll have to work round it officially, and see Mrs Cura to make sure Deirdre didn't go there after work on the Saturday. We may already know she didn't from Shelley, but we still have to do it by the book. We'll have to ask at Crayshaw's, too, the estate agents, to see whether Deirdre was there on Saturday afternoon, and if so what time she left work. And whether she seemed normal. After that, we need to find out whether anyone at all saw her after that Saturday . . .'

Maybe it would turn out to be just another missing teenager run off to London. There were plenty of them, after all.

But surely she would have told her best friend? And why hadn't her mother, at least, reported it?

Chapter 3

'I want to go to Crayshaw's first thing – Oh shit, that's a ladder in my new tights, and just where it shows!' Jane unpeeled both legs in exasperation, then rooted around in a jumbled drawer with urgent fingers. 'Purple – what the hell did I buy those for? Black . . . no, too much like uniform. Ah, don't say this pair's intact? As I was saying, I want to do all the follow-ups before I get deflected. Otherwise it's going to get classed as "just another runaway teenager to put on the list", you know?'

As usual she was carrying on this conversation with Matty through an open door, her voice pitched to reach her invisible flatmate. One missing schoolgirl, whose absence hadn't even been reported by her parents. It was a hard fact, but without more to go on, Jane was likely to be instructed simply to file it. Since they hadn't even received a formal complaint.

So many teenagers did take off for London from all parts of the country, so why did she feel in her bones that Deirdre's case was different?

'Have you got time for some toast?' Matty's voice floated through from the kitchen.

'Not when I've just slept through my alarm!' That was what came of sitting up late over a bottle of Greek brandy with several of Matty's friends who were for once not on call. 'Oh God, and I'm always meaning to set it even earlier and go jogging!'

'Cagney and Lacey stuff? Whichever of them it is who does all that running around in a tracksuit behind the credits.'

31

Jane appeared in the kitchen halfway through Matty's comment, still rapidly buttoning her skirt. 'Tell me that kettle's just boiled,' she said imploringly. 'Tea I must have!'

'That kettle's just boiled,' Matty said obediently.

'Thank God for that. And now I come to think of it, I can stop finding excuses for why I never go jogging. That guy from orthopaedics last night was telling me all about stress fractures. Do you have to look so revoltingly chipper?'

'I've had more than two hours' sleep for once,' Matty pointed out cheerfully. She looked blooming in her silk wrapper, which was covered with vivid flowers in colours which would have drowned anyone else's skin tones. 'You look OK – the smartly neutral look? By the way, I noticed you and Daniel seemed to be getting on pretty well.'

'No, Daniel's hypnotised by you. He just finds it easier to talk to me because I'm not the princess in the tower, just the princess's friend.' Jane grinned at Matty's grimace. 'Never mind, that's better than the ones who fall into acute silence the minute they hear I'm a cop. Ouch, why did I swallow that tea too hot? Well, I'm out of here. See you when I see you!'

One of these days she might find a circle of friends of her own in this place, instead of being dependent on Matty's. The trouble was, if you ruled out colleagues (which she did, knowing warily the effect the wrong relationship could have on a police career) who else did she meet? The criminal fraternity. And members of the public who saw her in her police guise. If she did happen to meet someone otherwise, even the most innocent new acquaintance seemed to develop a look in the eyes as if hastily wondering about unpaid parking tickets the minute her job was mentioned . . . She was used to that by now, but it still gave her narrowed options. In London there had been one or two old friends when she wasn't too busy herself to see them; but here she was still a relative newcomer.

Never mind, that would change. And no doubt there were advantages in living like a celibate nun – if she could think what they were. Sublimation, perhaps? She bit back a snort of laughter, and straightened her thoughts for the interview she was on her way to conduct. Crayshaw's, Estate Agents, should have opened its doors by now.

It had. Mr Anthony Crayshaw, FICS, was there in person. He was in his middle forties, with hair marginally beginning a retreat from his brow and the smooth plumpness of someone who might be a regular attender at Rotarian dinners. On hearing who Jane was he swept her to the rear of the property showroom and into his private office. It had discreet but thick-pile carpeting, an expensive-looking antique desk, and good water-colour paintings of local scenes against elegant Georgian-striped wallpaper. There he fussed about ushering her into a chair, which was also antique. Noticeably, he left the door wide open, and Jane somehow had the impression that it was to show he had nothing at all to hide.

'Now, Sergeant, what can I do for you?' he asked heartily. 'We haven't got squatters in one of our empty properties, I hope! No? Oh, that's a relief! Well, what little problem can we help you with?'

'I'm just making some routine enquiries about a teenager called Deirdre MacArthy. I believe you employ her here on Saturdays?'

'Saturdays. Deirdre MacArthy. I'm not sure, my office manager deals with . . . Oh yes, I remember now, one of our very part-time staff.'

Jane took him through her list of questions. Had Deirdre been in the office last Saturday? Well, now it was mentioned he believed she hadn't; he seemed to remember his office manager complaining the girl hadn't turned up. Yes, he was right, and it had been annoying. But that was the trouble with teenagers, wasn't it? Thoroughly willing and keen to start with, then abruptly bored with the whole idea!

The previous Saturday? Yes, he supposed she had been in then. He wouldn't necessarily have been aware . . . He would have been seeing clients and taking them out to show them round houses; Deirdre's work took place in the back offices: filing, photocopying, making tea or coffee. As far as he knew, she would have left at her usual time, six. She certainly hadn't been here when he had locked up the office at six forty-five. As to whether she had seemed normal that day, he really couldn't say. If it was important he could ask his Saturday staff, though none of them was actually in today.

Oh dear, was the girl in some kind of trouble?

That seemed like an afterthought.

Jane let the implication float that it was merely a matter of the girl missing school. She received his instant assurances that there would never be, had never been, any question of his office employing anyone of that age during school hours. It had been a Saturday job only, and he had given the girl a job because she seemed keen to have some office experience, and earn some pocket-money at the same time. Since how long? Oh, three or four months, he supposed.

Jane murmured something reassuring, and managed to elicit that Deirdre had seemed a reasonably good employee, as far as he knew. Mr Crayshaw then told Jane again that teenage attention-span was short, so he had not really been surprised to learn that the MacArthy girl had stopped coming in. At that age girls did tend to be unreliable, didn't Sergeant Perry agree?

Winding things up, Jane let him encourage her to come to Crayshaw's if she ever decided to buy a property herself. There really were some very good bargains on the market . . . His eagerness suggested his firm was as badly hit by the recession as any other, though he certainly didn't look as if poverty were about to get up and bite him.

He shook her wringingly by the hand and she left him. Walking back to her car, she tried to assess what she had made of Mr Anthony Crayshaw. He had certainly seemed the picture of innocent candour . . . though had she sensed a very

34

slight flicker in his eyes at her first mention of Deirdre MacArthy's name? And while he had claimed to find the girl singularly unnoticeable, he did eventually find himself able to give quite clear details of the girl's hours and duties.

She let a faint query arise in her mind: had her employer fancied the girl? A little bit of sexual harassment, maybe? Enough to make him so keen to stress that teenagers were not to be trusted?

It was probably nothing. Deirdre would surely have shared something like that with Shelley – her best friend – and Shelley had seemed certain there was nothing at all in Deirdre's life to make her run away. The girl had been almost vehement about that.

And then on the other side there was Jimmy, Deirdre's brother, so sure she had run away; the parents, claiming to have sent her to Ireland; Mrs Cura, Shelley's mother, already visited and positive about the fact that Deirdre had not come to her house seeking refuge. Mrs Cura would have no reason to lie. So there were a lot of pieces which didn't quite fit together.

But, anyway, Jane had made all the enquiries she could decently make at this stage from Crayshaw's. She could make a note that Deirdre usually left the premises at six and had definitely not been there when the place was locked up at six forty-five. If things did proceed further Jane could probably go back and interview Crayshaw's Saturday staff, to see what mood Deirdre had been in that day, but that was all.

To convince herself that she had done everything possible, Jane made a detour via both the rail stations to show the staff a snapshot Mrs Cura had provided, out of a collection of Shelley's. No one had seen a girl resembling the slightly blurred image . . . 'But then we wouldn't really notice, would we, I mean, just one passenger? There's kids catching trains all the time!' The answer was much the same at the coach station.

It was time for Jane to return to her desk. There was plenty of other work calling for her attention. Those lost or stolen credit cards, for instance . . . though that seemed to be a cooling trail. And collating public complaints about graffiti vandals – Morland's latest stimulating brainwave to occupy Jane's time. She would simply have to write up what little she had on Deirdre and leave the information on an open file.

Back in the CID room, Jane found a surprise. Vern Harris was busily clearing his desk and loading the contents into a cardboard box. He was looking exceptionally pleased with himself and offered a wide grin when he noticed her raised eyebrows.

'Yes, that's right, I'm off! On my way!'

'Really? Where?'

'I got on the Advanced Course. I thought it was a turn down when I didn't hear, but apparently it was just that the paperwork got sent somewhere else – or someone else fell out of the course, *I* don't know – don't care much, either! Anyway I'm expected pronto, I only heard late last night.' He was too excited to hide behind his usual who-am-I-to-care attitude. 'You know what it means – promotion at last! So maybe coming up through the ranks does count for something after all . . . Ah, nothing against you personally, Jane.'

'Nothing personal taken. And congratulations. They might have given you a bit more warning, though! And us. We'll miss you.' Like a hole in the head when he was in one of his more conceited moods, but she was genuinely pleased for him just the same. 'Where's the course being held?'

'The centre just outside Manchester. A new place, purpose-built. It'll be a change going north again, I used to work up that way.'

'Well, great.' Not for his wife, left abruptly with two young children and in an advanced state of pregnancy, but Jane forbore to cloud his satisfaction by mentioning that. Police wives were supposed to take whatever the force handed out, anyway. 'I wish you all the best, I hope it goes well!'

'I'll see that it does, believe you me! Now, I think that's the lot. Oh, Morland was asking for you. Something to do with some old ladies in a home, and he wants you to look into it.'

That sounded very likely. Anything to do with the old, the halt, or pet-owners wanting missing cats traced. 'Thanks,' Jane said drily.

'Cheer up, I'll leave you my unfinished files to follow up and perhaps he won't notice,' Vern said, out of competition enough to be generous and flashing her a smile. 'Oh, and there's that snout of mine who's trying to get a sniff on whether there's some steal-to-order car racket going on . . . No, I reckon the guv'nor'll think Gary ought to take him over. Right, that's it, I've got everything. I'll do a quick go-round to say my goodbyes, and then I'm away!'

The door banged behind him, a man in a hurry. Jane glanced round the temporarily empty CID room, and knew that they would miss him. She might personally find him a pain sometimes, but he had a good nose for villains. His sudden departure would certainly leave them all busier . . . They'd be one short on CID sergeants, however they changed the reliefs round.

That could be useful as far as she was concerned. She was tempted to have a quick flick through the files Vern had left now instead of waiting for Dan Crowe to reallocate them. Morland could hardly sideline her now – not with a hole in the department until such time as a proper replacement could be found. That might take a while, too.

This thought put her in a good enough temper to go and see the man himself about the old ladies Vern had mentioned. It transpired that the DCI had been reading through the back files and found that three residents of a local Retirement Home had got into a panic because they thought their pension books were being taken away from them. Kenny Barnes had already sorted it out; it had merely been the home's matron being helpful about getting their pensions cashed. Now, Morland wanted Jane to go back and check again, to see that nothing dubious was happening, and that there had been no cause for complaint since.

'Certainly, sir, if that's what you want, but DI Crowe did think DC Barnes' judgement was to be trusted—'

'One can't be too careful. Old people too easily lay themselves open to being cheated – and mistreated! – and I think it's a good idea to show we're keeping a close eye on things. A woman's touch here, I think. Now, what else did I see . . . Oh yes, this question of a missing girl who isn't actually missing at all, but merely gone away to Ireland. I think you can close that one, Sergeant Perry. It was just a piece of hysteria from her friend – typical of a teenage girl.'

'DI Crowe thought it was worth checking, sir. And I did a bit of following up this morning, I went to see Crayshaw's where the MacArthy girl used to do some part-time work. I spoke to Mr Anthony Crayshaw, and there's a slight—'

'You bothered Anthony Crayshaw personally? Don't you realise he's a member of the same Rotary Club as the Chief Superintendent? It can't have been necessary to bother him with such a routine enquiry!' DCI Morland gave her a minatory frown, and if there had been a set of advertising lights above his head, their message would definitely have flashed a yearning to put her somewhere harmless. Like in uniform directing traffic. 'If you'd been here for the planning meeting at nine, you would have known we concluded it was a false alarm. The girl will no doubt reappear shortly, and her parents told you quite clearly she was on holiday.'

'I know, sir, but . . .' No, she was damned if she was going to pass on what they'd heard from Jimmy MacArthy, and get an official reprimand for both herself and Kenny for questioning a minor without his parents present. She hadn't even told Dan Crowe yet, waiting to catch him at a good moment. DCI

38

Morland ignored her attempted interjection and was steamrollering on.

'You may be aware that Sergeant Harris leaves today, and without any of the warning we should have had. I'm making it a priority to consider who should step in as acting sergeant – DC Lockley, probably. It won't really be your concern, except to give every assistance to whoever may move in from uniform to take Lockley's place. That's all, then, Sergeant Perry.'

Jane went away simmering, as always, and as always conscious that she disliked the man from the top of his high-domed bald head to the tip of his over-shiny shoes. Let alone his self-importantly picky manner and his endless lists, charts, checks, and extended planning meetings. She could only decide that some other regional force had probably used a glowing recommendation as a way of getting him out of their hair. And why wasn't it supposed to be her concern who became the new sergeant in CID? Answer – undoubtedly – because he hoped she'd become invisible. Well, he certainly had another hope coming on that one . . .

She went off to fulfil the task of enquiring into the old ladies and their pension books, leaving a note in the still-empty CID room to explain where she'd gone – where *was* everyone this morning? An hour later she came back with notes to prove that everything had indeed been sorted out and that there were no further complaints. It was some consolation for her time-wasting visit to find that the fat fraud-file Vern had been working on had landed up on her desk. It was a slow one and needed a lot of computer checking, but if she could unravel it properly it might turn out to be big. The DI was just in the process of handing out assignments.

'Gary, you'd better take over the motor-theft stuff, since Vern suggested you already knew his snout. See if you can get something a bit more useful out of him! Kenny, you can go on looking into the query arson but report back to me. Mike – no,

I'll give this one to the only proper sergeant I've got left. It's a spate of minor burglaries Vern was keeping on the back-burner.' He flung the file in Jane's direction, adding, 'You can use the woodentops to help with the enquiries. They've got half the information anyway. Mike, you can have the last two – the assault, and the pending prosecution for dog-fighting. Everyone happy? Right, scatter, you've all got plenty to do and so have I!'

'Guv?'

'Yes, DC Lockley, I *have* been asked for my opinion about you becoming acting DS. I'm still thinking about it.' Dan Crowe beetled at Mike's hopeful face, though something in his voice suggested he was merely delaying his agreement so as to keep the DC in line. 'Now, I've got people to see, and so have all of you: get busy!'

This was not the moment to talk to him about the Deirdre MacArthy case, or tell him why she wanted it kept open. Jane made a point of typing up her own report, and put the file in her pending basket, before she picked up Vern's burglaries file and looked to see which of the woodentops (or uniform, out of slang) she would need to talk to about it. There was something still nagging at her about the missing girl. Not just the different versions she'd been given by Jimmy and Michael MacArthy. There was something else, like an echo . . .

She put it out of her mind and went to look for the uniform sergeant who had been in charge of booking in a burglary suspect – later released because he'd found three friends to alibi him. Then she picked up on a call-out to a shop break-in, not connected but worth CID presence. It was late afternoon when she was back at her desk with the chance to delve into the fraud file and familiarise herself with it. She was soon deeply immersed in the endless columns of figures, merely keeping one ear cocked towards the desultory conversation going on between Kenny and Mike who were both at their own desks. Mike had put his feet up on his the moment Dan Crowe was safely out of the way on a summons upstairs to see the Super.

'If we're all going to do extra work, let's hope they give us overtime instead of just calling it part of our general allowance! I could do with the extra dosh, and my girlfriend's not best pleased even now by the number of evenings I've been working late!'

'You and your girlfriends,' Kenny retorted. 'You'd do better to keep your mind on the job, my lad! Overtime's a fine hope anyway. It's hard enough to get our expenses OKed, nowadays. Some people should try what it's like with a wife and four kids and a mortgage!'

'Some people don't reckon to. Not for a while yet. By the way, have you seen the new uniform girl, the one with the tits – oops, sorry, Sarge!' Mike said as Jane lifted her head. It was something that he bothered to say it, even with an unrepentant grin.

'Don't mind me!' she said sweetly. 'I just wonder sometimes how you fellas would like to be described by nothing by your anatomy, that's all!'

'Dunno, you should hear some of the things my sister says when she's been out on a hen-night to see one of those male strippers!'

'Round *here*? Heavens, and here was I thinking it was a quiet cathedral city!'

'Oh, it's all seething sex behind closed doors,' Kenny pronounced. 'You should hear the stories my wife tells about what goes on on our estate – Ahem, sir!'

The door had opened unexpectedly on Superintendent Annerley, down from his administrative office on the second floor and as suave and tidy as always. He had Dan Crowe with him. Mike's legs were down from his desk with the rapidity of a contortionist, and he and Kenny were suddenly extremely busy, though with an alertness to show they were poised to spring to their feet if required. Nominally Jane was in charge, and she bit her lip, but found herself rescued by the Super's deadpan ability to ignore minor infractions.

'Sergeant Perry, Detectives – all catching up on your paperwork, I see? Good. Sergeant Perry, if I could have a word?'

'Yes, of course, sir.'

'No, no need to get up, I just wanted to tell you personally about the new colleague who'll be joining you tomorrow. Detective-Sergeant Ryan is being sent to us to fill Vernon Harris's place on a temporary posting. I've asked Inspector Crowe to put you on to work together, since Sergeant Ryan won't be familiar with anything we've been doing. If you won't mind showing him the ropes, and keeping a general eye on him while he's settling in . . .'

Keeping an eye on him? What was he, a geriatric called back for duty? 'No, of course not, sir,' Jane agreed, and glanced at Dan Crowe. Now what was *he* looking so bad-tempered about? Having a strange sergeant pushed on to him just when he'd reorganised Vern's work, or what?

'Good,' the Super said again, and stepped back to show he had finished all he wanted to say. 'I'll leave you to it, then, carry on!'

The door closed behind him. 'You two, your desks look as if you've been collecting from the nearest tip, and isn't one of you supposed to be out?' Dan Crowe asked explosively, with a glower at Kenny and Mike. 'Or have you just decided between you that Gary doesn't need relieving from outside that villain's last known address?'

'Sorry, Guv, hadn't noticed the time.' Kenny moved as quickly as his round bulk would allow. 'Just going now!'

'Right. And DC Lockley, it seems they've found a new ranking sergeant for us before we'd expected, but maybe that's fortunate considering where you had your feet when I came in! This is a working office, not your lounge!'

With that he banged off into his own small cubby-hole of an

office and slammed the door. Cross as hell. Maybe it was just an untidy CID room and an apparently relaxing staff when the Super happened to wander in which was at the root of his bad temper.

Still, it definitely was not the moment to talk to him about Deirdre MacArthy.

Chapter 4

The new sergeant certainly wasn't geriatric. He arrived in Dan Crowe's wake in the CID room just after Jane had come back from lunch, and Jane's first impression was, thirty-ish, tight but well-fitting jeans, a brown leather jacket. He also looked tough and self-contained and very much at ease with himself – and quite unmoved by the fact that the DI was still clearly in one of his snappier moods.

'Good, you're here,' he greeted Jane on a growl. 'This is Sergeant Ryan – Sergeant Perry. She'll show you round. He can have Vern's desk, you can start there. And you'd better give him a tour of the whole station so he doesn't waste everyone's time by getting lost. Otherwise, take him round with you, you heard what the Super said!'

'Yes, Guv.'

'He can meet the others when they bother to trail back in, if they can remember I'm not running a holiday camp. There isn't anything urgent you want to see me about, is there? Good, get him settled in, then!'

He gave the newcomer a noticeably dispassionate look and headed off into his office. Jane found herself being regarded amiably by a pair of ruefully amused grey eyes, and a hand was held out for her to shake.

'Hi. Steve Ryan. I think I'm in the doghouse already for turning up late, but then nobody told me exactly when I was expected . . . Sorry to be thrust on you like a lost sheep, but if you won't mind giving me the low-down on everything in sight?'

'That seems to be my job. Jane Perry,' Jane told him, returning his handshake. It was extremely firm, a quick grip of muscular fingers. He certainly didn't look as if he would easily feel lost. No more than a couple of inches above Jane's own height, he was compactly muscled and stood with a boxer's easy balance, weight poised for movement. Perhaps it was boxing which had broken his nose at some time, leaving it very slightly crooked and with a small scar on the bridge. It didn't detract from his good-looking competence; not handsome, but a long way from being ugly. He had very short hair, almost an army cut, above neat ears.

Not someone who looked at all as if he would need nursemaiding. Jane realised abruptly that he was aware he was being comprehensively inspected – and, in the same breath, that he was attractive. He probably knew it, too. She moved rapidly back to the official line, coolly friendly.

'So – where are you from?'

'London. Born there thirty years ago, bred there, worked there – Docklands area, last. This'll be a change.' It was the other side of London from Jane's former haunts; it wasn't even worth asking if they had any common acquaintances in the force. There was no London twang in his voice, which was straightforwardly classless, and she wondered what sort of a background he came from. And why he was floating and available to fill in sudden vacancies. A moment later he answered that question, with an easy stretch of leather-clad shoulders. 'I've been on leave for a while after stopping a bullet, and now I'm back and fit for duty someone, somewhere, seems to have decided there isn't anywhere to put me for the moment. Hence . . .'

'They've sent you out here for a quiet life?' Even as she said it Jane was amused to recognise how quickly she'd picked up local defensive attitudes, the Met versus the provinces. It had taken her a good month after her arrival to convince people that she was not automatically expecting things to be quiet

46

and dozy after the capital. 'Have you left a family behind in London?' she asked politely.

'Nope, no ties. Maybe that's why they decided I wouldn't gripe about being used as a hole-plugger. What's it like here? Easy to find somewhere to live?'

'No, hard, the city's got a lot of students. They'll probably be able to find you something in the Section House.'

'No thanks!' The answer was prompt and he pulled a face at her. 'I'd rather take my chances!'

'I'll start showing you round.' She wondered suddenly whether he outranked her: she must ask him, as casually as possible, how long he had been a sergeant. Morland would love it if he could establish the new DS as her senior. Not that that was Steve Ryan's fault. And the Super had seemed to suggest he would be working to her, at least to start with. What was the position on temporary postings, anyway? 'That's your desk there, the empty one. That, in the corner, is the coffee-machine, when it works, though what it produces is warm and wet rather than coffee. Which will be no surprise . . .'

'None!'

'It's better in the canteen, they haven't gone automated yet. That's the day-to-day chart, on that wall; that's the shift chart next to it. Filing cabinets over there, current. Phone extensions for CID are 196 and 197. The guv's office, through there, 198. There's a list on the wall of all the others. Tell me if I'm going too fast for you!'

'I've got a good memory.'

'Good. We might as well go out and do the whole tour, then, and I'll show you where everything is. It's probably much the same pattern as you're used to. Communications is central, and the charging area. Interview rooms are all down one side. The cells are – well, never mind, you'll see. And I'll introduce you around to uniform and the civilian clerks – unless the guv's already done that?'

47

'No, he just collected me from upstairs, where I was sent when I arrived . . . Am I interrupting something you were doing?' he asked, his eyes on the file she had left open on her desk. 'I could probably find my own way around.'

'It's all right, I was only going over some computer print-outs. A fraud I've taken over from Vern Harris, the sergeant you're replacing.' And she wasn't passing that file over to him, he needn't think so. 'It's been chuntering on for months, it'll keep!'

'Sooner you than me, I hate columns of figures. DI Crowe said you and I would work on the same cases until I'm settled; well, you can keep that one!'

She would. And whatever else came her way. Morland permitting. 'You've met DCI Morland, I gather?' she asked, glancing towards the stairs as she led the way out of the CID room.

'The thin Humpty-Dumpty who looks as if he's got to keep counting the bricks on the wall to stop himself falling off?'

It was so beautifully apt that Jane had to swallow a sudden choke. Oh, Steve Ryan was going to be worth having around, if only for that! 'The DCI's only been here a few months and he's still settling in,' she managed, though not without a tremor in her voice.

'And I ought to be more careful what I say?' A glance at him showed an innocently enquiring expression, and he added, 'Now that *does* take me back, who was it who used to say that to me all the time when I was a rookie?' His look of mischief changed to a friendly grin. 'I liked the look of your guv, though – our guv? – in spite of the way he was growling. A good copper?'

'Yes, he is.' She was beginning to get the feeling that Steve Ryan was a deliberate rebel – floating because he'd got on the wrong side of someone in authority? Maybe Dan Crowe knew that, and was feeling dumped on. Interesting.

It wouldn't necessarily mean the new sergeant wasn't a

good detective. They would just have to wait and see on that one.

She showed him all round, and let him make his number with the duty officers. There was some surprise that a replacement for Vern had been found so rapidly after his last-minute departure, and the usual assessing looks which said silently, What's this one going to be like? They were making their way back to the CID room when a WPC put her head out from Communications and summoned them with an urgent wave.

'Sergeant Perry! A smash-and-grab has just come in from Herne Bay and they're asking for CID back-up. The DI wants you two to go, straight away, he said!'

'Right. Just give me some details.'

They were in her car moments later, armed with a map-reference for the street and a quick print-out of the name of the jewellery store, also the name of the officer in charge to whom they should report. 'There are sub-stations in most of the coastal towns, but this lot are near enough to come under us,' Jane explained to Steve Ryan as she took a back-street route to avoid getting snarled up in traffic, then joined the main north road out of the city. 'Herne Bay's only five or six miles from here. It's a seaside tourist place – there's a strip of them along the estuary coast. On a clear day you can just see Southend opposite, so I'm told. Or am I telling you things you already know?'

'No, this part of Kent's new territory to me.' He sat easily in the passenger seat beside her, glancing with apparent interest at the farmlands they were passing, a criss-cross pattern of flat fields with neat hedges. 'D'you get the same sort of troubles as Southend?'

'No, luckily, it's quieter this side. The bikers haven't picked on it as a place to gather. There's just the odd teenage fight around the amusement arcades.' They crossed the Thanet Way with its flat surroundings and a glimpse of ugly, shed-

49

like industrial buildings spread out behind, then turned into the outskirts of the small town – bungalows, Edwardian villas to show a once-fashionable history as a watering-place, then the sudden glare of plate-glass and neon-scrawled signs which was a shopping arcade. The sea was abruptly visible through a gap ahead in a thin line along the horizon.

The jewellery shop was in the modernised pedestrian precinct, all pattern-laid brick paving and bollards to make parking impossible. There was a jagged hole in the shop window and bright shards of glass everywhere. Jane caught up with the uniformed sergeant in charge, one she knew.

'Hello, Ron, someone's got a nerve in broad daylight, haven't they? Did they get away with much?'

'A display of rings, a couple of necklaces, a handful of gold chains. The owner's just trying to give us a list. It was one perp, white, male, twenty-ish. We've got a couple of witnesses prepared to give a description.' He glanced curiously at Steve and gave a friendly nod as Jane introduced them. 'He ran away on foot, and no one seems to have had the nous to try and stop him. One of the witnesses is almost sure he was bleeding, though. And the other one says she's "sure he's not local".'

'She got a good look at his face? That should help. I suppose she means "local" as *here*, not that he was actually a foreigner.' Jane was used to the insularity of this part of the country by now. As often as not someone was classed as 'coming from outside' if they lived more than three miles away. 'OK, we'll talk to both the witnesses, and see if it sounds like anyone we might know. Anyone hurt – apart from the perp?'

'No, luckily. There's a bit of blood on the glass over there which is probably his. I've asked for a SOCO to come and dust for prints, since it looks as if he wasn't wearing gloves. We'll be round the streets keeping our eyes open for anyone likely wearing a bandage, but it looks as if he's slipped through for now. Jeavons, keep those people back, will you? No, Madam,

I'm sorry, I can't let you through to the baker's just now. If you wouldn't mind waiting ten minutes we should have cleared a path for you by then!'

He moved away and Jane went to talk to the shop owner, and the two witnesses. Steve Ryan went with her, and she soon noticed that he had an easy way with elderly ladies eager to tell someone what they had seen. Also, the ability to charm them patiently into remembering. A useful talent, if surprising from someone she would have thought the old lady concerned might have viewed with suspicion as looking like a tear-away.

Driving back, trying to sort out her assessment of what she'd seen of him so far, she asked him casually how long he'd been in the Met – and how long he had been a Detective Sergeant. Twelve years and three years respectively, he said. Three years – damn, that did make him technically her senior. 'You must have joined up straight from school,' she said.

'A uniform seemed a good cure for boredom, and for some reason I fancied doing the nicking rather than being nicked. Where I come from you could call that the basic choice. Half the people I was at school with took the opposite route.' He sounded amused about it, and she wondered again about the classless voice. A deliberate attempt to distance himself from his origins? 'How about you, Sergeant Jane Perry? I'll tell you what I guess. You're a force high-flier, fast-promotion stream. I bet you came in from university.'

'Are you one of those who objects?'

'Not in the least. Ambitious?'

'I want to get somewhere, yes. Not necessarily in a hurry, though.' She glanced across at him and saw an amused interest in his eyes which made her feel she might have sounded defensive. 'Nothing wrong with ambition, is there? And, like you, I prefer to do something interesting with my time!'

'I'm surprised you aren't with the Met. That's where I'd have expected to find you.'

51

'That was where I started. Got tired of big city life, though, and thought there might be more variety out here. As there is, from time to time. *Damn!*'

'Something the matter?' He must have been aware of her instinctive move to stamp on the brakes, though she had changed her mind almost instantly. 'Have we left something behind?'

'No, sorry.' Coming to a dead stop had been her first reaction to a sharp memory, but would have been pointless. 'It was just that something came back to me. About another case I'm working on. I knew it was setting up echoes . . . There's a missing schoolgirl, and I've had an uneasy feeling about it.' And a reason, a recognition, had abruptly come to her.

'Share it?'

'It was a case when I first joined – when I was still on the beat. It involved a Turkish family . . .' With a young daughter who had vanished as abruptly as Deirdre had. And parents who had claimed the girl had merely gone away on a visit to their homeland. It was a young male teacher that time who had stuck his neck out by insisting on having the girl's disappearance looked into – at some cost to his career when it turned out he'd been having a close relationship with the seventeen-year-old. But he had been right. They had found the girl's dismembered body in the freezer of her parents' home, waiting to be disposed of, and her strictly Moslem father and uncle had stood trial for her murder. 'It's not necessarily the same situation, but I know now why I was getting warning bells,' Jane told the man beside her. 'Still, we can leave it for now.' And she went back to negotiating her way through the traffic, thickening now they were approaching the city again.

Reaching the station, she made her way back inside, with Steve behind her. She paused at Communications to tell them there was a SOCO report she would want, please, when it came in, and found there was another message for her.

52

'The Duty Desk civilian was asking if you were back yet. About five minutes ago.'

'Oh, right. Did he say what he wanted? Don't worry, I'll go round that way and ask him. Can you remember your way back to CID?' she asked Steve, noticing meanwhile, with a philosophical cynicism, that one of the WPCs had taken off her headset and was combing her fingers through her hair, probably so that the new sergeant could notice how prettily it curled.

'Yes, I'll manage. I'll tell the DI you'll be along in a minute, shall I?'

'OK, do that . . .'

The station's reception area was fenced off behind protective glass and had another glass panel behind it so that anyone on the desk could communicate with the office behind without having to move. Jane tapped on it to show she was there, and the Duty Desk civilian slipped the locking catch and slid the panel back to speak to her. 'Oh yes, Sergeant Perry, there's someone asking for you – won't talk to anyone else. She said she'd wait. I think she's still here.' He moved back to lean over the desk and peer round the corner, then came back to her. 'Yes, she is. She wants "the lady detective". She wouldn't give her name.'

'All right, I'll come round,' Jane told him. Maybe it was one of the little old ladies worrying about her pension book still. She hoped that whole thing wasn't going to start up again. Jane let herself out through the security lock into the front area and glanced across to see who was waiting for her.

Then she was moving quickly, her breath caught. If she had come in even a minute later . . . The figure had already got up and turned away towards the exit, moving like someone who had lost heart. Dear God, don't let her have changed her mind. Jane reached Ruth MacArthy just as she began to push the door open, and laid a gentle hand on her arm.

'Mrs MacArthy? I'm sorry you've had to wait. I've only just

heard you were here. You'd like to talk to me? I'm Sergeant Perry, remember?'

'I . . . It doesn't matter. I'd better be—'

'Yes of course it matters, if you've bothered to come all this way! Shall we go inside and talk over a cup of tea?'

For a moment it seemed as if Ruth MacArthy might refuse. Then, with an air of gathering her courage, she nodded. She had no children with her today; a glance outside showed no pram or push-chair. She allowed Jane to lead her back to the inner door and waited while it was opened; she let herself be ushered into the nearest free interview room. A quick word ensured that two teas would be brought.

As soon as she was seated, Ruth MacArthy lifted her chin and spoke, softly but with a surprising firmness.

'I've come to report my daughter Deirdre missing. She's been gone from home almost two weeks now. I'm sorry we lied to you, but Michael thought—'

'Your husband thought?' Jane prompted as she broke off and didn't continue.

'He thought she'd get herself a bad name . . .'

The tap on the door came at the wrong moment, but it was the tea, brought by a young policewoman in uniform. As she handed over the steaming cardboard cups and offered sugar, Jane signed to her to stay. Ruth MacArthy looked immediately apprehensive, but Jane fixed her with a deliberately reassuring gaze.

'If you're reporting Deirdre missing, we'll need to get it written down. And Constable—'

'Welsh, Sergeant.'

'Yes, Constable Welsh, sorry.' It was due to working with the men that she could only think of the girl as 'the new uniform with the tits', which swelled her regulation jacket noticeably above an otherwise trim figure. 'Constable Welsh can write it all down for you, and we'll get you to sign it. And then we can start looking for Deirdre. All right?'

Ruth MacArthy nodded again, with only the barest hesitation this time, as if, having taken the plunge, she would now accept whatever that brought.

'You were saying?' Jane prompted. 'Deirdre's been gone from home almost two weeks, and you don't know where she is? So you didn't actually send her off to Ireland for a holiday?'

'I'm sorry about the story. Michael cares about her, and she's a girl after all, so it matters if she gets herself a bad reputation. So he thought . . . we thought that it was better . . . And that she'd come home! I was sure she would – she's not one to frighten me like this! And anything could have happened to her by now, couldn't it?' The worn hands were suddenly twisting in Ruth MacArthy's lap. 'You read such things . . .'

'Yes, you do, so it's much safer to report someone missing and get her looked for. I'm glad you've told me and I think you're very wise. I expect your husband agreed that you should; did he?'

'He doesn't know I've – Only, he won't listen when I tell him! And I'm her mother, aren't I? And there's her friend coming round asking for her so she can't be there – and Jimmy saying she'll have run off to London. And I can't just go on waiting to hear from her, can I? She's not a bad girl, whatever Michael says! She wouldn't run off with some man and get him to buy her new clothes and everything!'

'So she hasn't taken any of her own clothes with her?'

'Not a stitch but what she was wearing to go to work. There's nothing missing from her room. And . . . and then today I found this!'

She fumbled in her pocket and pulled out a thin blue booklet. A Post Office Savings book, Jane saw as it was handed to her. With Deirdre MacArthy, name, address and signature, written along the side of the cover in a rounded hand under the clear plastic.

'She was saving her wages,' Ruth MacArthy explained on a tremor, 'so she'd only have the one day's money with her,

55

wouldn't she, if she'd left without this? And she wouldn't have left it if she'd meant not to come home? So when I found it I thought – I *had* to come, didn't I? No matter what it means, I *had* to tell you.'

'Yes, of course you did. Let's get all the dates and times written down properly, and then we can start trying to find her.' Jane reached out a hand to touch the other woman's, tightly clenched on the table.

No, this wasn't the same as the case with the Turkish girl, whose mother had known what had happened but accepted it as the male world's justice to an erring daughter.

All the same, as soon as Ruth MacArthy's statement was signed and made official, the first person Jane would want to talk to would be Michael MacArthy, who hadn't wanted his stepdaughter reported missing. And who still didn't, since his wife had had to come here without his knowledge.

It was a proper case now.

And, since no young girl sensible enough to bank her wages would run away without them, probably a nasty one.

Chapter 5

'We still shouldn't jump to the conclusion that it's anything more than a runaway, though I agree there are certain worrying features.' DCI Morland tapped a pencil against his desk, looking sour. 'Sergeant Perry and DC Barnes should obviously have tried to talk to the mother alone at the start!'

'At that stage she wasn't ready to co-operate. Now she is, so we can go on from there,' Dan Crowe said.

They were at a hastily convened case meeting in Morland's office – Jane, Dan Crowe, and Kenny Barnes, with Steve Ryan included.

'I'd be in favour of pulling out a lot more of the stops and checking all the girl's last known movements,' Dan Crowe went on. 'It may not come to anything, but we don't want to lay ourselves open to accusations that we didn't even look for her.'

The DCI gave a noticeable twitch, which Dan Crowe took as agreement. 'Sergeant Perry's already covered a bit of the ground, fortunately, by talking to the girl's employer, on my say-so.' He put that in without a flicker. 'But we'll need to ask again. Family, friends, anyone else she might have talked to. Stick up her picture and we might just be lucky enough to find someone who saw her after she left work. And noticed which direction she was heading, whether she was with someone, whether she got into a car . . . What was her usual route home, do we know?'

'Mrs MacArthy thought she always took the bus from just beyond the roundabout, then walked through the short cut at the back of the estate. I've put it down in her statement.'

'That means the woods,' Kenny put in, offering his knowledge of the neighbourhood. 'The short cut. Daylight, though, if it was what, six-thirty? And there are always kids hurtling about up there pretending they're on trail-bikes, even at that time of day!'

'I'm going to need extra manpower if we have to start searching those woods. But I reckon we might look closer to home first and have another go at the stepfather. Don't you agree, sir? We've already caught him out in one lie, and there's been a whisper about domestic violence which is worth following up.' Dan Crowe said it without elaborating on where the whisper had come from, though Jane had given him all of it now. 'Pull him in and see what he's got to say about wanting the girl's absence kept quiet?'

'*Invite* him in. It's all still speculation at the moment, but I agree we ought to start pursuing enquiries. I suggest you put—'

'I'd like Sergeant Perry to stay on it, sir. She seems to have got the mother's trust. I'd reckon putting her in charge – reporting direct to me, of course.'

'If the stepfather has a tough reputation—'

'It's sometimes better to use a woman to defuse it, yes, I agree, sir. Anyway I'll give her Sergeant Ryan as back-up – the Super suggested they worked in tandem until he gets to know the district.'

Jane had known Dan Crowe could finagle, but she had never seen him cut the ground from under somebody's feet so blatantly before. He was leaning back in his chair as if it was settled. He glanced across at her and added, 'It's your weekend on duty, isn't it? Good, you won't have any plans you have to cancel, then. If it was me I'd see the stepfather tonight before he's had time to think up too many answers. Then start checking everything else tomorrow. You might find the kid somewhere safe and well; let's hope so! OK to go ahead, sir?'

58

'We seem to have wrapped up the general outline. Very well, make your enquiries, Sergeant Perry. And keep me informed. That seems to be all, and I've got an inter-departmental meeting in five minutes . . .'

'Thanks, Guv,' Jane said when the door was safely shut behind them.

'Don't thank me yet. Wait until you've done all the miles of trudging. And probably for nothing. God, if there's one thing I hate it's missing kids! Give me a straightforward robbery blag any day. As to that, I'll give Ron Dellow a ring and tell him I'm going to look into his smash-and-grab case myself. I've got all your notes, haven't I? Don't imagine I'm taking anything else off your desk, though. Well, get on, then!'

He had just stuck his neck out to stop the Deirdre case being taken away from her, so Jane certainly wasn't going to complain about being growled at. As the DI stamped away, Jane turned her head to the others.

'Steve and I may as well go straight to the Ribden Road estate. Mrs MacArthy promised to find me a good photo of Deirdre. Kenny – how are you fixed, are you going to have time to help with this one?'

'I'll do what I can. I've got several other things on, but I don't mind being involved in between.'

'Good. I'll probably want to know the names of some of the kids who play in those woods. I'm going to check with all the bus drivers first to see if there's one who can remember if Deirdre caught her usual bus that evening. Someone might if she was a regular. Anything else you've remembered about Michael MacArthy before I go and talk to him?'

'Nothing comes to mind. He's long-term unemployed and living on benefits, but we covered that before. Want me to try the Central Computer to see if he's known in any other manor?'

'Thanks, that'd be a help. I wonder if he's doing any kind of undeclared money-in-the-hand job? Put the word round and see if anyone knows. It could be useful to have something to threaten him with!' They had reached the CID room and Jane paused briefly, looking across at Kenny. 'By the way, were you serious when you said that any car left unattended up there might get vandalised?'

'Well, I'd certainly leave it where you can see it!'

'Thanks, I'll remember. I've had it under a year and I'd rather not get the paint scratched or wipers ripped off!' She glanced across at Steve and added, 'I suppose you don't want to take *your* wheels, whatever they are . . .?'

'We could. My transport's very second-hand, but it's got a Porsche engine, so I don't want that cut out and taken away either! I like to feel a bit of power under my foot,' he added, grinning at Kenny who had raised an eyebrow.

'We'll take mine,' Jane said, cutting off a possible discussion on the value of high-powered car engines. 'Shall we go?'

Speed under the bonnet of an ordinary-looking car – that somehow fitted with the rebel-image she had got of Steve Ryan so far. His air of controlled toughness might be a help with Michael MacArthy . . . as long as he stayed in the background unless or until she wanted him to use it. They were on the road before he spoke again.

'What has Humpty-Dumpty got against you?'

'That I'm a woman, and therefore only fit to make tea and soothe fevered brows!'

'Bad judge of character, that man. So Humpty-Dumpty wants you to stay in the background and be a traditional female, does he? A frustrating boss to find yourself lumbered with?'

'Luckily his predecessor was my gender, very good at her job, and earned herself a lot of liking and respect. So that means we start about even.' She wasn't going to begin sharing gripes with him. 'You'll have gathered the background to this case from the meeting, yes? Girl missing, reported by friend initially. Parents unco-operative until now. There's a brother, about a year older, who let it out to Kenny and me that the stepfather took his fists to the girl the night before she disappeared. How badly I don't know, the boy considered it mild. So now we're going to ask the stepfather for his version!'

'This is the man who lied about why she was missing? Hm. Standard reason?'

'You picked up that he'd been suggesting she was a bad girl, and that she might have gone off with some man? That said possible sexual abuse to me, too.' Jane paused, her eyes narrowing thoughtfully as she waited for a break in the traffic so as to turn into the estate. 'It does give a reason for Deirdre to take off. But without money or clothes . . . If it's true that she stayed out later than she's allowed on the night before she disappeared, and wouldn't say who she was with – the mother's version – that brings someone else we haven't heard about yet into the equation too. But I'm targeting Michael MacArthy first, obviously.'

'More often than not murder's close to home. You think the girl's dead, don't you.'

He made it a statement rather than a question. 'My instincts say so, though I'm hoping not,' Jane answered him, after a careful moment. 'Oh well, now we've got the mother's statement, we can at least start looking!'

And without letting any more time go by, either. Enough had already: almost two weeks since the girl had last been seen.

Jane pulled up at the end of Meadowtree Avenue, noting the dead-eyed blankness of the houses. It was the time when they were probably all about to eat tea in front of a flickering telly. Her eyes took in the visible strip of woodland too – where the short cut must be? Deirdre's usual route home . . . if, that night, she had ever got that far.

They were barely at number twenty's short front path when they heard the shouting from inside the house. Two voices rose and fell at high volume, male and female; if audible from here, surely deafening through the partition wall of the

61

adjoining semi. Not a front curtain twitched, however.

Jane lengthened her stride rapidly. Her finger pressed and held the door-bell and its continuing shrillness cut across a woman's brief scream, and a thud which could he heard clearly through the thin front door. A baby began an abrupt wailing somewhere above. The other voices had stopped, but there was a movement in the hall and the front door swung furiously open.

'Will you mind your own . . .'

The sight of them did at least stop Michael MacArthy in mid-snarl. He was breathing heavily. And Ruth MacArthy lay beyond him on the floor, sprawled clumsily like a badly-jointed doll and with a rapidly reddening mark across one cheek. Jane was past him with one arctic blue stare, and bent over to help the woman as she began to struggle to her feet.

'It's all right, Mrs MacArthy. It's Sergeant Perry again – I said I'd be round.' She steadied the woman and turned an icy gaze back on Michael MacArthy. 'If your wife wants to make a complaint against you, Mr MacArthy, Sergeant Ryan and I are right here and ready to hear it!'

'I – I don't—'

'I should think about that for a moment or two if I were you. Mr MacArthy, we've come here to ask you some questions about Deirdre, and to enquire why you lied to us about her whereabouts. In fact, we've come to invite you to come down to the station with us and answer a few questions. I imagine you'll be willing to do that?'

'Why should I?'

'Because we're asking you,' Steve Ryan put in from behind him, smoothly casual. Jane saw Michael MacArthy turn his head to size him up. For a moment Jane feared a macho confrontation, and she resumed the initiative with a deliberate coolness.

'If you want Deirdre found as much as we all do, Mr MacArthy, you won't mind answering some questions to help us. Though, of course, if your wife does care to make a complaint against you—'

'It's only that he has a temper,' Ruth MacArthy interrupted quickly. She shook off Jane's supporting hand and moved to her husband to lay her own hand pleadingly on his arm. 'Michael, I told you, it was the only thing to do to tell them the truth. It's for Deirdre's sake, I couldn't leave it any longer. I want her *found*. Michael . . .?'

'Oh, all right, woman, I'll answer any questions they want. I never said I wouldn't, did I?'

There was something like a bull on a tether in the way Michael MacArthy swung his black-curled head. For a flash of a second there was even a tiny fraction of shamefaced apology as he looked down into his wife's face and the rising bruise across her cheek. Whatever had been in his look was gone, however, as he raised his head again to look directly at Jane, with a narrow-eyed hostility which he seemed to be trying to mask.

'I was only trying to protect the girl, if she's got herself into some trouble! Can I be blamed for that? So what is it you want to ask me?'

'I'd like you to come down to the station and give us a full statement.'

'Then I will, for all the good it'll do. I haven't seen her any more than my wife has. But I'll come now and get it over with, if that's what you're asking.'

'Good. Sergeant Ryan will show you to the car. Mrs MacArthy, do you think I could see Deirdre's room? And did you manage to find me that photograph?'

'Yes, I did, it's the one she had taken at school. I'll fetch it after I've showed you her room . . .'

There was nothing much to be gleaned from Deirdre's room. A poster on the wall of a current pop star, and another smaller one of Patrick Swayze. A bag with school-books sticking out of it, wedged into the small space between the dressing-table and the bed; a hairbrush and comb set at random on the otherwise empty dressing-table top. A small wardrobe held a couple of cotton dresses and her school uniform. A teddy bear, old and battered and one-eyed, sat neatly at the head of the bed on top of a faded patchwork cover . . . Jane studied the room, then let Ruth MacArthy lead her out again and shut the door behind her. All the doors up here were shut and one of them had 'Shaun and Mina and Patrick' stuck on to it in crayoned and cut-out letters. Mrs MacArthy put her finger to her lips as they passed that, and the baby which had let out a cry earlier couldn't be heard now.

'Deirdre did that for the children's door . . . They're all sleeping, if you'll come down softly? And I'll fetch you that photograph now.'

Jane followed her downstairs and through into what must be the family sitting-room. It was shabbily furnished but clean and tidy, a playpen stacked full of bright toys in one corner, a giant television set with a video on the shelf beneath it in another. The video looked new and the most elaborately expensive model. Tucked away behind a settee there was a brand new sounds system too, still only half unpacked from its box. There must be money coming into the house from somewhere . . . Jane had her eyes guilelessly on Ruth MacArthy as the other woman turned back to her with a photograph in her hand.

'It's this year's and it's a good likeness . . .'

It was the standard school portrait, set into an oval of cardboard and showing a shy-looking girl with a round face, dark eyes, light-brown hair falling in a curly cascade to her shoulders. She was in school uniform, white shirt and neatly-tied striped tie, with the silvery gleam of a small medallion pulled out to lie on top of it. 'You don't mind if I keep this?' Jane asked. 'I'll get some copies made to circulate.'

'Yes, keep it. That's her St Christopher medal round her neck, she always wears it . . .' Ruth MacArthy's mouth was suddenly tightly buttoned as if she was holding back tears, but when she put a hand to her cheek she gave a small instinctive wince as her fingers touched the bruise. It gave Jane the lead she wanted.

'You know you don't have to put up with domestic violence, don't you? There are places you and the children could go—'

'Oh no, I wouldn't leave him! Michael's not a bad man, Miss – Sergeant – you mustn't think so! Tonight was just . . . he'll never raise a hand to the children, and not to me either in the usual way!'

'Really?' Ruth MacArthy's mutinous expression showed Jane she wasn't going to get anywhere, but it had been worth trying. 'When you say "the children", do you mean Jimmy and Deirdre as well?'

'He'll discipline Jimmy if he needs it. Deirdre's never—' She broke off, her eyes sliding away, and when they came back to Jane they were defensive. 'There's times a teenage girl will need a smack, but he'd never give her more than a small one! And not often, it was only the once – I mean, there's never been more than once or twice, and they were always on as good terms as ever after. You asked me that before, this afternoon, and I told you no!'

'I'd forgotten. Right, thank you for the photograph, and we'll do what we can. Oh – does Deirdre have a passport?'

'No . . . They just had a general one when they went on a school day-trip last year. She's never had one of her own. You don't think . . .?'

'I'm just covering everything,' Jane said reassuringly. She paused as she turned towards the door. 'Don't forget, if you ever do need anywhere for you and the children—'

'I won't. And please don't keep Michael long. He hasn't had his tea yet!'

For all her worn and frightened appearance, Ruth MacArthy could bite back quite sharply when she chose. 'We won't keep

65

him any longer than we need,' Jane replied politely, and let herself be ushered out. Past the kitchen. It wasn't big enough to hold a large freezer, anyway . . . Michael MacArthy was waiting in the car, in an apparently bored silence, to be taken to the station.

'We didn't get anywhere with him, did we?' she asked Steve much later, tapping the tape of the interview against her finger with weary exasperation. 'Is he very clever, or very stupid? Or sly mixed with stupid? There's *something* he's covering!'

'I agree. And if it's anything else he'd be stupid to conceal it, wouldn't he – when he must be able to see what we're going to suspect him of.'

'That's just it, isn't it? He doesn't seem to realise that we might suspect him of Deirdre's murder! I can't think of any approach I missed, can you?'

'No, you're good.' He said it without flattery, merely as a straight statement. 'Leave it for tonight? Show me a pub where we can get a drink?' He glanced at his watch. 'Hm, that'd have to be somewhere with a late licence by now. Do you have such things out here?'

'On a Friday night, yes, but they're full of disco-ing yuppies, so I think I'd rather give that a miss. Is it really that late? You won't have found somewhere to stay!'

'No, but I expect there *is* a bed in the Section House. Or someone can point me at a B and B where the owner keeps late hours. Unless you're offering me a piece of your floor?'

'Sorry, can't I'm afraid. My flat-mate's also my landlady and I can't lend out her floor unasked.' It made a good enough excuse not to let him get any ideas. She'd found him easy to work with tonight; his mind moved with the same quickness as her own. He was watching her now, sprawled at his ease, a roughening of stubble shadowing his chin and making him look more like a villain than a villain-catcher.

'No husband and no full-time boyfriend you're living with either? You said "landlady",' he added, as she raised an eyebrow.

'Someone I was at university with, who happens to live down here. She's as careerist as I am.' That should make things clear. 'Do you always ask so many direct questions?'

'When I want to know. The next one wasn't going to be, "Are you a lesbian?" I've got beyond those teenage tricks!'

'So I should hope. It wouldn't be your business if I was, anyway, would it?' And then she was caught into a sudden laugh, almost a choke. 'Though there'd be a lot of people—'

'A lot of people what?'

'A lot of people desperately disappointed if my flat-mate was! Nothing – a private joke.' What had made her laugh was the sudden vision of Matty's pining cohort of admirers. 'Why should you think I ought to be living with a man, just as a matter of interest?'

'All right, it was a stupid thing to say. Just a way of finding out, that's all!' He raised a hand as if to defend himself, grinning, not a whit disturbed. 'I'd be bound to want to, wouldn't I? Considering the packaging!'

'If that's meant to be a compliment, I'll tell you your packaging isn't too bad either. But I never mix work and play. Now we've got that cleared up, shall we leave it there? I wish to hell we'd got Michael MacArthy cleared up,' she added, brooding back on to tonight's interview. 'Half the time it felt like trying to drill a hole into a block of wood!'

'Tomorrow may give us something.' They both began to move. They had come back into the interview room to clear it after they had let Michael MacArthy go, and Steve reached out his hand to pick up the tape recorder. 'I'll take this back to the equipment room and log it back in. Yes, I can find the way!'

'I'd have thought you could by now. You've been thrown in

67

at the deep end ever since you arrived, and you seem to have survived! We're not always this busy. Like everywhere else, it goes in phases.'

'And you did warn me the provinces aren't necessarily the place for a quiet life.' He said it with an easy grin, his eyes lingering on her again, in a way which made her gather up the tape and her notes with a determined briskness.

'I'm just going to file these, and then I'm going home!'

She wasn't Steve Ryan's nursemaid, and had no inclination to behave like one, so she wouldn't show any more concern about where he was going to sleep. Let him sort that out with the duty sergeants.

Over the weekend they arranged to get out the fliers carrying Deirdre's picture and description and *'Have you seen this girl?'* They talked to Crayshaw's Saturday staff, who said Deirdre had seemed exactly the same as usual, quiet and willing. The Saturday manager said she had paid Deirdre out of the safe at her going-home time, and she supposed the girl had left the office straight after that. She couldn't be absolutely sure because a client had come in just then, and Deirdre would have gone out at the back, via the car park. She had been surprised when Deirdre hadn't turned up the following Saturday, and might have rung her home number to see if she was ill, but she had been busy and let the chance slip past. She might have asked Mr Crayshaw what to do about it if he'd been there, but he was out all that day playing in a golf tournament with his son. He was expected in today, but not until later. The only thing which differed from Mr Crayshaw's own account was that Deirdre had worked in the office for five months, not 'three or four'.

Jane gathered that Deirdre had been liked by the other staff, but no one had known her particularly well. She left them to buzz in muted excitement and round-eyed concern, promising they'd report anything they thought of.

At the bus station, next, Jane learned that the driver who

covered Deirdre's regular route home had gone away on holiday three days earlier.

And Michael MacArthy had no previous record anywhere, according to the Central Computer.

Who had Deirdre been out with on that last Friday night? Not Shelley, who had been at a swimming gala. Not a boyfriend Shelley appeared to know about, because she had shaken her head and then burst into tears and been beyond further questioning; Jane had had to let Mrs Cura lead her away. Shelley had already said she 'couldn't remember' what they had talked about on the Saturday lunch-time, but it wasn't any plan for Deirdre to run away . . . There was no pub, club, or teenage disco which could remember seeing a girl resembling Deirdre's photograph on the Friday night, when Jane and Steve tried all the ones she could think of within the city limits.

'We've got three people who say she was out that night, and half a hundred who saw no sign of her,' Jane remarked sourly, pulling off a shoe to rub her aching foot.

'So she went somewhere private. Or somewhere outside the city, by car. At least I'm getting an orientation tour; I reckon I know my way round pretty well by now.' Steve cocked an eyebrow at her. 'Back to the office?'

'May as well. I'll write all this up. Let's hope the posters bring something in over the next few days.'

'Show me somewhere we can have something to eat tonight on me?'

'Thanks but no thanks. I've got things to do at home. Try Mike, he knows all the best haunts. Oh no, he's off this weekend. Well, ask around.'

'Are you really going to refuse to socialise with me outside working hours?'

'I don't socialise, I just work and sleep. No, sorry, I'm not just giving you a stand-off. I really do have things to do tonight. And you'll see quite enough of me, if we're going to be trudging through this case together.'

'And the others. Anything else you're working on, that I'm supposed to help you with until I find my feet,' he reminded her.

'Oh, yes. Well I'd say you'll be sent out on your own pretty quickly, or with one of the DCs. You seem to be pretty quick to fit in!' She had already seen him in easy conversation with several people around the station. His silence made her turn her head to look at him across the car in which they were sitting, and she studied his expression. 'Oh no, you're not going to play little boy lost! With what I've seen of you since yesterday, that won't wash!'

'I was afraid it wouldn't, but you can't say I don't try.'

'And a bit too bloody quick off the mark, too!' But she was unable to keep from laughing. Damn the man, he really was attractive – better than she'd seen for some time. Amusing, quick, up-front but with an air of hidden depths, interesting – and making it obvious he was interested. No, she would *not* fall into that trap, just for a pair of quizzical grey eyes, a sexy grin, and a body which moved like a cat. 'Go and set tongues wagging by cutting a swathe through the uniform girls, if you must have company!' she told him.

'I thought the civilian secretaries looked more promising, myself. Unless they're all married or spoken for!'

'Goodness, do you draw the line? No, forget I said that! And just don't make waves; otherwise I won't enquire what you're getting up to! Now, didn't we say we were heading back to the office?'

Sparring with him was more amusing than it ought to have been, but she would stick to work, thanks. Reputations could end up in tatters all too easily around any station, and Morland would love to have his prejudices justified. Jane spent the rest of the afternoon at her desk, and went home for the evening to wash her hair.

* * *

Sunday brought them nothing. They looked through what they'd got so far, and went out to talk to a student who'd been roughed up, but refused to make a formal complaint. He was gay, Jane assessed. They came back to an office which seemed preternaturally quiet. Jane busied them both by taking Steve through the current files. He was percipient and quick to catch on, she found. Well, she would have expected that, from what she'd seen of him to date . . . How long would he be with them, she wondered – and then was annoyed with herself for wondering. OK, so she liked him, his rebel-streak included; that still didn't mean she was going to succumb to his suggestion that she might help him, tomorrow, in his hunt for a flat or a room. Nor would she take him up on the casual suggestion (again) that she should show him a place where they could both eat tonight. No socialising – and ignore his amused, rueful look, and her own hastily suppressed feeling of regret. Working hours were the only time she was going to spend with Steve Ryan, and if her Monday off in lieu of the weekend seemed suddenly to yawn with a boring emptiness, maybe something in the Deirdre case would break, to call her back in.

Nothing did. There was no instant response to the posters, strategically placed around the city by Monday morning; no one came forward to say they'd seen her, or anyone looking like her. It was as if, on the night before her disappearance and on the Saturday evening itself, Deirdre MacArthy had moved through other people's lives as invisibly as a ghost.

It wasn't until Thursday that the body of a girl was found, in a ditch next to a lay-by on one of the side-roads leading out towards the coast.

Chapter 6

'She must have been dumped from a car, but there aren't any relevant tyre tracks,' the SOCO told Jane. He was in his thirties and practical-looking: since the Scene-of-Crimes-Officer job had been civilianised all sorts of people had come into it, but they all had the same air of detached competence. 'I shouldn't come too close if I were you. The pathologist reckoned she's been dead at least a couple of weeks.'

'The pathologist's already been and gone? That was quick.'

'He lives in one of the villages near here and they caught him on his morning off.' The SOCO picked up something with tweezers and dropped it into a small plastic bag. 'Be finished here in a minute.'

'Is she still identifiable?'

'Oh yes, she's not that far gone, and her face hasn't been damaged.' He turned his head to look up at Jane. 'You've got someone missing? Well, have a look when I'm through. We've covered the immediate area, but I'm just getting samples of the dust and threads off her clothes for forensic. The body's been kept somewhere dry before she was wrapped up in the black plastic sacks. Brought out here some time before the rain on Tuesday, though, as the ground's dry underneath her. It's lucky we're not having a wet summer, it makes the timing easier to pinpoint.'

'Is she wearing a St Christopher medal? On a chain round her neck?'

'Haven't seen one. She's young – does that fit? But no jewellery at all. Half a mo, I'll look again, but the dog didn't

73

disturb anything much . . . No, nothing round her neck, or fallen in amongst her clothes. All right, you can see her now, and then we'll get her bagged up and taken in.'

The body had been found by a Mrs Harcourt who had stopped her car in everyday innocence to let her corgi out for a pee. She was back at the police station now, white and shocked. Jane stepped across the taped barrier and moved carefully down the steep incline of rough grass and tangled weeds. A sickeningly-sweet stench made her hold her breath as she bent down to look at the face surrounded by brown curly hair. Yes, it was recognisably Deirdre, even with the sunken cheeks and the half-closed eyes; a bony travesty of the girl in the photograph, but her none the less. In contrast to the sunken face, her body had begun to bloat under the white blouse and short pink skirt. But the face looked almost tranquil – apart from a heavy dent surrounded by dark bruising above one temple.

'The pathologist thought that blow on the head could be what killed her,' the SOCO said, 'not that they ever like being definite until they've had the body in for full examination. You can see there aren't any strangulation marks, anyway. And she's still got her knickers on. Seen enough? At least she hasn't been slashed about like the other one—' He glanced up at Jane's exclamation and added, 'The Dover girl? You haven't had a report circulated on her yet? Well, she was only found two days ago, though she'd been dead longer than this one.'

'Dumped like this one?' Jane asked sharply.

'No, found in the cellar of a half derelict factory between Dover and Folkestone. She'd been there a few weeks, to judge by the state of her. Hands and feet tied before death, knife slashes in her clothes as well as on her face and body, but she had been strangled as well as cut. They're pulling in known sex-offenders, I heard, though they don't know of anyone with that particular MO. She'd been pretty thoroughly roughed up. Have you finished here?'

74

'Yes. Thanks. And thanks for the info about the other girl.' Two girls, that put a different complexion on things, and she'd have to get on to Dover fast for their report. Different, or the same perpetrator?

The ambulance men came clumping down as Jane withdrew; a lot of moving feet in regulation wellingtons, manoeuvres with a stretcher and a body-bag. A young constable set to guard the taped area turned his eyes away with a forced casualness in an attempt not to look as queasy as he felt, apparently absorbed in studying a fluffy white cloud high above, almost as if he expected a clue to appear from it in sky-writing. Jane didn't let her breath out until she reached her car, and even then the sweetness of decay seemed to linger in her nostrils.

At least two weeks dead . . . The autopsy would tell them more, but it seemed her fears had been right. Deirdre had been dead all along.

And so had another girl, only a few miles away, left in a cellar with multiple knife slashes. A coincidence, or a double killing?

In Deirdre's case, it appeared someone had kept the body hidden and then – when her absence became public? – when it was obvious a search was beginning? – had brought it out here to get rid of it somewhere public and anonymous. Had not even tried to bury it, just dumped it rapidly, wrapped up to look like any other unwanted rubbish.

Jane drove steadily back into the city, trying to concentrate on the road. A young girl, quiet and ordinary, who kept an old teddy bear on her bed and drew coloured letters for her little brothers and sister . . . It was no use to let judgement be clouded by anger; this was just another case, to be worked on like a jigsaw puzzle, each small piece needing to be found and identified and fitted into place.

By afternoon she had rung Dover with an urgent request for a copy of the written report on their murder case, and had made promises to pass over information on Deirdre in return. And by the following morning a lot of other practical things had been organised, too: space had been made for an Incident Room, a VDU was in place and a card carrousel, maps and photographs and lists of Deirdre's last known movements had gone up on the walls, and there were specially manned telephones *in situ*.

Someone in public relations was seeing to the press, including the local television station, because Mrs Harcourt had told a friend who had told another friend who had known someone who was a TV reporter . . . Dover was still managing to keep a press clamp-down on their murder, but it was unlikely to be long before that leaked out too and set up a baying in the local papers; possibly even the nationals, unless they had too many juicy news stories in other parts of the country to distract them. Ruth and Michael MacArthy had been to the morgue to identify the dead girl, and had been seen briefly on the morning news, both of them in tears. There had been shots of the school too, and an attempt to interview some of the pupils going in until the headteacher had stepped in to stop it.

DCI Morland had dropped into the Incident Room but had soon gone away again, and it was Dan Crowe who addressed the assorted company pulled in to work on the case.

'Right, we're waiting for the autopsy report which should be in today – I hope – but we do know we've got a body.' He pointed to the photographs. 'That's our victim, and that's what she looked like when she was found. DS Perry's been in charge of things so far, and she'll go on organising the legwork along with DS Ryan – you all know Sergeant Ryan by now, don't you? They'll both be reporting to me, and I'll pass things on up to the DCI and Superintendent Annerley. So – Sergeant Perry?'

Jane took up a position at the front of the room and glanced at Dan Crowe, waiting to start on his nod. 'OK. What the DI didn't tell you was that Dover's got a body too. Also a young girl, almost certainly killed some days before ours. They may or may not be connected. Until we can be certain, it's been decided that we're going to pursue our own enquiries as if they're separate incidents. There's enough that isn't the same and that's the way we're playing it. Now, to tell you what's been done so far, we started out by investigating Deirdre MacArthy as a missing person . . .'

She ran through everything they knew, what questions had been asked, who made up the cast of characters. 'What we need to find is anyone who saw Deirdre after she left work that evening,' she summed up. 'And, of course, we need to identify this A.N. Other she's supposed to have been out with the previous evening. She may have arranged to meet him again the following day. If he exists at all. We want a house-to-house in Watt Street and on the Ribden Road estate, to find out if anyone at all saw her on the Saturday evening. So far the last sighting of her was at Crayshaw's office just before she left work. We also want anything known about the stepfather's movements, for obvious reasons. Yes?'

'Would his wife cover for him?'

'It's hard to tell. So far I've had to conclude no, not if she actually knew he'd harmed the girl. I think she'd defend him against anything else, but not that. She did collude in covering up Deirdre's absence in the beginning, but she seems genuinely to believe it wasn't anything to do with her husband. We've had him in a second time, as I've said. And we've gone over his car with a fine-tooth comb. We still got nothing. Guv?'

'I got no more out of him than the sergeants did on the first interview – except an admission that he did give the girl a smacking on the Friday night. Otherwise, just a lot of noise and angry innocence, and a lot of alibis for any time of the day I cared to mention. Too many, if you ask me, and he was sweating blood by the time I'd finished! But nothing we could hold him on.'

'If it's a sex attack, are we going to look at known offenders?'

'We won't know until we get the autopsy report,' Jane answered the questioner. 'She was found fully clothed. That would make it unusual. When the report arrives, if there's any mention of signs of rape or attempted, we'll certainly want to look at anyone local with a record of sex offences. However, for the moment, we particularly want to establish three things. Where and when Deirdre was last seen. Where she went on the Friday night, and with whom. And where her body could have been hidden after she was killed, and before it was dumped. An empty house or a lock-up? A car boot for the whole time? Some derelict building? There has to be someone, somewhere, who noticed something unusual: let's try to find that someone!'

'Sergeant Perry?' It was the uniform girl, Rachel Welsh, who had put up a hesitant hand. 'Are we assuming the murd . . . the perpetrator's someone local? I mean, if she was kept somewhere after she was killed, and then dumped, it would have to be someone local, wouldn't it?'

'That's how it looks. If it was a casual pick-up by someone passing through – offering her a lift, say – they'd have to come back to dump her. We don't know that someone didn't do that, of course. A lot of people are very mobile nowadays. Dover, by the way, know their girl was killed where she was found. That's one of the differences between the cases. Now—' Jane looked round. 'Any more questions from anyone? OK, that's all we've got for now. Guv?'

'You all know what to do, so let's get on with it,' Dan Crowe said, bringing things to a close. 'Anything you find out, bring it back here to be collated. Thanks, everyone!'

Kenny drifted over as the team was leaving. 'You said this morning you wanted to ask me something about Crayshaw's?' he asked, raising an eyebrow.

'It was just something which made me wonder. Background stuff. The Crayshaws – well off? Happily married? All that?'

78

'Mrs Crayshaw's wealthy in her own right. She put her money into the business but has plenty left over. I can't remember which family she comes from; something county-ish . . . They won't be short of a bob or two whether the property market's high or low, and the kids go to private schools. That's all I can tell you about them, really.'

'Mm. It wasn't that important, just a detail. Oh, you won't forget to see if your snouts have anything on where Michael MacArthy might be getting extra cash from, will you?'

'This "legacy" he tried to persuade the guv he'd inherited? That stuff in his house isn't listed as stolen, but someone's certainly been paying him off for something! I'm on it, and Mike and Gary are listening out too.'

The first day wound its way through. Jane and Steve went to Crayshaw's again, where Mr Crayshaw was absent, the staff subdued, the office manager defensive.

'Mr Crayshaw's had summer flu all week, and this isn't going to make him feel any better, is it? I really can't see why anybody thinks it's anything to do with us, just because he was kind enough to give a young girl a job. I didn't even know her myself, as I don't work weekends! And I'm sorry if you think I'm unsympathetic, but the local press is going to blow it out of all proportion, and give us a bad name!'

'Funny how some people react,' Steve said drily as they left the estate agent's with a short list of empty properties, various sets of keys, and the bristling assurance that no one would have had access to them anyway, but since a phone call to the Crayshaw home had confirmed they should be handed over, here they were. 'Did it strike you that she was angrier because Mrs Crayshaw had been in this morning than she was about anything else?'

'She doesn't like her employer's wife interfering, certainly. But otherwise . . . oh, she's probably scared, like the rest of them. It's a reminder of being at risk, isn't it?' The office manager had been young, and good looking in a rather over

79

made up way, and her hardness had definitely struck Jane as being put on.

'I'll be as surprised as she is if we do find Deirdre's body was stashed in one of these,' she added as they approached the first property on their list. 'It'd be a lot too obvious, wouldn't it? But we still need to rule them out.'

There was nothing to be found in any of the empty Crayshaw properties. Nothing amongst bare rooms, or rooms left partially furnished, or rooms with violent-patterned carpets and garish wallpaper.

'Would *you* buy anything from someone with that kind of taste?' Jane asked Steve at one point, gazing in appalled fascination at an artificial stone inglenook decorated with sea shells. Nothing in cellars or attics, and no sign that anyone had recently cleaned any empty room too thoroughly either. Jane hadn't thought there would be; it was merely a place to start. The first rule of detection: cover all the bases, see what it isn't, see what you're left with.

The MacArthy house had already been searched, politely but thoroughly, with the explanation that the police were merely looking for any clue Deirdre might have left concerning her private life. They had drawn a blank, with no diary or note to be found amongst Deirdre's things.

The autopsy report, commendably quick, arrived as the day was ending. Jane ran through it, frowning, picking her way through the medical details, then handed it to Steve.

'No bruising to thighs or stomach, no signs of forced sexual congress,' he read out, flipping through. 'Not a virgin, however. Not pregnant. Not strangled. Not asphyxiated. It's giving us mainly nots, isn't it? Death caused by a blow to the anterior something-or-other causing internal bleeding to the brain, administered in an upward direction . . . a heavy instrument, probably metal, with a sharp corner on it. Difficult to strike upwards with something heavy.'

'Just after that it says, query wound caused by *fall*.'

'She fell and hit her head? But someone else must have been there . . . Had probably been having sexual intercourse regularly, but not immediately before death. Hadn't eaten for several hours before death, estimated date . . . yes, that fits in with when she disappeared. Pooling of blood shows the body was kept in a folded position after death. So. What have we got that we didn't have before? That it wasn't a rape, though it may have been an intended one except she died first. That—'

'That I'll need to talk to Shelley again! Deirdre's not supposed to have had a regular boyfriend. But according to this . . .'

'She either did, or it was long-term abuse. She probably wouldn't have told even her best friend if it was that – they usually don't, from what I've read. Are we getting Michael MacArthy even more squarely in the frame? No point in questioning him again yet, though.'

'Comparing this with the Dover case, the only thing that's the same is that neither of them were raped. I suppose you could call it a common factor. And they've decided the other girl was also killed by a blow, after being slashed before and afterwards, and then strangled as well for good measure . . . I wonder. If it is the same guy, could he have been interrupted when he was with Deirdre? Didn't have time to do any more to her, simply shoved her in the boot of his car, say, and left her there for several days? I wish the forensic report on the samples the SOCO took from her clothes had come in. It might give us some clue as to where the body was kept!'

'You're turning away from Michael MacArthy again?'

'No, just keeping my options open.' It would be all too easy to let her dislike of Michael MacArthy colour her thinking. And there was a part of her which said he was too obvious – against the other part which told her that murder, in the main, often did come down to the obvious suspect. 'They know who the Dover girl was now, by the way. Eighteen and living in digs, looking for work. Not reported missing because her landlady thought she "might have found a chambermaid job or something". There doesn't seem to be any connection with Deirdre or with any of the MacArthys. No, we'll have to go on treating the cases as separate.' Jane sighed, a frustrated gust of air. 'What we need is a sighting!'

'But we haven't got one, and it's packing up time for today.' Steve came to his feet and reached out a hand to pull Jane to hers. 'The collators haven't got anything more for us, so it's time to drop it for tonight, right? You know what they say – don't take your cases personally, and don't take them home with you?'

'I'm not a rookie,' Jane said drily.

'I didn't say you were.'

'But that I was taking this one personally? I'm not. Shall we go out and eat? Or have you got something else planned?'

'No, and I was just going to suggest it.' He didn't make a point out of her change of heart, either. Jane knew it had been an impulse; they had been together all day, why should the evening matter? 'What do you fancy?' he asked. 'Pizza? Italian? Indian? Chinese? One thing I have noticed about this city, it's got a fair variety of places to eat!'

'Thai,' she said, grinning, because it was one he hadn't mentioned. 'It's only just down the road and it's not expensive! No, seriously, if you don't fancy it, pizza's fine by me.'

'Stop imagining I might only have commonplace tastes, or I'll insist we drive to the coast and look for a winkle stall!'

They went to the Thai restaurant, and ate cracked crab and ginger in the dim interior with its small, silent, oriental waiters. They didn't talk about the case, though they did slide into shop – which district she had worked in in the Met, what had made her choose police work when she might have been a lawyer instead. She challenged him to describe his childhood, so that she could see if the child was father to the man. He gave her an easy thumbnail sketch of football played around the concrete pile of a block of council flats, the automatic 'borrowing' of any unattended bike to see who could do the highest wheelie on it, a pilfering ring to see who could lift most out of the local corner shop . . . Winter days which started well before dawn because his father's work as a meat-porter started at four a.m., but the advantage of getting taken to afternoon dog races when his father got home at two.

'When you weren't at school?'

'Before I was old enough to go. Watching the greyhounds and hearing about their racing form is one of my earliest memories.' He grinned at her. 'It occurs to me, if you'd grown up where I did we'd probably have sat next to each other in infant school. At least in mine they always insisted on putting us alphabetically by surname, so P and R would have been together. I'd have been the one pinching your crayons and pulling your hair. What's the joke?'

'The thought of you in my first school. You wouldn't exactly have fitted. It was all-female, and full of very small Saudi princesses.' She saw his eyebrows lift, and knew she'd have to explain. 'My father was seconded to Riyadh at the time as a military adviser. And after that we were in Sweden because he was doing something for the UN, and then after a brief spell in Italy on NATO liaison we moved to Germany. We were quite a while there because it was a senior posting. We did move around quite a bit.'

'A travelling childhood. Did you end up in a posh boarding-school?'

'No, I went to international schools wherever we were. As a result I seemed to take half my classes in French as a first language, but that's another story. It was my little sister who drew the boarding-school straw, once she was eleven or so. She's ten years younger than me and approaching A levels.' And flew out to New Zealand only for the long summer holidays, spending other vacations with their mother's numerous Scottish relatives. Jane was guiltily aware that she hadn't seen Chloe for innumerable months, but the age gap between them did yawn. 'Do you have brothers and sisters?'

'Several, all married, and all of them keep giving me nieces and nephews, whose birthdays I always forget.' He leaned back, watching her curiously. 'You know, after seeing you work, I'm more and more mystified that you didn't stay with the Met – where all the ambitious ones are? What happened, did you get on the wrong side of someone?'

'All right, if you really want to know, I just got tired of the hidden agenda! You know, the one which says women are all right in the Domestic Violence Unit, or in Rape Crisis, or just about OK in collating if they can get their pretty little heads round the computers, but not in real CID work! Not in undercover, unless of course you happen to want to use one as a decoy – nor, heaven forbid, in any of the special units. All right, you may well raise an eyebrow considering I shifted myself out of the Met only to end up with our present not-so-beloved DCI!'

'Far be it from me to point out the obvious.' But he was giving her a wicked grin, fair enough when she had let her own wry exasperation sound clearly. 'You actually thought it would be better in the provinces? Why? Less competition?'

'No, simpler than that. There was a female DCI in charge then – well, the rest is history.' She pulled a face. At least he hadn't tried to deny that the force did operate on a system of male brotherhood which guarded itself against female inclusion in every petty way it could. 'What are you going to say,' she challenged, 'that all that men's locker-room stuff is perfectly fair, because what women really want out of life is to get married and raise children, so there's no actual point in promoting them? Don't even start on that hoary old myth!'

'I've known some very good married lady cops,' he said mildly, and put up a hand as if defending himself. 'Don't shoot at me, I'm not the enemy! I won't even call you a raging feminist—'

'No, don't: I'm a human-ist.' She began to calm down, and gave him a grin. 'You asked . . .'

'I did. What special unit in the Met would you like to have got into? Drugs? Armed Response? Counter-terrorist? – oh no, they're still deciding whether SO 13's going to stay with us or go over entirely to MI5, aren't they, so no openings there. What would you have fancied, given the chance?'

'None of them particularly. I'd just like to have known I could join them, without being blocked. Other than that, I'm happy getting my head down in CID – but with the chance of being taken seriously! Come on, you know perfectly well how it works!'

'I suppose so. I've never had to think about it.'

'No, you wouldn't!' She gave him a resigned look, half-humorous, aware that she didn't really want to quarrel with him. 'So what about you? Any particular ambitions?'

'Staying out of disciplinary hearings.' He grinned at her as if the thought didn't actually trouble him much, then added, 'Working on the ground – not getting lumbered with too much paperwork – not landing up behind a desk. Can't say I'm too likely to get promoted behind a desk, that's for sure! Carry your bags, ma'am, when you're made a Superintendent?'

'Thank you, Sergeant, I'll remember the offer when I get that far.' Her eyes met his amused ones. 'Very little bothers you, does it?'

'Oh, some things. You know, when you were being so militant just now, I could really see you as a daughter of the army! What rank did you say your father was?'

'I didn't. Anyway I'm not at all like him. I'm supposed to look exactly like my mother did when young. But she was no slouch either, she can knock spots off most people when it comes to getting things done her way!' Jane grinned, then glanced up, suddenly aware of someone hovering not too distantly. The place had nearly emptied, only themselves and a couple in the corner left, and a lurking waiter was trying not to look hopeful that he could soon close. 'Oh, it's late, isn't it? I'll split—'

'No you won't, this one's on me. You can do the next one,' Steve added, 'so you can stop looking as if it's male chauvinism!'

He was laughing at her. Jane decided not to argue, since he was brandishing a wallet full of notes and she only had a small amount of cash with her, and a credit card would have meant a lot of fiddling around. And she wasn't unwilling that there should be a 'next time', or an excuse for it. What was happening to her sensible principles?

Out in the dark night air, among the smells of summer and street dust, they strolled through the patches of light from uncurtained windows and decoratively antique street lamps, moving in an easy silence towards the street where they had left both cars. A scattering of stars could be seen high up between the buildings, and the dryness of the night caught Jane in a reminder. Rain rare enough this year so that the SOCO had been sure Deirdre MacArthy's body had been dumped before Tuesday . . . The thought sobered her to an infinitesimal sigh, and she glanced at the man beside her.

'It's a weird job we do, isn't it? We spend most of our time seeing human nature at its worst. But we're told, and trained, to switch off. D'you ever feel it's not so easy to do that and stay human too – that one day you might end up with no feelings at all?'

'Who doesn't? No, I'll put it another way. Anyone who doesn't carry that kind of concern could be heading for psychopathology. Keeping the balance takes practice. So they say.' He turned his head towards her. 'You know what your voice reminds me of? Cut glass – that really good, fancy kind.'

'It does not!'

'Oh yes – when you're not deliberately toning it down! There's no need to bristle, it's not a criticism. I like it. Wouldn't do you any good under deep cover, though,' he added mischievously. 'But then, neither would the cut-glass looks, much too hard to disguise!'

'Whereas you could go anywhere and do anything? Are you

by any chance being classist now, as well as sexist?'

'No, just appreciative.' His hand brushed her arm, a casual move, but a sudden warning about where his thoughts might be heading. Towards a pleasant end to a pleasant evening . . . A wistful twinge reminded her of sexual starvation, but bed was not going to be the final item on tonight's menu. Definitely, absolutely not. Even though she had to crush a treacherous thought which said that was a pity and a waste.

'Thanks for tonight. I've enjoyed it,' she said with deliberately calm friendliness as they reached her car. 'By the way, I've never asked you, how did you get your bullet? The one you've been recovering from?'

'Oh, that.' He paused, his eyes catching the light as he studied her. 'It's actually rather a different story. I shot someone rather than getting shot. A security van heist was going down, and we'd been warned, so we were carrying. Unfortunately the man I got was the one who wasn't tooled up. There's no argument about whether he was one of the villains, but they're still trying to decide whether I jumped in too fast. Shocked?'

'No, of course not, it happens. That was what you meant about disciplinary hearings? You're threatened with one?' Perhaps that was why Dan Crowe had reacted so grumpily to the new arrival: he must know about it, and probably didn't like the idea of their force being used as a dumping-ground for someone else's mistakes. 'So you've been on a suspension rather than a convalescence?'

'Yes. I think they must have got tired of arguing about it, since they sent me down here for this temporary posting – out of sight out of mind? The guy didn't die, anyway, I only winged him rather badly. So, anyway, here I am – which does have its advantages . . .'

Maybe he'd had to confess in case they moved on to a state of intimacy where he'd have a lack of scars to explain. Jane kept her face deadpan, despite a flicker of amusement. 'I'll keep shtum,' she assured him, then added sweetly, 'Unless

87

you were hoping I would mention to the civilian secretaries that you're not an invalid after all? Let me know if you've got a particular favourite into whose shell-like you want me to drop an innocent word. Goodnight, Steve. Sleep well, and thanks again for this evening!'

'You're more than welcome.' He sketched her a salute as she opened her car door, his expression suggesting he was accepting defeat quizzically.

If only temporarily.

As she drove away he was still standing there beside his own car, and gave her an amused and mocking wave.

Chapter 7

Shelley had been in a constant flood of tears ever since Deirdre's body had been found. She had also, according to her mother, been refusing to speak at all. 'I've tried to get her to talk, it seemed the best way,' Mrs Cura told Jane worriedly; but even Jane's most gentle questioning had elicited nothing but tightly closed lips, and then another collapse into tears. There was nothing to be learned from her on whether Deirdre had actually had a boyfriend, or even (very carefully) on whether she had ever mentioned 'that sort of trouble at home' – though there had been a very sharp-eyed look from Mrs Cura after that question, and a tightlipped promise to see if she could get any more out of her daughter. That was where it had to be left. It was frustrating, when there was something about Shelley which made Jane suspect she did know something. Surely there had been the beginnings of a sharp shake of the head at the question about sexual abuse? But it was impossible to force an answer out of the child. Why wouldn't Shelley help?

The forensic report came in, but that gave them little that was helpful. There were no fingerprints on the black plastic sacks, which were standard issue. The body had been kept somewhere dry. There were some threads of sacking on Deirdre's clothes, also dry earth and traces of chemical fertiliser dust. There had been a small piece of straw or 'treated vegetable fibre' in her hair; an inch-long yellow strip with rough ends, it was sent with the report, in a small sealed plastic bag.

'There's an old barn in the woods behind the Ribden Road estate!' Kenny said, snapping his fingers. But a search team, sent up there, found the barn no longer had any doors, and was used all the time as a play-area by the local children. There was nowhere inside it that a body could have lain without being found. The MacArthy house possessed no garden shed which might have held chemical fertiliser, and neither did any of its neighbours.

'I still think a car boot's the most likely.' Kenny again. 'I keep an old sack in mine, for putting under the wheels if I'm bogged down somewhere. You could find garden fertiliser in a boot if someone had been buying it sometime, and it'd explain the body's folded-up position, too, wouldn't it?'

'Yes. But what car, is what we want to know! And wouldn't there be something else – a trace of oil, rubber-dust from the spare wheel, anything . . .? Sorry,' Jane said, knowing her voice had been too impatient. 'It's still a good suggestion, and I'm grateful for any input you can give. Steve, what did the guv say about my going to see Mr Crayshaw at his home? I know Morland won't like it, but Crayshaw's still away from work, and there are a few more things I'd like to ask him!'

'The DI says OK, but handle with care. I told him we would – extreme caution for the local nob!'

'Let's go, then – you'll come? It'll look better with two of us, and you can see what you think of him, too.'

She wasn't ruling Anthony Crayshaw out completely: even respectable Rotary Clubbers and personal friends of the Chief Super could have their weaknesses. And things to hide. Not that she could quite see Anthony Crayshaw hitting a young girl on the head – hitting anyone . . . Her remembered impression brought out a softness about him under the hearty bluster.

'We'll just say we're checking Deirdre's times of work again,' she told Steve as they drove up the hill towards the smart southern end of the city. 'It's worth taking another look at him – though I certainly wouldn't dare ask if I can examine the boot of *his* car. Not without very strong grounds, anyway!'

90

'Or search his garden shed, if he's got one? I wonder what he's suffering from to keep him away from work this long? Summer flu, did his office manager say?'

'Yes, but I'm hoping he'll be out of bed by now.' They pulled up outside the house Jane had been looking for. 'Hm, not as large as I'd have expected him to have, though perhaps it's described as "a gem". Get those beams – genuine Tudor? And it all looks very just-so, doesn't it?'

But in the best of taste. Set back from the road with a prettily-paved, rose-bushed front garden – and no front hedge, perhaps to show it off – the Crayshaw house had the restrained elegance of something very well maintained, looking superior even to its neighbours in the quiet residential road. A double-garage had been added to one side, but was built in muted, rose-tinted old brick so as not to spoil the overall effect. The garage doors were open with one car visible in the shadows within and another, an expensive and sporty-looking model, standing on the tarmac area which lay in front.

'Here we go, then.'

She had almost expected the front door to be opened by a maid. It wasn't: to Jane's discreet pressure on a small white bell-push the finely carved wood swung back to reveal against the dark interior a figure whose well-cut skirt and silk blouse instantly said 'couture'. Grey-blonde hair, short and casually upswept but obviously cut by a top stylist; an aquiline face discreetly made up to show off high cheekbones; piercing and rather bad tempered hazel eyes, slightly narrow-set and with a line graven between the brows.

'Mrs Crayshaw?' Jane asked, guessing.

'Yes?'

'Good morning, I'm so sorry to disturb you . . .'

She introduced herself, and then Steve, and stated their business. For a swift moment she felt an inclination to glance at Steve as if to say, '*All right, I'm using my cut-glass voice, but this is the kind of occasion when it helps!*' It did, too. Mrs

91

Crayshaw cast her a sharply sizing-up look but appeared marginally less inclined to take exception to their arrival. 'So you want to see my husband about this ghastly business of the girl he used to employ?' she said in one of those nasal county voices which seemed designed to carry halfway across a grouse moor. 'Yes, all right. I suppose you wouldn't bother us if it wasn't important. Though I'm sure he won't be able to tell you anything! You'd better come in. He isn't up and about yet because he's still convalescing from this damned flu-bug, but I'll see if he'll come downstairs.'

'Oh dear, I really am sorry to disturb him,' Jane said again, opting for sounding hesitantly charming. 'We really wouldn't have bothered you, except that I need to confirm a few details.'

'Anything we can do to help, of course. Wait here, then. I'll see if he'll come down in his dressing-gown. Presumably you don't actually want him to go anywhere.'

There was the distinct inference that people like the Crayshaws didn't get asked to go anywhere by the police, helpful though they were prepared to be as public-minded citizens. She had ushered them into a sitting-room – spotlessly tidy save for one newspaper flung across a chintz-covered chair – and left them. French windows looked out on a garden which was surprisingly small for this kind of property, reaching only about the depth of the house before it ended in a tall clipped hedge. The garden area was paved again, with tubs of flowers. The Crayshaws didn't apparently believe in having anything as troublesome as a lawn. Jane looked at Steve, who raised an eyebrow and then glanced round the room thoughtfully.

'Not your average cluttered home,' he murmured. 'Childless?'

'Kids away at boarding-school, I think Kenny said.' The only photograph on display showed Mrs Crayshaw in sporting gear with a large fish on the end of a line, with a background of water and misty hills. It was, almost predictably, in an antique silver frame. 'Maybe they're untidier and more comfortable somewhere else,' she suggested, keeping her voice as low as his. There were no sounds of Mrs Crayshaw returning yet, but the walls seemed thick enough to supply sound-proofing. 'She seems to have found our arrival bearable.'

'Once she realised we weren't evangelists or double-glazing reps,' Steve said, his lips quirking in a brief grin. 'They're taking their time, aren't they?'

'They're the kind of people who do. No, *she* is. She's rather a different kettle of fish from – I think they're coming!'

Mr Crayshaw did look ill, though he had partially dressed himself in honour of the call: he wore trousers under the paisley silk dressing-gown he was sporting. He looked pale, with a greenish tinge, as he followed his wife into the room, and there was an unhealthy dullness in his eyes too. Nevertheless he tried for the heartiness with which he had greeted Jane before.

'Virginia tells me you've got some more details you'd like me to clear up. Of course, if there's anything at all we can do in this dreadful business . . . It's been on the news now, and in the local paper. What a terrible thing! How can I help?'

'Sit down, Tony. They know you're convalescent. And I'm sure there isn't much we can say, so let's keep it as short as we can, shall we?'

Virginia Crayshaw's drawl somehow managed to sound impatient too. Did she always address her husband as if he were a recalcitrant child, Jane wondered? There might have been affection in the way she perched on the arm of his chair, but it wasn't very visible.

Jane launched into a series of polite questions regarding Mr Crayshaw's memories of Deirdre; and a request to be told again exactly when he had last seen her (he couldn't remember), whether he knew if she had any friends (no, he didn't), whether she ever dealt with the agency's customers (no, never). Eventually she had run out of possible queries, and began to wind things up.

'That's all?' He made to rise, but his wife's arm pressed him back into his chair. 'Yes, well, only too glad to have been of help. My goodness, it's quite unnerving being questioned by the police! No, only a joke, of course!'

'I'm only sorry to have had to disturb you.'

'Yes, well, I don't suppose you'll need to again.' Virginia Crayshaw's drawl wasn't quite rude, though it came close. 'No, don't get up, Tony. I'll see them out. Honestly, men don't have the sense they were born with, do they?' she said in Jane's direction – the first sign of a friendly comment she had shown, and delivered with a sudden and surprising smile. It made her look distinctly more attractive. She ushered them back into the hallway. 'I'm sorry we couldn't be much help, but of course, Tony hardly saw the girl except in passing. Employees aren't the sort of people one actually *knows*!'

'Mrs Crayshaw, if you wouldn't mind one last question, do you go into the office yourself?'

'No, it's my husband's occupation, not mine. I've looked in occasionally – but I couldn't even have told you which one the girl was. That's it, then. Goodbye, Sergeant – what was it? Perry? I'll remember the name.'

She didn't dignify Steve with a farewell, obviously having seen his silent presence in the background as relegating him to a minor role. Jane glanced at him as they went back down the paved front path, and saw an amused gleam in his eye.

'One tough lady! What did you want me to notice – apart from the fact that they don't have a potting-shed in the garden to hide a body in? No countrified places of concealment at all, in fact.'

'Oh, anything which might have suggested he could have fancied the girl,' Jane answered his question. 'It was a small hope, anyway . . . and he wouldn't have been likely to give anything away with his wife there. He was too sick to see if anything special made him nervous, besides, wasn't he.'

'Or too nervous to do anything other than look sick. With

that kind of wife he's probably got a mistress on the side, and lives in terror that the harpy's going to find out. I'd lay money on his office manager, the one who was so protective about him, remember?'

'Goodness, yes, could be. I hadn't thought of that.' Jane took the idea in. 'Yes, that could be a possibility. And it would explain why having us rootling around his business asking questions makes him uncomfortable, too. It doesn't get us any further with Deirdre, in fact it rather rules him out, but then I wasn't seriously considering him as a candidate. Just plodding through every possible lead.

'Mm. And getting your name remembered.'

'She did make a point of that, didn't she? To pass on to the Chief Super's wife, no doubt, next time the four of them get together!' Jane spoke ruefully, but without any serious worry: she'd had Dan Crowe's OK for the visit, after all. And she was only doing her job, on a murder enquiry.

Another name to strike out, though: the visit had revealed a certain amount about Anthony Crayshaw (and some guesswork) but not that he was a likely murderer. Back to looking and hunting and asking, then. Door-to-doors had produced nothing so far. Michael MacArthy couldn't be proven to have done anything – besides lie. Somehow, and sometime soon, they would find the thread which unravelled everything, though, wouldn't they?

Walking back into the station with Steve behind her, Jane was unprepared for the tall, elegant figure which suddenly obtruded itself into her line of sight. As fair as she, but six foot two of well-tailored muscle, apparently concluding a conversation with one of the uniform inspectors. Then, his blue eyes lighting up at the sight of her, and, 'Janey!' delivered in ringing tones as he waited for her to come up to him. 'I hoped I might run into you!'

'*Dennis?*' She let him give her a smacking kiss on the cheek, and had already reached up automatically to give him one in return before she remembered where she was. 'Good God, what are you doing here? And how did you know I was down here?'

'Word filters back. You didn't know I'd left the army, I suppose. Did it six months ago, and joined Special Branch instead.'

'You're Special Branch?' Wonders would never cease. 'Oh, this is Steve Ryan, one of my co-sergeants,' she added as his eyes went past her with a sudden look of interest. 'Steve, this is Dennis Dalkeith, a very old friend of mine.'

'We've met before. In fact I was just going to ask you what you were doing in such bad company!' Dennis said cheerfully, reaching across to shake Steve by the hand. 'Is everybody deserting London for this neck of the woods? When we last saw each other you were around the Docklands area. When did you switch?'

'Recently,' Steve said easily, while Jane was still trying to absorb the fact that the two men knew each other. He gave Jane a quizzical glance and added, 'If I'd known the kind of welcome some people rate even in the middle of a police station, I'd have come down armed with an introduction . . .'

'I've known Dennis all my life, in fact we're cousins of some sort,' Jane said hastily, annoyed to feel heat in her face and know it for a blush. 'Look, let's not stand around nattering in the corridor—'

'No, I was just going to say, I've finished chatting to the people I came to see for the moment, and it's coming up to lunch-time. Why don't you both come out for a pie and a pint?'

'No reason why not.' It was Steve who answered while Jane was still opening her mouth. 'You can tell us what Special Branch wants with our humble services, too. Or is it hush-hush?'

It was just what Jane had been about to ask. 'No secret, I'm just doing a preliminary vet for the protection of some foreign royal,' Dennis said cheerfully. 'You've got one arriving here, but not for another month – and only for the day. That's what I'm here for. But let's go and look for a pub – Janey?'

'Yes, OK. Just give me a minute to dump some stuff and I'll be with you!'

The Incident Room had nothing to hold her back, and she joined the two men a moment later. They walked up the road and round the corner to the Sea Rose – the more civilised of the nearby pubs and not quite the closest, therefore less likely to harbour anyone else from the station. The Sea Rose had done itself up lately to attract smart custom and had turned its back half into a bistro. Dennis looked round it with amiable appreciation, bought Jane a shandy without asking her what she wanted, and plonked it down in front of her saying with a grin, 'There you are, lovey, your usual sarsaparilla!' Steve looked at her sidelong with a raised eyebrow, but it was an old family joke. The pub wasn't full and they had a quiet corner to themselves, with the three Ploughmans they had ordered due to arrive in front of them at any minute.

'I was telling Steve while we were waiting for you that you and I used to share a bath when we were three,' Dennis said, grinning at Jane. 'Funny how something like that stays with you!'

'I was three and you were five. Seriously, Dennis, if you're going to produce embarrassing memories I shall pour this drink down your neck!' Jane pretended to frown at him, but was very pleased to see him. 'Come on, start catching me up. When did you leave the army? And why? I thought you were firmly settled in it, for good!'

'It's less interesting than it was in your father's day. Too full of cut-backs and joint policing operations. I decided on a change. By the way, it was Henry who told me where you'd moved to – you know, Henry? Legal-eagle Henry? Hangdog and pining Henry, last seen—?'

'Not when I last saw him. He was in a temper. Excuse us,' Jane said quickly to Steve, abruptly aware of his attentive listening, 'we'll be through exchanging news in a minute! Leaving other things aside, Dennis – you, in Special Branch? It's just bodyguarding, basically, isn't it?'

'Oh, it has its interesting aspects. And I knew all the right people to get into it!' Luckily Dennis seemed prepared to leave the subject of Jane's former boyfriend alone; or perhaps he felt he had already embarrassed her enough in front of a colleague. To make sure, she kept him on the subject of his Special Branch duties.

'When you said your VIP would be here "only for the day", did you mean you'd be here then, too?'

'Yes, but I'll be on escort duty. One of the young Spanish royals is hopping over to attend a society wedding in your cathedral – and, while here, dutifully opening a Spanish Studies Centre at your university. I'm to be the official security presence to escort the princelet to and fro while he's on our soil. I've just come down today to make my polite number with your uniformed people. Letting them know when we'll be arriving and leaving and all that.' Dennis stretched, shifting his broad shoulders comfortably. He cast Jane a quizzical look. 'Do I detect an air of disappointment? What were you hoping for, a crowned head with one of our own royals along for company, and a full-blown walkabout to keep you busy? Sorry, but apart from asking your traffic department to clear a road from one end of your city to the other through the Saturday jams so that he isn't late for the wedding, I doubt if you'll even know we've been here!'

'Sounds fine to me if you're going to be Traffic's problem not ours. I still think it's a waste of your talents to quit on the army!' Jane added, returning to her earlier attack and giving Dennis a reproachful frown. 'Oh, I've no doubt Special Branch was glad enough to recruit you – what with your army record, and of course, the famous Dalkeith charm – so useful for keeping high-ups sweet! But you, just doing endless VIP hand-holding? Honestly, Dennis! Don't tell me you won't end up bored out of your mind! Or have you picked up some brainless aristocratic girlfriend who's talked you into settling down?'

'Not currently. I'm looking round for a suitable candidate, though . . . You remember that exotic brunette I had in tow last time we met?' he said to Steve, with a sudden reminiscent gleam in his eye. 'When you were on the watch for villains in the Docklands Development area, and I got under your feet?'

'Yes, do fill me in on how you two met!'

'There was some fancy do going on in one of the new buildings.' It was Steve who answered for both of them, coming into the conversation at last. 'And there was I, on a stake-out because we'd had a tip-off about something that might be going down in the next building, when I ran into this character in the full black-and-white penguin suit, right where he shouldn't be. Furthermore he was wandering around with some bint on his arm who was stoned out of her mind. I was more than tempted to take both parties in and demand to know who her supplier was. Anyway . . . We unsnarled that, and since my villains plainly weren't going to show with so many people tramping about—'

'We repaired to sink a few jars together. More than a few, I seem to remember. I'd got rid of Annabella by then – boring girl, if stunning. By the time we'd finished we were drinking in places we shouldn't have been as law-abiding citizens, let alone as law enforcers!'

Dennis grinned happily. Jane was well aware that there must be more to the story; also that she wasn't going to be told. Both men had fallen silent with an exchange of expressions which suggested a veil being drawn. Before she could let this demonstration of male solidarity irritate her, Dennis was speaking again, and making a swoop on her plate. 'Janey, if you're not going to eat your pickled onion, I will. Does anyone want another round? No? Come on, then, tell me how life's treating you both down here!' They all had to get back before too long; Dennis still had some details to see to before he returned to London, and there was duty to summon the others. It was a cheerful threesome, however, which arrived back at the station.

'Pity you can't stay for the evening, or you could have seen Matty.'

'I know, but tell her I send her my undying love, and that I'm as always eternally her slave! Ah, if only she'd have me, I'd lead a blameless life . . .' Dennis produced a theatrical sigh, a grin, the sketch of a wave, and then he left them. Jane tried to pull herself together into a suitably official mood of sobriety, but glanced at Steve before it took hold of her entirely.

'Just for the record, I don't get addressed as "Janey" by anyone else!'

'Would I dare?'

'Not if you're interested in survival. Dennis isn't the idiot he likes to pretend to be, but you probably know that.'

'Yes, I'd already sussed that he's a long way from being a chinless ex-guardsman.'

'He wasn't in the guards, he served in the twenty-first, just to be technical. And to be accurate and fair, the guards don't deserve that reputation; they're bloody good fighters. Sorry . . .' She gave a sudden grin. 'Automatic defensiveness!'

'Daughter of the army,' he said mockingly. 'So the dashing Major Dalkeith is your cousin Dennis, is he? Well, well . . .'

'A kind of cousin, yes. But, look—'

'No names, no pack-drill, my lips are sealed! Come on, let's go and see if the collators have got anything new for us.'

He was already pushing the Incident Room door open. At the moment they practically lived in there instead of CID. As Jane followed him in, Rachel Welsh looked round quickly from the phone she was manning and raised an eager finger.

'Yes, hold on a minute, would you, sir.' She shifted the microphone away from her mouth and spoke urgently. 'Sergeant Perry, I think we've got a sighting! For the Friday evening – Yes, sir, if you could just give me that again?'

Jane moved quickly to pick up the extra headset. Even before it had reached her ear, she saw the WPC's face begin to fall. Then the girl's voice politely cut across the quavery elderly tones which sounded in her ear.

'I'm afraid that's the week after she went missing, sir, though it's very good of you to ring us. If you're sure about the date . . . Yes. Yes, we were asking about the Friday before. No, that's all right, and thank you for taking the trouble to call!'

Another blank, after the sudden leap of hope. Just an old man sure he'd seen the girl outside the disco – well after she must have been dead.

Why were there no callers who had actually seen her? Deirdre MacArthy must have been somewhere: why could no one tell them where?

Chapter 8

'You really like this guy Steve, don't you?'

Matty's face was upside-down from where Jane was lying, and gave the effect of hanging over her with the ceiling lightshade as a halo. Constant fitness was a requirement for the job, and since Jane hadn't made it to a gym recently she was running through her own special routine, a mixture of yoga and callisthenics. At the moment that had her arching her back muscles off the sitting-room carpet, then raising both legs very, very slowly. 'All right,' she said, on a difficult breath. 'Suppose I do? He doesn't hassle me – phew! – which I like. But at the same time he makes it clear – phew! – that he's ready, willing and able . . .' Distinctly able, she would lay a fair bet. 'And – phew! – he's quiet, but in that lazily dangerous sort of way, if you know what I mean. And he's funny – funny humorous, not peculiar – and we strike sparks off each other. He's nobody's fool, either!'

'He does seem to have got you magnetised.'

'No he hasn't. I didn't say that. Blast, now I've lost my rhythm!'

'Along with your cool,' Matty said with a chuckle, her eyes amused.

'You can stop laughing, it isn't funny!' Jane abandoned the straight leg-lifts and put her hands behind her head to begin, determinedly, on sit-up twists instead. 'The trouble is he's so damned fanciable! And just when—' She didn't bother to finish the sentence. It *was* beginning to feel like a long time. Since Henry, in London, who might have had his stuffily conventional moments, but had been surprisingly good in bed.

'The question is, dear girl, are you going to do anything about you and Steve?'

'I can't, can I? I've always said, no way, no mixing it with work. Far too many pitfalls for the ambitious career-girl. And people always find out, even if they're not supposed to. Oh damn the man, I've only known him five minutes! But then, to quote a joke in bad taste, love's like murder, you either know who straight away or you may never find out.' A joke in very bad taste, considering another week had gone by and the Deirdre case was still stuck down a deep hole . . . No, she wasn't going to carry work home with her. 'Not that we're talking about love in this case,' Jane said with exasperation, 'just damned bloody violent sexual attraction, that's what!'

'But you also like him,' Matty pointed out.

'And I also have him on the forbidden list!'

'Or why else would you need to do such vigorous press-ups?' Matty was still sounding amused, if sympathetic too. 'Hm, I think I should meet this Steve! Ask him to dinner and I'll vet him for you!'

'What, and have yourself called out halfway through the evening leaving us alone together in far too inviting circumstances? Oh no!' Jane sat up again with a snort, and settled herself to do some nice calming deep breathing. 'I shall . . . simply . . . be my usual cool, calm, and utterly controlled self . . . Dennis likes him, I could tell. Utterly different types, but they'd obviously hit it off like a bomb. Mind you, *men* . . . It's funny they should have met, isn't it? Met in the Met. Oh God, I'm not going to start making corny jokes now, am I?'

'I'm sorry I couldn't have seen Dennis while he was here. If I could have had a brother – well, a white brother – it'd be him.'

'Don't tell him that, you'll break his heart. No, it's all right, I know the messages he sends you aren't meant to be serious.

104

He's been a brother-on-loan to both of us, hasn't he? In between the acres of time when we don't see him at all. You won't get the chance to see him next time, either, he'll be too busy shepherding his royal about. Oh dear, I should have remembered to ask him if he'd seen Chloe,' Jane added guiltily, but absently. 'Remind me that I will write to my little sister, will you? I really don't seem to have seen much of her since she was four, and even then she was always in the charge of the au pair, the one time we had one. She had a Marine Sergeant as a nanny for a while after that, I can't imagine what that must have done to her consciousness!'

'Made her fancy Marines for ever afterwards, maybe,' Matty suggested flippantly. 'What a worry for your mama! Jane . . .'

'Mm? Is something up? You look serious.'

'Well, if you've finished burning off your excess energy, there's something I might ask you.' Matty tilted her head on one side, her deep brown eyes unusually troubled. 'It's difficult ethically, that's the problem. Suppose I were to ask you to talk to someone unofficially, could you?'

'Possibly. Probably? Can you tell me more about it?'

'It's a student I've got in as a patient. He's been badly beaten—'

'We had one recently who'd been roughed up and wouldn't make an official complaint. Art student, probably gay – is yours?'

'No, I wouldn't say so, and mine's at the university, not the Art College. And he's been more than roughed up. Nasty head injuries, that's why he landed up with me. He's post-operative now and conscious, and I don't think there's anything wrong with his memory. But he's been into drugs. We're having to give him substitutes so's to keep him stable while his head heals.' She frowned. 'He definitely doesn't want to talk to the police, and a friend brought him in, so your lot were never involved. I'm stuck in this bind. I think you ought to be involved, but he's my patient, so I can't go against what he wants. He's pretty scared, though, so I just wondered . . .'

'If I could come and visit him off the record and see if I can get him to talk?'

'Something like that. Otherwise, supposing it happens again after I let him out, only worse next time?'

'If he's been in trouble for not paying his drug supplier, and he still can't pay up? Yes, I see.' Jane nibbled her finger. 'It's not an easy one. If it turns out there's a pusher in the university – or a pusher with a heavy getting to the Uni students – and I hear about it, then I'll have to pass it on. In fact even from what you've told me I'm going to have to pass a nod and a wink in the right direction. I won't say where I got it from; I can call it a rumour. But if I talk to this student off the record and he tells me something important, I'm going to have a job not making it official. I'm sorry, love, but you see how I'm fixed, don't you? I'm not really the best person to ask.'

'Will you think about it, though? I'm sorry to bother you when I know how busy you are.'

'Stuck in a rut more than busy, as far as my murder case is concerned. And don't worry, I can see your ethical dilemma and I won't jump any guns. How long can I brew it? I mean, is he due for discharge?'

'I'd say he'll be with us for at least another couple of weeks. He was quite badly hurt.'

They agreed that Jane would think the problem over, and Matty would let her know if anything changed. They didn't go back to the subject of Jane's troublesome hormones, either (thankfully), since Matty was bleeped by the hospital before there was any chance of them drifting back to it – though next morning, when Jane left in her usual rush for work, she received a slanted glance and a teasing, 'Keep on with the deep breathing!'

She would. It was just proximity, after all, and a temptation to be resisted with exasperated humour. She had the question Matty had set her to mull over, a quiet word to pass on about the drug scene, and the fraud figures to get back to in any quiet moment. There had been an inquest on Deirdre, opened and adjourned. Her family wouldn't be allowed to bury her yet; that must be hard . . . Dover hadn't got any further with their case, either. With the murder enquiries at a frustrating standstill, Dan Crowe elected to send Steve off to see a known fence with Mike, trying to track down some of the Herne Bay smash-and-grab loot. There had been another break-in, too, to add to Jane's list, and she was beginning to see a pattern in them, enough to ask the uniform patrols to keep an eye out in certain directions.

It was half past one before she looked in at the Incident Room again, to flip through the card carrousel and see that one new report had come in. The bus driver on Deirdre's normal home-going route was back from his holiday. He did remember Deirdre since he lived on the Ribden Road estate himself, and could recall that she had not taken his bus on that last Saturday night. He had noticed it particularly because she usually sat at the front and chatted to him.

It was something, if only another negative sighting. Deirdre hadn't caught the bus home after work. That must mean what – that she was meeting someone, or had been offered a lift?

The internal phone buzzed beside her and she reached for it. 'Incident Room internal line, DS Perry here. Yes, sorry, I was in the CID room a moment ago but now I'm here. What? Who? Somebody called Crayshaw? Asking for me by name? Yes, I'll come. Ask him very politely to wait in an interview room, I know who it is!'

Anthony Crayshaw? Coming to the station in person and asking especially for her?

It wasn't Anthony Crayshaw. This was a slighter, finer version, just as tall but narrower all over, and with a distinct family resemblance. He was very young – seventeen, perhaps. He stood tensely in the interview room as if barely noticing

107

the uniformed PC who waited inexpressively by the door. The boy's hands were balled into fists, while the eyes – brown where Anthony Crayshaw's were blue – were dark pools of grief. Jane made a rapid guess before he even spoke, though his words came out quickly and jerkily as soon as she came in and identified herself.

'I've just heard about Deirdre. I'm David Crayshaw. I – I didn't know . . . Nobody told me . . .'

'You haven't seen any news bulletins?' Jane asked drily, looking into the agonised young face.

'I've been away, on a school trip! We only got back last night, and if Shelley hadn't come today and found me—'

'Shelley?' So Shelley knew him. 'You've got some information for us, haven't you?' she told the agonised boy. 'We'd better ring your parents. That's Anthony and Virginia Crayshaw, isn't it?'

'Yes, but . . . please don't ring them. They don't . . . I'd rather . . . Do you have to?'

'It depends. How old are you?'

'Seventeen and a half . . .' Adding 'a half' showed just how young he was. 'Please, couldn't I talk to you privately first?'

'All right. But at some stage I'll have to let them know you're here.' She glanced at the constable, then moved to ask him quietly to buzz the CID room. If either the DI or Kenny Barnes was in, could he ask one of them to join her? It was Kenny who came, a moment later, murmuring, 'The guv's gone out . . .'

'OK, you'll do. David, this is DC Barnes. And this is David Crayshaw, who has come to tell us something. David, I have to caution you that you have the right to remain silent, but anything you do say may be taken down and used in evidence. Do you understand?' Jane said, since he was over seventeen and old enough for the statutory warning. She added quickly as she saw his frozen horror, 'That's just something I have to

108

say for formality's sake, all right? Now, what is it you want to tell me?'

'You want to talk to people who saw Deirdre before—' He broke off, gulping. 'I . . . I took her out on the Friday evening before I went away. Shelley says she hasn't been seen since the day after, I didn't know, I swear I didn't!'

'And when did you go away?'

'Monday the eighteenth. We've been in Norway studying fiords for four weeks. It was a special geography field trip. I couldn't even send her a postcard.' There was something infinitely forlorn in the way he said that, before he swallowed and went on bleakly. 'She . . . wouldn't have got it even if I had, would she? Shelley told me that – that . . .'

'That Deirdre was probably murdered the weekend she went missing. I'd like your movements during that weekend, please – since you didn't go abroad until the Monday.'

She saw it hit him, and could only judge his reaction as genuine. Unless he was a brilliant actor. He pulled himself together with an obvious effort.

'I was at school all Saturday morning. We had a meeting about travel arrangements for Monday,' he began, swallowing, his adam's apple jumping. 'Then—'

'Wait a moment, please. Which school?'

'Kent College. It's not all boarders, about half of us are day boys.' It was up on the north side of the city, near the university; the Crayshaws hadn't sent their son away, then, only to a private day school within the city's bounds.

'Right. Go on.'

'Saturday afternoon I was with my mother. Then I went back to school for the concert. Then I went back with a friend to spend the night at his house. He'd broken his ankle so he couldn't come on the trip, and we were sorting out all the notes he wanted me to take for him . . .' He broke off and added carefully, 'His name's Giles Robertson, I expect you'll want to know.'

109

'Thank you. I'd like his address too, please.'

He gave it, his face paler than ever if that were possible. When she nodded to him to go on, he swallowed again, and said, 'I went home from Giles's at midday on Sunday. We had lunch—'

'You and your parents?'

'Yes. And then we . . . sat around reading the Sunday papers, I think. Unless my father was gardening. No, he wasn't, I remember, because he had the radio on to listen to a play . . . Then I packed. And went to bed. We went off early on Monday, on a coach. And I got back late last night . . .'

And his parents hadn't mentioned Deirdre to him. No . . . Jane had already guessed they knew nothing about the connection. 'Employees aren't the sort of people one knows', Mrs Crayshaw had said; and no doubt that was supposed to go for her son too. Jane let it pass without comment, for now.

'And today, what?'

'I went to school. Shelley found me in the lunch-hour. I saw her hanging about outside. She's . . . a friend – Deirdre's friend – and she slipped out of school to find me. After she'd told me,' he said, blinking hard, 'I thought I'd better come straight down here. I mean, if there's been an . . . an appeal to know where Deirdre was, and . . .'

'Yes.' She wasn't going to give him time for emotion. 'Could we come to your relationship with Deirdre, now, please?'

'What do you want to know?'

'Did you take her out regularly, or just on that Friday evening?'

'Regularly,' he said faintly. 'I met her first in Dad's office. We've been going out together for three months. Only, you see—'

'Yes?' Jane prompted as he broke off.

'My parents don't know about it. They wouldn't approve. Hers wouldn't either, they wouldn't approve of me any more than mine would of her.' He said that defiantly, almost as if it

110

was a point of principle. 'So we used to meet in secret. I'd leave her notes in a phone box we'd agreed on, taped under the shelf. And she'd send me notes back.' His hands balled themselves into fists with the tension of grief. 'How could anyone harm her? She was so sweet and quiet and *real*! I loved her . . .'

'Did you have a physical relationship?' Jane saw his flush at her cool question, and added drily, 'Let's forget for the moment that she was under age. Did you?'

'Yes . . .'

'And where did you go?'

'We went out in my car. I'd like to have taken her to ordinary places in town, but we had to make sure no one saw us,' he said, making a plea out of it. 'It really was her family as much as mine. She's Catholic and her parents are strict with her . . .' Jane saw him realise that he had used the present tense, and what that realisation did to him. He was intelligent, she had noted; intelligent enough to have given a careful record of his movements when she asked for them, and to realise why he was being asked, even against his emotional turmoil. There was a moment's pause, then he spoke again with a dull flatness. 'You wanted to know where we went. Blean Woods sometimes . . . The other woods near Chartham . . . just places where no one would see us, and we could be together!'

Young lovers, with their secret to add intensity. 'How often did you go out together?' Jane asked him, keeping her voice formal.

'It was usually Fridays. There was a school club she could pretend to be at. Sometimes I could get away on a Sunday, and if I could I'd leave a note in Dad's estate office, somewhere she'd know to look.'

'I see. And where did you go on that particular Friday?'

'Just out to the woods. We were late back, though, because I got a puncture. I was worried about that, her parents would

111

have been angry. It wasn't that night, was it?' he asked with sudden painful entreaty. 'After I dropped her near home? It wasn't – I took her as near as she'd let me. And Shelley said . . .'

'Deirdre spent Saturday doing her usual part-time job in your father's office. Whatever happened to her was after that. We heard she got into trouble for coming home late the night before and for refusing to explain where she'd been. Did she ever talk to you much about her family? Her stepfather, for instance?'

'She said he had a temper, and that he used to get drunk and hit her mother sometimes.' He added, firing up, 'If I thought he'd ever hit Deirdre . . .'

'What would you have done? She was an under-age girl, with whom you were having an illicit affair.'

'It wasn't just an affair, I *loved* her! She wasn't like anyone else. Just because she came from a poor home—' He broke off again, looking somewhere between defiant and sick, and there were actual tears in the corners of his eyes. 'I did love her. And she loved me. I can't believe she's dead, that someone – And I didn't even know!'

Hadn't he? His face made it appear believable. Every inch of his story could be checked, and would be, but it didn't seem as if he would have had time . . . Not unless he had managed to contrive alibis more carefully than she could believe. Jane watched his face, and picked up on an earlier point.

'You say you drive a car? Your own?'

'Yes . . . I was given it for my seventeenth birthday. I haven't got it at the moment, my father's using it. His was stolen while I was away.'

'Really? I must see if we've got a report of it.'

'You will have. He said the traffic police found it miles away, burnt out. If you want my car, would you be able to get it without telling my father why – I suppose it doesn't matter now. Except that I couldn't stand what – It'll be my mother, really, not him. I just couldn't stand it if she starts saying . . . I suppose I have to tell them, don't I?'

'Yes, you do,' Jane told him, picking her way through that jumbled outburst. 'They'll need to know. Particularly since we'll want to talk to you again. Now then, David, is there anything else at all that you want to tell us?'

'No. Except that whoever . . . hurt her ought to be damned to burn in hell. And if she was – I mean . . .'

'She wasn't raped. The autopsy confirms that.' Let him have that; one less horror for him to dwell on. 'But it also told us she'd been sexually involved with someone, and now we know it was you.' Jane looked at the desolate young face in front of her, and decided to call a halt. There seemed nothing more she could gain from him – for the moment. 'I think you should go home now, David, and talk to your parents. We'll be in touch when we want to see you again. You know we'll have to check all the facts you've given us, don't you? So I'd like you to warn your parents that we'll need to contact your school. Oh, and next time I see you, I'll want you to make an official statement, and sign it. We won't bother about that formality today. All right?'

'Yes . . .'

'Then you can go now. I'll have you shown out.'

When he had gone, Kenny raised an eyebrow at her. He had sat silently by to one side of the table, and the notebook open in front of him was covered with his rapid scribble. 'When he makes his official statement we can compare it with what you've taken down today,' Jane told him. 'Then we can see if there are any significant discrepancies. What did you think, genuine?'

'He came forward on his own bat and as soon as he heard. A right little Romeo and Juliet situation, wasn't it?'

'Except that one thing she didn't do was commit suicide.' Jane set a finger against her lip and let out a sigh. 'Well, we've found the missing boyfriend, but it doesn't seem to have got us any further, does it? If he's told us the truth . . .'

'We know where she was on the Friday evening. We'll probably get a break now and hear from someone who saw her after work on the Saturday.' Kenny sounded chirpily optimistic. 'Get one break and the others sort!'

'I hope so. All we'd really had till today is the usual nutters wanting to confess and getting their facts wrong. And you know what they say, the longer it goes on the harder it gets.'

'If you don't mind my saying so, I'm a bit surprised you let him out on his own and didn't send him back in a squad car.'

'I wanted him to have time by himself to think.' She'd believed him, and she also hadn't wanted Mrs Crayshaw offended by a squad car on her doorstep. Moral cowardice, perhaps. 'We know where to find him; he won't be going anywhere except home. Can you get what he told us typed up straight away?' she asked Kenny. 'I want it ready for when we have him back, and I'll want the guv to see him next time, if only to keep the DCI from . . . No, forget that bit!'

'Forgotten, Sarge. You know, my money's still on Michael MacArthy – even more, now. He's got a history of violence, right? So how about this: he found out about the posh boyfriend, hit the girl again in a rage and too hard this time, found he'd killed her so had to do a cover-up? Once we've found out where he kept the body hidden, we'll have him!'

'Maybe,' Jane said. But she had grilled Michael MacArthy, and so had the guv. Was the man really so much cleverer than the brute he seemed?

'Well, I reckon we'll see,' she told Kenny, smiling at him to show she was going to share his optimism. 'It's either going to be Michael MacArthy or someone we haven't found yet, I'd guess. And murder's more often than not domestic – a lousy comment on family life, that, isn't it! – so you're probably right. We'll have to check David Crayshaw's statement down to the last inch, but after that . . .' She paused, then went on, her voice hard.

'I'll tell you one thing, if it was that poor child's stepfather, I'm going to get him – and tied up so tight that the CPS has a watertight case against him!'

PART II

The Dover Immigration Officer in the Arrivals booth held out his hand for the woman's passport, and she handed it up to him through her open car window. The small folder showed she was Mary Waldstein, a British subject but resident in the Netherlands. He glanced at it briefly, then handed it back and casually waved her on, indifferent to just one more arrival on the early morning ferry. No doubt his replacement would be just as indifferent when Mrs Waldstein returned this evening from her day trip to Britain, irreproachable in her quietly smart clothes and her air of respectability.

He would have no idea that his country had been entertaining the Widow, known and wanted all across Europe.

Mrs Waldstein, who was also the Widow, smiled pleasantly as she received the return of her false papers, uttering a pleasant good morning as she let out the clutch. Her voice was soft and educated, her English faultless. It had, after all, been her first language. It was only later, with Gerhard, that she had learned to speak German like a native, adopting it as her main tongue, using it as her first preference. She felt herself more German than English nowadays.

England. She shrugged off a faint sense of unease almost before it came to her. Who could remember or recognise her, anyway? Nobody. Certainly there was no need to let her thoughts drift into the distant past, to a girl from a dull Midlands home who went to a dull school which took it for granted she would not be clever enough to do anything of interest, so left her to kick her heels in aimless frustration . . . The only lesson that place had taught her was how, chameleon-like, to feign stupidity and mediocrity.

A more valuable lesson than they knew, since the practice showed her she could readily mimic anything: accents, voices, manners . . .

Her thoughts came abruptly back to the present as she entered the stream of traffic mounting the hill which curved away from the sea and followed the signposts which would take her inland. She had work to do: plans and details needing her full concentration.

Out of all the contracts her group had taken on in the past months, this one merited extra careful planning. No quick in and out this time, even though that was their usual pattern. For this one, they must be there in advance, already established. So the Dutchman (who, for all his occasional nasty habits, could be trusted with this) had been sent over to look round quietly; to check if there were houses to rent, while she and Simeon worked on what they would need. On the Dutchman's return Simeon had come over to lay the next piece of groundwork. His false papers were ready by then, hers shortly afterwards: they were to be 'Mr and Mrs Frederick Waldstein', he an American architect working in Europe, she a British national who was simply his wife.

Simeon had telephoned last night to say he had already found the two houses they needed, and had arranged the rental of one of them, to start in a week's time. Today, Mr Frederick Waldstein would visit the university to admire its modern design and extensive campus. This evening, he and his wife would be returning to Holland together on the evening ferry – with vital information to exchange, decisions to finalise.

The Widow glanced ahead at the secondary road she had taken out of Dover, following Simeon's instructions. She began to look out for the signpost he had specified. A left turn into a minor road . . . yes, here it was. She turned into it and soon came to a fork, where she took the even narrower side-road. The house she sought was set a mile distant from the nearest village, standing on its own behind a belt of trees. She found it easily after winding along the narrow lane. Good: it was only five miles from their main objective, but nicely isolated. It had also lain empty for some time and the agent who had shown Simeon round had seemed discouraged about the idea that it would be let in the near future. She saw that a telephone line ran to the house, but Simeon had established that it was disconnected. They knew how to fix it, but on balance, better not in case it was noticed. A large barn next to the house allowed room for two cars. Also good.

It had not occurred to the agent that Mr Frederick Waldstein might be someone who would make a wax impression of house-keys even as he wandered round holding them in his hand. The copies he had subsequently arranged were now concealed just inside the empty barn.

Letting herself into the house itself, the Widow saw that it was barely furnished. No matter, what was here would do; this place was only an emergency bolt-hole which should stay looking empty from the outside. There was a petrol generator in a locked outhouse in case they needed lights, Simeon had said. That too would be better left unused, in case some passing farmer or villager was made curious by a glimpse of light through the trees. There was a full Calorgas tank to service the cooker in the kitchen. Yes, it would all do very well.

It was time to move on. This time for a more official inspection, with keys she would collect from a different letting agency. Mrs Waldstein's identity would be clearly established. The dark blue Citroën had acquired a splash of country mud from a puddle near the barn, and she wiped that off to leave the surface gleaming. Then she was negotiating the short bumpy track again; pausing only to close a leaning gate. She turned smoothly into the lane, then back to the main road.

The tall, fretted towers of the cathedral pointed the way. The massive building was clearly visible across the flat landscape, *reaching high above its surrounding buildings. As she drove into the city itself, into narrow streets curling round the pedestrianised centre, the cathedral became unexpectedly lost again, mere glimpses of soaring grey stonework appearing occasionally through gaps or above ruddily tiled roofs.*

'Mary Waldstein' found a car park, consulted a streetmap in the booklet she had bought on the ferry, and headed for the street Simeon had named, where the estate agents Markham and Riley were located.

Fifteen minutes later Mrs Waldstein had the keys to a small house within the city itself, on which 'Mr Waldstein' had already paid a holding deposit.

'My husband's not with me today, he's too busy. But I wanted to see the house for myself. What luck that he could find us something so quickly! No, you don't need to accompany me, thank you. I'll drop the keys back as soon as I've looked. And we'll pick them up again next week when we actually move in.'

Markham and Riley seemed to feel it necessary to reassure her that she would find the house in excellent condition: it was only empty because the owners didn't want to let it to students for fear of the damage they might cause. But the street wasn't noisy, in spite of being very central. However, they did have other properties on their books in case she should change her mind . . . She smiled again politely to cut off the sales patter, hiding her impatience and promising to return the keys after lunch.

The street itself was tucked in amongst the back ways of the centre; a quiet residential oasis of small terraced and semi-detached houses. She guessed the road's other residents to be young working couples, some students (one house, shabbier than the others, had stickers on its windows) – the kind of fluid, incurious population where new neighbours went mainly unnoticed.

The house, when she let herself in, appeared respectably furnished, and had a convenient rear exit through the small

122

garden, leading on to a footpath by the river. Yes, this would do very satisfactorily as a place for Mr and Mrs Waldstein to take up their quiet residence. And who would suspect that people taking on such a house for three months would actually require it for only two weeks – just until one particular day?

Now she could go out for a stroll, to orientate herself, looking like any other visitor.

The city fitted with what she had already seen from the map: small and centralised, in size barely larger than some market towns. Part of it lay within the remains of a high encircling wall, with newer residential areas extending beyond until they petered out in surrounding farmland. The pedestrianised centre comprised the old High Street, wide and straight with the giant towers of an old city gate at one end. A bridge, barely recognisable as such except that it gave a brief glimpse of water with beamed houses alongside, formed part of the same wide thoroughfare. Mary Waldstein strolled, paused, strolled on. Narrow side streets fanned off here and there; one, barely wide enough for more than a bicycle, gave a glimpse of a highly ornamented stone gateway at its far end, leading into the cathedral precincts. She turned her steps that way as if casually, pausing for a moment to glance back along the main thoroughfare. It was June, tourist season, the city's visitors forming a sea of bobbing heads all along the wide street.

Back there, up the hill which lay beyond the looming arch of the ancient city gate, would lie the university and its campus: modern buildings surrounded by woodland and open fields. Simeon would be up there now, mapping out the place in his head. Later a final choice would be made: where was the best and most vulnerable point for action? Up at the university, or down here, at the cathedral?

Anyone watching might have supposed Mary Waldstein to be particularly interested in cathedral architecture. She spent some considerable time studying the main doorway which led out into the precincts, and inspected with interest how open this

123

side of the cathedral was. It was laid out to grass and paths in the main, with a row of tall, narrow, pastel-painted houses closing off one side. Two of these houses had been turned into the Cathedral Gift Shop.

Inside the cathedral itself, where her steps led her a few moments later, Mrs Waldstein seemed less interested in the beauty of the soaring arches than in the many doors which led outside again – to the cloisters and chapter house; to and through the Thomas à Becket Chapel, down a flight of steps, and thence to the famous King's School which provided the choir for the cathedral; down into the crypt and out through the door which led outside from there . . .

At last she turned back through the main body of the cathedral, and went out the way she had entered. She paused again to make a further study of the porched south-west doorway, the one most generally used.

Finally she seemed to have seen enough, and strolled away, by a different route, up a path through the precincts which led to the Queningate.

This took her to the top of the town. The ring road surrounding the grey flint city walls was busy – and uninteresting, it seemed. She cut away from it and took the next right turn to lead her back towards the centre. Soon she was near the cathedral precincts again, she realised, though this time outside them: they were rendered invisible to her from here by a street of shops backed up against their surrounding wall. She began to walk down, then saw a coffee shop in a side street. It was commonplace, with plate glass, small indoor tables, tea or coffee offered in plain white cups and sold along with cardboard-looking pastries. In this street cars were allowed to pass on their way round to the top of the town. It seemed a good place to pause for a while and sit over a cup of coffee with her tourist guide book open on her knee, and the street immediately outside to look over.

She took a seat at an empty table and was brought her order.

A handbill pinned up on one wall, its curling edges suggesting it had been fixed there for some time, asked for information about a missing teenage girl. She turned her eyes away indifferently and gazed out through the wide window. A young policeman in uniform had paused to give directions to a passer-by, and a tiny curl of scorn stirred in her mind. If he knew who sat within twenty feet of him . . . But the English were so insular that the Widow's reputation probably had not even reached them. Well, it would before long . . .

She watched while someone else came up to the helmeted constable, standing hidden behind him for a moment. Then a movement brought her into view, and at the same time she turned full face.

The Widow froze, disbelief hammering like a blow through her brain.

The Brigadier's wife . . .

It wasn't possible. But the memory, vivid, almost hallucinatory, came roaring out of the past – that face, that slim figure, that short sweep of blonde hair falling across the forehead . . .

It couldn't be so. It was almost thirteen years ago! The woman wouldn't even look like that now. It must be a chance likeness – or her imagination! She found she was automatically shading her face with her hand – but beneath it her eyes were fixed on the girl across the road, who moved a little, asking the constable another question. Then she raised her eyebrows, smiled, prepared to move briskly away. Now she looked younger than the Brigadier's wife had been, even then; only by a few years, perhaps, but it was definitely a more youthful version of the same face. Yet it was still that face, shockingly recognisable, too clear to mistake; her gestures and movements catching the echo too.

Who—?

The older daughter? The one she had disliked so much, though secretly, for her easy social manner, for the attention she could always command without even trying, for her endless friends?

The young woman outside had gone – no, she was just a bit further down the street, and leaning in through the window of a police patrol car. Familiarly. Then she pulled open the back door and stepped in, as if that was familiar too.

Could it be the daughter? She must be about the right age ... Gone now, driven away. But what was she doing here? She might well be living in England now, why not – but in this county, this city?

A trap ... No, reason reasserted itself; nobody could know that much, or have enough inside information for a trap to be set. They had been too careful.

But this was no random likeness either. The Widow could already feel it in her nerve-ends; against all probability, the sense of recognition. And recognition could go two ways.

Even the slightest risk was unacceptable. Nothing could be left to chance now, when a safe invisibility was vital to the success of the contract!

The Widow's mind was suddenly working again, ice-cool and steady. She must act on the supposition that there was an ill coincidence, and the girl actually lived here. That meant everything would have to be replanned ...

The girl had gone off in a car, so it should be safe enough for the Widow to walk back along the pedestrianised main street, amid the covering crowds.

Mary Waldstein strolled back the way she had come, with the same apparent interest in all around her. Behind that, however, her brain was clicking rapidly through the things to be done. She could make no radical alteration to her appearance, since it had already been established with the estate agents ... Her first task must be setting someone to discover exactly who this girl was. Just in case there had, after all, been a mistake. A trick of the light. Though the Widow was sure she had been right, it was necessary to check. And at the same time, find out *how much danger the girl might represent to the Widow's plans.*

She would send Arne.

And when he had found out the information she sought, she would know how best to deal with this new contingency.

Chapter 9

'Thanks for the lift, fellas! There's nothing much going on down in town today, is there: here's hoping your shift goes on being quiet!'

Jane gave the patrol which had brought her back a cheerful wave as they left her in front of the police station and departed to continue their tour round. She made for the front entrance, since it was a quicker way in than going round the back. She was without her own car because she had lent it to Steve, his being temporarily out of commission. (What was the use of having a posh engine in his old jalopy if it didn't always go? Just something to boast about, presumably. Men!) Something, oddly, was making her feel as if a goose had walked over her grave . . . No, it was nothing; or more probably the constant background nag of wondering if they were ever going to get anywhere with the Deirdre murder. David Crayshaw's information had filled in a hole, but it had done little else.

The DCI had leapt into action himself on hearing the Crayshaws were further involved. No one lower in rank than a DI should have interviewed David – 'Tact, Sergeant Perry!' he had said with annoyance. 'I really can't imagine why you didn't call *me* in as soon as the boy presented himself, if Inspector Crowe was unavailable! There are ways of handling these things!' Dan Crowe had been despatched to re-interview David in his own home but Morland had stated his intention of taking David's official statement himself. At the Crayshaws' convenience, of course, since it would mean their calling at the station . . . Well, let him get on with it, she thought, since there was small danger he'd take over the whole case once he discovered that Deirdre MacArthy was in no way important to the Crayshaws senior. Only to their son. And no doubt with his parents' (at least his mother's) outraged shock and disapproval, now that the young people's friendship had been discovered.

All the things David had said had already been checked and confirmed: no solution there . . .

Jane paused to let various members of the public emerge from the station entrance, and switched her mind resolutely back to the shop-owner she had just been down to see. His case offered little help to her other burglary investigations. The door of his shop showed signs that someone had tried to force it overnight, but he thought it was only kids after cigarettes. And since they hadn't actually managed to break in, he had reported the incident only to get the repair done on the insurance. It had certainly looked amateur and showed no match with the MO of the other break-ins on her list. Those seemed to have come to a stop for the moment, which suggested that her instructions to the night-duty patrols might be having an effect . . .

Jane's train of thought was broken by catching the sound of her own name as she came through the outer door. That loud drawl asking at the desk for 'your Detective-Sergeant Perry' was surely familiar? Virginia Crayshaw was at the reception counter with David in tow. It was almost a week since Jane had last seen the boy, but he was still looking pale, with dark lines under his eyes. It must be today that his parents had found it convenient for their appointment with Morland. And the DCI must have been hanging about in readiness, since he appeared now like a jack-out-of-a-box, beginning a flutter of apology and obeisance which plainly annoyed Virginia Crayshaw even more thoroughly than she was already. At that moment Mrs Crayshaw turned her head and saw Jane, and she promptly switched her attention, ignoring the DCI.

'Oh, there you are, Detective-Sergeant Perry! Is this going to take long? David ought to be back at school, if he'll just pull himself together!'

'I'll be handling this case myself now,' the DCI put in rapidly.

Virginia Crayshaw turned to regard him as if he were an overactive species of insect. 'I thought the gel was the one in charge of all this?' she enquired rudely. 'For goodness sake, we've already had that other detective. Do we really have to deal with so many people and say everything three times?'

'Sergeant Perry merely handles the routine aspects—'

'Well that's all this is, isn't it? Oh well, I suppose if we're not going right to the top, it doesn't matter which of the Indians we speak to!' A faint but visible flush spread up across DCI Morland's bald pate, as she swung round on Jane again. 'But you stay! David's already talked to you, and he must be tired of repeating himself!'

The DCI was ruffling up as he came back into the conversation, and if the stiffness of a voice could kill, someone – Jane, undoubtedly, from the poisonous glance he threw her – would have a lance straight through the heart. 'I'm sure no repetition will be necessary once David's statement has been properly recorded, and in your presence,' he said. 'But Sergeant Perry can remain, if you wish! I suggest my office. Will your husband be joining us?'

'No, I told him not to bother. It's not as if David's in trouble – except for some silly association, about which he should have known better!' The dismissiveness of her tone was so cruel that Jane almost winced, but the boy just stood numbly by. Mrs Crayshaw fixed DCI Morland with a disbelieving eye and adding scathingly, 'Good God, you're not going to suggest he has to have his father here? What is this place, the last bastion of male supremacy? If so, I really must have a word with Priscilla Gray about it – your Chief Superintendent's wife. Now, could we please get on with it?'

She allowed the DCI to lead the way upstairs to his own office – no ordinary interview room for the Crayshaws, apparently – and Jane trailed along behind, as she had been instructed. A tremor of amusement was catching at her behind her carefully deadpan face, though to find Morland's obvious discomfiture funny was undoubtedly unwise. Once they were seated he took the boy through the typed notes of his previous interview, now transferred to a statement form. Virginia Crayshaw lapsed into an impatient silence, her aggression merely channelled into a sharply scornful, 'No, indeed we did not!' when David confirmed that his parents had known nothing about his friendship with Deirdre.

Glancing covertly at Virginia Crayshaw, Jane wondered if the woman knew how rude she had sounded ever since her arrival at the station. Probably she did, and didn't care. She might at least show a grain of sympathy for her son . . .

One young and tragically sad boy. His answers were practically monosyllabic. It seemed unlikely that his air of acute misery could be feigned. No murderer? Surely not. Besides, every account of his movements tallied, and all his time, except those few hours spent with Deirdre on the Friday night, had been vouched for by others.

DCI Morland reached the point of asking David to read through his statement thoroughly, then sign it on each page. The boy did as he was asked, listlessly, while his mother shifted irritably in her chair behind him. The DCI cast her a glance.

'Thank you, Mrs Crayshaw, and as you see, that didn't take long. We simply had to—'

'Yes, yes, all right! That's all, then, is it? What about you, Sergeant Perry? Is there any other routine matter you want to ask about, so that we can be sure all this is thoroughly finished?'

'Just a couple of things.' Jane knew she was being rash when DCI Morland was beginning to puff himself up like a pouter-pigeon, but Mrs Crayshaw had given her an opening. There was an omission Jane had made which had only just occurred to her. There was also something minor but puzzling which had come up when she checked her notes, so she might as well go the whole hog and cover that as well. 'David, did Deirdre give you anything that Friday night? A keepsake, maybe, for while you were away?'

'No. No, she didn't. We never . . .' He broke off with a glance at his mother and away again, but Jane could guess the rest of the bleak little sentence: they never exchanged presents for fear of their being noticed.

He hadn't been given the missing St Christopher medal, then. 'Thank you,' she told the boy, and then raised her next question. 'I was told by someone that Mr Crayshaw was out playing in a golf tournament with his son on the Saturday after Deirdre disappeared. That must be a mistake, I suppose? Considering that David was abroad?'

'David has a fourteen-year-old brother. He's retarded and lives in a home.' Virginia Crayshaw's voice was suddenly very crisp – but she recovered herself quickly, and went on with something like her usual scornful drawl. 'Very thorough of you, Sergeant, but that would have been our younger son Jeremy. Mind you,' she added with a curl of her lip, '"golf tournament" is an exaggerated term for the simple game they would have been playing. But then Tony's no golfer anyway!' She came to her feet in a neat angry movement, a touch of colour in her cheeks. 'Now that really is all, I imagine? Oh, David's car – we drove here in it, since you made that request to search it or something. It's parked on your forecourt with the keys inside. Presumably someone downstairs is capable of calling us a taxi home!'

'I don't think we really need to look at David's car, since everything seems to be perfectly satisfactory,' Morland began, looking piqued, and glancing at Jane to show she must be responsible for this unnecessary detail. 'Really, Sergeant, there's no call for that in the circumstances—'

'No, do search it, by all means. After all I've bothered to bring it!' Mrs Crayshaw had interrupted him before he could finish. 'I can't imagine what you think you might find in it, and anyway Tony's been driving it since his was stolen by some wretched joy-riding vandals. But do by all means look at the thing, then we can be finished with all of this and forget it! I assume you'll deliver it back to us in one piece. David, come along. We've spent enough time here! Oh, and Inspector whoever-you-are,' she added nastily, 'try not to get this bloody car stolen. I've presumed it won't be, since it's parked right outside your door!'

She swept out of the room with the boy in her wake, making it clear she didn't care to be escorted from the station. Jane would have liked to make her own escape by following her, but she had not yet been dismissed so she simply got to her feet. An unexpected sympathy for the DCI after Virginia Crayshaw's verbal onslaughts prompted her rashly into speech.

'She's a rather difficult woman, isn't she, Sir?'

'Mrs Crayshaw is a valued member of the local community!' DCI Morland snapped. 'And you really must learn not to put yourself forward with unnecessary and intrusive questions, Sergeant, when I'm conducting an interview! Your behaviour in front of senior officers – Oh, go away. I really have no patience with you!'

'Sir!' Jane came to attention with a positively new-recruit smartness but a bitter taste in her mouth. She wheeled out of his office at her best march. Serve her right for thinking of the man for just one moment as a fellow human being. Dan Crowe would have responded to her comment with a rueful beetle of his eyebrows; even Superintendent Annerley might have cleared his throat and agreed deadpan that some members of the public were less easy to deal with than others. But not Morland, oh no. She should have been wary enough to expect that he would take his bruised dignity out on her. He probably would again, once he had thought up some further reprimand—

Oh, forget it. He wasn't worth the energy!

She made her way downstairs. So the Crayshaws had another son . . . and one his mother plainly didn't like mentioned. Poor David, if all his mother's expectations rested doubly on his shoulders for that reason. To be fair, maybe poor Virginia Crayshaw, too: how could Jane know what pain lay behind that abrasive and dismissive manner?

She wasn't exactly likeable, though. Or motherly. Her attitude to David's heartbreak seemed as harsh as a punishment. No, not even that – it was more as if she simply didn't believe in it. As if Deirdre's death was no more than some inconvenience to be lived through, and its touch on the lives of the Crayshaw family merely an impertinence.

Even Michael MacArthy seemed more human than that – unless of course . . .

'Talking to yourself?' Steve said behind her. 'Or just swearing under your breath?' He came up cheerfully beside her, and pretended a look of meek apology. 'If it's about your wheels, they're back. Oh, and look, about the dent in the nearside wing—'

'What?'

'Gotcha. No, it's all right, there isn't one. I was just getting my own back for that nasty remark you made this morning about men being in love with their cars. I've treated yours with every propriety, I promise, and thanks for the loan!' He dangled her keys in front of her and dropped them into her outstretched hand. 'What are you brooding about? Has something new come up on the murder scene while I've been out hunting villains?'

'Nothing at all, but since we're into the subject of cars, we've got David Crayshaw's in now for examination. Not that there's likely to be anything to find in it.' The boy had certainly voiced no objection to having it searched. David's car was another place where the St Christopher medal might, innocently, be lost. The absence of Deirdre's only piece of jewellery was still their only tentative clue: find that, Jane thought – unless it did turn up under a seat in David's car – and it could lead them to where her body had been kept. 'Oh blast, there was one more thing I wanted to know from the Crayshaws! Exactly when Mr C's car was actually stolen, as opposed to reported. Just in case . . .'

'In case the boy was using that rather than his own car on the Saturday night? A bit convenient that it was nicked and burned out afterwards? I thought you'd just about ruled the boy out, though?'

'I have. Almost. Almost definitely. If everything else wasn't producing such a frustrating blank . . . Oh well, back to all the other blanks on our books! The guv hasn't managed to track down the perp for that smash-and-grab so far, did you hear?'

'But they've nabbed the arsonist, so that's one under the department's belt. Caught in the act with a can of petrol and several oily rags, so he had no choice but to cough. To all of them, I gather. He said he "just likes fires!".'

Steve held open the door for her and they both passed into the CID room. Kenny was behind his desk, the room otherwise empty. 'Hear you've got the fire-merchant, well done!' Jane told him. 'Where's Mike? Out?'

'Canteen having an early lunch. And Gary's in court. Likely to be a long hang-about, too. He's rung to say the case before his seems to be dragging on.' Going into court to give evidence always seemed to take up an inordinate amount of time, as well as all too often ending up with some judge deciding to put a villain back on the streets 'for lack of evidence'. And that was when the Crown Prosecution Service had let them get even that far. Sometimes all the effort they put into catching criminals seemed singularly pointless, when society appeared bent on weighting things in favour of the villains. Jane pulled a face in sympathy for Gary's plight, and then remembered there was something she had wanted to ask the guv – whether they should wind down the house-to-house queries about Deirdre, or plod on with them, since nothing had come of them so far. His cubby-hole office was empty so she would have to catch him later. She was abruptly aware that Kenny was looking up at her with a query.

'Yeah, sorry, what?'

'That rumour you heard about a drug scene at the university – have you got any more on it? Sergeant Clay was asking.'

'Nothing more than the bare bones I gave him. Sorry.'

'I'll pass that back if I see him, shall I?'

'Thanks . . .'

That was one more thing she hadn't managed to solve yet: the question Matty had asked her. How far could she risk going, unofficially? Since she was a long way from being Morland's favourite person – and double that after the interview just now – she would really be sticking her neck out if she took too independent a line and then things went wrong.

She glanced across at Steve with the sudden realisation that he might be the one to ask. If there was a way round the rules he'd know it, and he knew how to keep shtum, too. Yes, she would ask him, next time she got him alone.

'Oh, there was another message for you, Sarge, sorry!' Kenny again, stretching a little, shifting on his chair. 'Let me just get it right. Inspector Grainger says, "Major Dalkeith says, hi." On the phone. That's it. Sounds a bit mysterious, doesn't it? Now wait a minute, Major Dalkeith, isn't he the one who . . .?'

'My cousin,' Jane said firmly, cursing Dennis and well aware from Kenny's expression that word had gone thoroughly round of their affectionate greeting in full public view. If there were comments, they certainly wouldn't stop if the idiot was going to start sending her messages via senior officers. 'I'm sure you know – since there are never any secrets in a cop-shop – that he's Special Branch. He happens to be a relative of mine as well. We grew up together and I hadn't seen him for ages. OK?

137

Just in case there are any other rumours going round!'

'Rumours, Sarge? In a place full of detectives? Never!'

'That'll be the day!'

Kenny gave her a grin. He was one of the easiest of people to work with, too pragmatic to care who gave him orders as long as he was allowed to get on with things in his own way. Which was usually slow but steady. 'Yes, I did hear it was a Special Branch visit,' he added. 'Some foreign royal coming next month, isn't it? Three weeks' time? Just when I'm off on leave. We're taking the kids out of school early to go camping in Dorset!'

'Sooner you than me, but we'll try to keep things quiet so you don't miss your holiday!' Jane knew it was the first year for ages that Kenny had managed to swing a summer break, instead of having to wait for a quieter time of the year when the city was less crowded and, therefore, less prone to crime. 'No, it's all right, I don't think they'd bother to put on extra security patrols for this visit! It's not as if there's going to be a street procession and all the pickpockets out—' The ringing of the phone interrupted her. She picked it up before Steve could reach for it. 'DS Perry, CID room. Yes, OK, give me the details and I'll take them down.'

A house break-in; CID presence requested, please, if anyone was available. It had to take precedence, even though Jane had been debating with herself whether to go to the Incident Room and simply nag some answer out of the meagre collected facts. She could delegate, of course . . . No, she would take this one herself, and fish Mike out of his early lunch to go with her. He was probably only flirting with the canteen staff anyway.

'Tell the guv this is where I am when he gets back from wherever *he* is!' she told Steve, and handed him the scribbled details. 'Tell him I've got Mike with me as well. Oh, and see that someone does look at David Crayshaw's car, will you? It's a specialist job, but somebody ought to be at it!'

She couldn't spend all her time on Deirdre. It might be the

most major case she had got, but already other things had to intervene so that it was like juggling, keeping all the balls in the air. Hercule Poirot never had that problem, she thought wryly. He was allowed to sit still and 'exercise the little grey cells'.

She soon found herself exercised in a different way. They had barely arrived, in a road of detached modern houses tucked away at the back of the St Stephens area, when a running figure darted out from behind a hedge with a uniformed copper in hot pursuit. Jane leapt out of one side of her car, Mike out of the other to offer a flanking movement as the figure sped towards them, swerved, and fled past Jane to dive down the side path of a house. 'Get round and cut him off!' she yelled to Mike, and saw the uniform change direction too as she set off fleetly after their quarry. He had made a bad choice, she saw, as she spotted him trying to hurl himself at a high fence at the far end of a well-kept garden. They believed in good, tall, solid fencing around here and there was no convenient rear gate, either. If she could get to him before he managed to scrabble his way right up and over, she would have him by the legs at least—

Mike got to him just before she did, his gangly form appearing over the side-fence near the end and his long legs taking him speedily the rest of the way. The uniformed copper arrived over the opposite side-fence just as Mike was pulling their quarry down. There was one vicious attempt to kick him off, but an expert twist from Mike had the young man down on the ground with the DC's knee across his thighs and one arm wrenched up behind him in a disabling armlock.

'He was hiding in an outside lean-to. We reckon he's the perp who did the break-in, then the householder came back and she must've disturbed him without knowing. He got out the back and hid . . .'

The uniformed copper was out of breath as he proffered the explanation. He pulled his handcuffs off his belt and passed

139

them down to Mike, who clipped them in place after yanking the second arm backwards to join the first. He kept a knee across their captive's thighs with a threatening growl as another kick was attempted. 'I suppose he's your collar now,' the young constable added, looking a touch aggrieved.

'No, you would have got him in another minute.' Uniform always seemed to think CID was out to grab all the kudos. Half of another uniformed figure appeared, puffing, above the fence from which they had just yanked their prisoner, to prove Jane's point. 'Or you can share it between you,' she added, in case Mike was feeling hard done by. 'Let him up, Mike, and let's see who we've got! Well, well. If it isn't the person who had all those alibis last time we had him down at the station! And a nice little record for petty pilfering too. You've landed yourself in it good and proper this time, haven't you, Darren!'

'Prove it,' the young man snarled defiantly, trying to shake the rat's tails of dirty yellow hair out of his eyes.

'That bag you left in the lean-to's going to prove it,' the uniform the other side of the fence told him, adding, 'With a pair of rubber gloves lying on top of it, too, which will have your prints all over them! You had to leave in too much of a hurry, didn't you?'

'All right, read him his rights and take him away. We'll follow you with this bag and gloves when I've had a word with the householder. It looks like everyone's lucky day – except Darren's!'

Taking over the mopping-up operations, Jane hoped the uniformed boys wouldn't take it amiss when they found CID monopolising Darren on his arrival at the station. Because it did sound very like the MO of that string of minor burglaries she'd been looking into, and about which Darren Smith had been questioned before. He had obviously changed his time of day, because there had been a regular trickle of mid-evening break-ins before, in houses where the owners had gone out for the evening. The change of timing could be because she had noticed a pattern and had instructed the patrols to make themselves obvious at certain times in certain streets. It would really be a turn-up for the book if she was right, and he could hardly rig an alibi this time.

She would stick to her guarantee that uniform could have the credit for the collar, but it did look as if her clear-up rate might suddenly have taken a turn for the better.

If it could just take a turn for the better over Deirdre too . . .

As soon as she walked into the station she knew by a buzz that something had happened. It was the sergeant in the charge-room who told her, when she went there first with the evidence for him to log in.

'DI Crowe's in the Incident Room and he wants you in there as soon as you're back. There's another dead girl. Another body.'

Chapter 10

'Tied up, slashed up, dumped from a car. They found her quite quickly this time. She was in a skip.'

'Where? On our patch?'

'No, Deal.' Dan Crowe fixed a marker into the map on the wall and drew a red circle round it. 'Three of them we've got now . . . It's a multiple, isn't it? And a nutter. Bloody fucking hell.'

Jane looked at the pattern made by the markers: a triangle with the city at its apex. Two near the sea, one inland, but all within twenty miles of each other. 'What's the exact MO this time?' she asked.

'What I said. Tied and slashed like the Dover girl, folded up and dumped out of a car like our girl. Must have been. The skip was on waste land next to a site where they're building some new houses. Must have been dumped at night. The ground's all churned up anyway with tyre tracks from the builders' machinery,' Dan Crowe added disgustedly. 'We haven't got much more than that yet. They just let us know straight away because they knew we'd got one too. Foreign girl this time. Elise something. Plenty of identification on her.'

'Can we be sure it's not a copycat? There's been plenty in the local press.'

'And they'll all be baying after us for sure, with this one! No, it isn't a copycat. One thing they did tell us, her face is marked same as the Dover girl. Two vertical slashes on each cheek.' That was a detail which had been carefully kept out of the press. The DI glanced at Jane. 'Yes, I know, not the same as ours, but we're going to have to reckon he was interrupted with our girl. We'll be coordinating all three from now on. It'd be too much of a coincidence if we had two men who liked killing young girls running loose in one area, wouldn't it? So let's just pray we can get this fucking nutter before he does it again!'

He was being unusually loquacious, for him. Had he got a daughter? A ten-year-old girl, Jane remembered, as well as two boys, one older and one younger. She gazed at the map again. Three points, that close together. Yes, it did look as if they'd got what was every police force's nightmare – a multiple, irrational, motiveless killer. Someone all the harder to track because he had no particular connection with his victims, so might strike anywhere. *He* – yes, it was surely a man. Somehow women didn't seem to go in for reasonless murder . . . or when they very occasionally did, the victims weren't of their own sex.

The new information made a nonsense out of all the careful checking they had been doing over Deirdre. There was a different aspect to things now . . . What they had achieved wasn't a complete waste, however: there were valuable facts there, eliminations. Besides, the killer might just as well be based here as at Dover or Deal. Or somewhere within easy reach of all three. It certainly made sense for the different divisions to coordinate and pass as much knowledge to and from as possible.

Work in the Incident Room was stepped up again, as what came in over the next couple of days gave them a clearer picture of the new victim. Elise Ducherain; French; nineteen over here to learn English. In fact she had only just arrived. She had been dead for four days by the time she was found. Her body had been wrapped up in blue plastic sheeting before it was dumped in the skip, but showed the same knife slashes and strangulation marks as the Dover girl. There were no immediate signs of rape. Her torn clothes and a small patchwork handbag had been bundled up in the plastic wrapping with her, the handbag making identification easy since it contained her passport. She was blonde, green-eyed, petite, and had been at least moderately pretty. There was no indication of where she had been killed, but it was estimated that she had been dumped very shortly afterwards.

The facts went into the computer, and on to a new set of collators' cards which had been widened to include details of all three killings. Jane set herself to study all of them and to check for comparisons. She was engaged in that in a quiet corner of the Incident Room, glancing up occasionally with frowning concentration at the three sets of details which Rachel Welsh was now reorganising into sections on the wall, when Steve hove up behind her.

'Thought you'd be in here . . . Well done about your burglar. I hear Darren Smith's going to plead to all sixteen, on the advice of his brief!'

'Mm, yes, I heard. It's good, isn't it? Oh, did someone take David Crayshaw's car back?' Deirdre's missing St Christopher had not been in it; there had been one long, curly brown hair in the crease of the back seat, but that was all. If it had been in the boot – but that was an irrelevance now, anyway.

'The car's been returned.' He seemed to be hovering, but while she was still wondering why, he pulled out the chair next to her and sat down. His head close to hers, he spoke with a deliberate quietness. 'Look, can we get certain things straight? There's something going on which certainly wasn't my idea, and—'

'What? Hang on a minute. Rachel, leave a space so that we can put lines between the three girls if we find anywhere they connect, will you? I want to go down to Deal and see the new girl's body for myself, I should think the guv will OK it!' she added, her attention returning to Steve. 'It might be interesting to have a proper look at what she had with her, too. She didn't know anybody over here, by the way. I've talked to the Police

145

Judiciaire in her home town and they were quite sure of that. Apparently her parents said—'

'Yes, all right, but can we talk about this other thing first?' Steve glanced round, but both the WPC and the civilian currently manning the telephone had their attention elsewhere. 'Jane. Listen. Humpty-Dumpty's come up with the fact that I was made up to sergeant before you were. So he's decided I'm technically in charge under the DI. He had me in and told me it should have been that way all along. I told him it wasn't—'

Jane had been staring at him. 'Don't stick your neck out,' she interrupted, tight-lipped, but with the beginnings of a seethe inside her. 'He's . . . even right, I suppose.'

'Is he hell! I'm only here on a temporary posting, for Christ's sake! You know damn well he's just doing this as a move against you! What have you done to him lately? Besides being a woman, of course!'

She had been there to watch while Virginia Crayshaw treated him like an annoying underling, and had even been foolish enough to show she'd noticed. It seemed a long time ago, though it was only two days. This was obviously Morland's petty revenge. Jane had been treated as Dan Crowe's senior sergeant ever since Vern's departure, and now the DCI was stepping in to decree a demotion. A minor one maybe since he was unable to manage anything better, but . . . She looked at Steve dumbly, but with a spark in her eye. However, since she had made no answer, he was going on.

'Anyway I'm just warning you, but it wasn't my idea, and it is not going to happen if I have anything to do with it. Fair do's, and I'm not going to have that stupid bastard playing out his hang-ups through me! So I went to the guv—'

'You shouldn't have. You're senior, so that's that.'

'No it bloody well isn't! Would I care? Come on, seriously! I was told to work to you from the moment I arrived, which was clear enough, and no sweat off my nose! You're local, I'm not. You were already in place, I'm the new boy. If you came on to

146

my patch, now . . .' He grinned at her, then sobered, looking tough. 'I wouldn't be passing this on except that you've got a right to know what's being said – and to keep your head down until it's over, if you're wise! The guv's up there with Humpty-Dumpty now, and having the devil of a row. You can hear raised voices even through closed doors. The Super's name is being bandied about, I rather think!'

She could see now why he was keeping his voice low. 'The guv's going out on a limb for me? Wow,' she said, her own voice equally quiet. But grateful. And a little surprised, too, although Dan Crowe had always been a good boss to work for, and a fair one.

'I think it was an explosion waiting to happen, don't you? And if you just chance to be the detonator . . . well, like I said, keep your head down!'

'Yes, it won't make me any more popular in certain quarters, will it? But thanks for the warning. And for – oh, not just letting it ride.'

'Are you crazy? I'm after your body, my girl, not your rank – given half a chance!' He said that deliberately, if even more softly, and with a wicked gleam in his eye. It was the most outright declaration of intent he had made yet, and, she thought, was said more to defuse her gratitude than to be taken seriously. It had the effect of making her laugh, anyway.

'Let's say I owe you one, but not that one, in case you should think otherwise!'

'I don't. And you don't. I don't play by those sort of rules!' He meant what he said, too, she could see, and was a little put out by her answer. 'If I can't get what I want by charm alone . . .'

'Then you go elsewhere. Bye bye! No, seriously, I *am* grateful – and you won't be the most popular person around either, will you!'

'Suits me,' he said with careless cynicism. He must have the reactions of a cat, as she had noticed before, because WPC Rachel Welsh had hardly moved into an orbit which might be within earshot when he was flipping over one of the collators' cards, and let his voice drift up to a normal level. 'So we're looking for any possible link between the three victims, right? Catholics? What was the Dover girl, do we know?'

'No, but Elise Ducherain was a French Protestant anyway. My Police Judiciaire contact happened to mention it. She was a regular churchgoer and the local minister, or whatever they call them over there, apparently came in with the parents. That poor child was away from home for the first time, and she'd only just got here . . .'

The only pattern at the moment was that the three were all young girls. There didn't seem to be anything else to tie them together; just three random victims.

No one sent for Jane when she finally emerged from the Incident Room. No one mentioned a change in the power structure of the department, either, though the guv was in his office flipping through some files. He glanced up at Jane through his open door but took no further notice of her than to give an acknowledging grunt. He must have won . . . She was too wise to try thanking him. It was better, as Steve had said, to keep her head down and look as if she didn't know anything. When she tapped on his door it was solely to ask permission to go and visit the Deal Incident Room on a bit of liaison, and take a look at Elise Ducherain's body while she was down there.

'Good idea. You can go now and take the rest of this afternoon. I'll give them a ring to say you're on your way.' His prompt answer made her suspect he thought it was a good thing for her to be somewhere else while things cooled off, though he covered it by adding, 'Saves us having to wait for the rest of their info if you go and look at everything first hand! Try to get something on what their full autopsy report's going to say. And see what they've got coming in from forensic. Oh, and bring back the photos they promised us, since they haven't turned up yet!'

'Right, Guv. Could I take Sergeant Ryan with me? Or do you need him here?'

'Both of you go. I can't see anything here to make either of you indispensable. Gary!' he yelled in the direction of the chunky young DC who was in the CID room for once instead of out doing legwork. 'Come in here and explain this one to me, will you? Go on, then, Sergeant, on your way!'

Jane gave the quiet Gary a smile as she passed him, and went to dig Steve out and tell him they were going on a trip to the coast. Maybe it was just as well for both of them to be out of the building for the rest of the afternoon. Flattering to think that two of the men she worked with had dug their heels in over Morland's campaign against her. Whatever Steve's stated motives, it was far more likely that his rebel streak had surfaced against petty bureaucracy. And he was probably right in thinking that the guv's reaction had been an explosion waiting to happen. All the same, the knowledge that she had backing was a comfort, and an acknowledgement that she had been doing her job.

They went in Steve's car – mended again – since he had opted to do the driving. They took the road out through the villages before circling to swing south; a pretty run, passing through village streets of beamed cottages, alternating with the tall poled greenery of hop fields nestling up to the road. Deal, when they reached it, had neatly pretty houses along its flat sea-front, looking for all the world like an advertisement for Quality Street chocolates. After that they had to backtrack into less decorative areas, and after several wrong turnings and a pause to ask directions – which made it fortunate, as Steve said with amusement, that they weren't in a marked police car, or where would the public's faith be? – they finally found their destination; the building site where this latest body had been found. A temporary Incident Room had been set up next to it, in a mobile.

Work was at a halt on this side of the building site –

probably unwillingly, Jane guessed, to judge from the sour look of a foreman in a hard hat who was wandering about. Trailing marker-ribbons were tacked up in relevant places, while some overalled coppers were doing another search of the ground.

They found a Chief Inspector Rivers from Dover in charge in the Incident Room, which showed the same proliferation of tacked up maps, notes and photos as theirs did, though here with a different victim.

'Yes, we had a call to say you were coming down,' the Chief Inspector said, welcoming them in. 'You want to see how much of what we've got ties in with yours? Our girl's body is at the mortuary in Dover: we've passed the word on that you'll be going there next. Nasty business, all of it, isn't it? I've got my men doing another search to see if they can find the weapon, but I'm not holding out any hopes. Come and have a look round, and I'll tell you our end of things as we go.'

The skip was back in its original place, though it was only when it had been moved to be emptied that the body had been found – the sudden glimpse of pale human feet protruding from a blue bundle as it was tipped with the other rubbish into a hole marked for infill. The man doing the tipping had promptly pulled back all the levers to stop the cascade, and yelled for his nearest mates to call the foreman. 'Lucky he was sharp-eyed or she'd have been under a heap of broken bricks and gone,' Chief Inspector Rivers said, adding, 'she was about halfway down in the skip, and they don't empty them until they're full right to the top.'

'How did he get her in there?' Jane asked, knowing the 'he' would be taken as she'd meant it – the killer. She looked at the size of the skip, measuring it with her eyes. A dead body, even of a slight girl, would be an inert weight. 'He'd have to be strong. That's quite a lift.'

'We've got a theory about that. A plank propped up to the side of the skip, and a wheelbarrow. There were plenty of both about. With the girl folded up as she was, and bundled up in the plastic sheeting, it's probably the only feasible way he could have done it. Then he threw an old door down on top of her, we think, and that protected the body from getting battered by all the other stuff which was put on top afterwards. Then – we suppose – he moved the plank away and got back in his car and drove off. Bastard,' the Chief Inspector added expressionlessly. 'The building site isn't fenced off, as you can see. There are only three houses going up, and the contractors didn't think the expense against the cost of pilfering was worth it. We've had all the men from the site in, of course, but they're all in the clear. Either our murderous friend is local and knows the area, or he simply drove up this road because it looked promisingly empty, then saw the skip as a handy place of concealment.'

'Does the plastic sheeting come from here, too?' Steve asked, looking round thoughtfully.

Chief Inspector Rivers shook his head. 'He must have brought her here already in it, we think. It's standard stuff that builders use, but definitely not from this site, according to the foreman. All theirs are yellow from a particular supplier. This was a blue one so he must have got it from somewhere else. It's obviously old and well used, too, with any number of different prints on it. We're following it up, of course, but . . .'

His shrug suggested there wasn't much hope to be had there: anyone who wanted to could probably pick up a discarded sheet like that almost anywhere. With Deirdre it had been black plastic sacks, Jane thought. He was clever enough, this man, to use things which were commonplace and untraceable. Except in the case of the Dover girl, left to lie where she had been killed, he also seemed able to find places to commit his murders which were untraceable too. So far. There was no point in asking Chief Inspector Rivers if his men had found any empty or derelict house with tell-tale bloodstains in it: he would have said so if they had.

There was other information, though, some of it new enough not to have been passed on yet. They knew Elise must only just have arrived in England; a Hovercraft ticket from Boulogne to Dover was found in her bag, with a date stamped on it which fitted the estimated day she died. She had been coming to attend a summer language course at Ramsgate but had never reached it. They also knew that she had asked at the Hovercraft enquiry desk how to get to Ramsgate from Dover – and that she had subsequently been seen out on the open road trying to hitch a lift. Seen, merely; no one was admitting to having picked her up.

A nineteen-year-old girl should have had more sense than to be thumbing lifts on her own.

'It's something, anyway,' Chief Inspector Rivers said. 'We're hoping we might find someone who actually saw her getting into a car or a lorry. She certainly never arrived at the school in Ramsgate: they just thought she must have decided not to come after all. So it looks as if that's how she met our killer. Your girl wasn't hitching, I suppose?'

'Not that we've heard or been able to establish. She wouldn't have, I think: she wasn't going far.' Or not that they knew. 'We haven't had any report of her being seen hitching,' Jane amended.

'Have you seen enough? That's all we've got for now – except for her body, which you'll find at the mortuary, as I said. The wounds look as if they came from the same knife used on the Dover girl, or certainly something similar. That's one reason why I don't hold out much hope of finding it here . . . Unless he keeps a set of them.' His voice was level, and trying hard to be dispassionate, Jane thought. He added, 'He's a real bastard, this one, as you'll see when you look at the body. Elise's clothes and possessions are still with our forensic people. You can call there after the mortuary. It's upstairs in the same building, and anyone will tell you how to find it.'

He handed over the packet of photographs Dan Crowe had

been asking for, and then Jane and Steve left him. Jane promised to pass on anything they learned in the Deirdre investigation, and then they were on their way. The next call promised to be the least pleasant . . . but had to be done. And if it was possible to coax answers out of a pathologist who had found no time yet to send in a written report, that had to be done, too.

The pathologist was in fact absent, having apparently been called away. A mortuary assistant took them into the emptiness of white tiles, glaring strip lights, and long working-tables from which Jane had to make an effort not to avert her eyes, although they were scrubbed and vacant at the moment. The air was chilly and held a whiff of some strong disinfectant. Their white-overalled escort consulted a list and then produced both Elise Ducherain and Catherine Jones – the Dover victim – out of the cold store which took up the whole of one wall. He slid the heavy metal shelves out with as cheerful an indifference as if he was showing off carcasses of beef. A daily exposure to death must have a hardening effect, and he flicked the sheets back with the same casualness, then simply stood by, whistling through his teeth.

Jane was aware of Steve's silence behind her as she made herself stare at the two corpses, then signed for the covering sheets to be replaced. She cleared her throat to ensure her voice sounded cool and official.

'Thanks. I suppose it's no use asking if the full autopsy report on . . . on the new one's been done yet?'

'Ducherain? I wouldn't know. The doc'll send everything in when she's finished writing it all up, I expect. All I do is work here!' he said, with a pointed glance at the clock as if it was approaching his going-home time.

'Right, then we won't keep you. Forensic's upstairs, we've been told. If you'll just point us the way?'

'Up two flights of stairs, first right, second left. Don't know if you'll find anyone's still there, though,' he said, with little interest, and was watching the hands of the clock and picking his teeth as they withdrew.

Forensic seemed less absorbed in time-keeping and felt more like a police department in spite of being a lab manned by white coats. One of these stopped what he was doing to come and greet them. 'The Ducherain girl? I can show you most of her things, though we haven't finished all the tests on her clothes yet. Come through to the office.' He led them into a small and cluttered room and pushed various police and medical manuals aside from the top of a desk. 'Have a look at what was in her bag while I fetch some of her clothing. We've gone over this lot thoroughly already, so you can touch if you want to!'

He fished a patchwork leather bag from a box and tipped its contents out on to the cleared space on the desk. Jane studied the small array. A handkerchief with an E embroidered on one corner. A maroon EEC passport, new looking, with no stamps in it – they rarely bothered on the ferries nowadays for European nationals – containing the details they already knew, plus the standard photograph which had caught the girl looking solemn and slightly anxious. A crumpled Hovercraft ticket; a half-smoked packet of cigarettes and a matchbook; a lipstick in a plastic cover with a French maker's name on it; an unopened tube of peppermints, also French. A purse with French money in one side of it and English in the other.

'She had forty pounds with her. She shouldn't have needed to hitch,' Steve said dispassionately.

'She just chose to save the fare, I suppose. Those are English cigarettes, I wonder when she bought them?' Jane stretched out her hand to pick them up, then lifted the small matchbook instead to study it with a frown. 'These are Dutch. See the writing? She wasn't on a Dutch boat, was she? No, by the ticket it was an English one. I wonder why Dutch matches?'

'Probably bought them on board. I expect what they have there is multinational. The kid didn't carry much around with her, did she? Perhaps everything else is packed away in her luggage. She was supposed to be coming for six weeks, wasn't she?'

'Where is the rest of her luggage? Somewhere here I suppose.'

'No, it's missing,' the forensic officer said, reappearing in the doorway with something bundled over his arm. 'We asked for everything, but this is all we got. There certainly was a suitcase, because she was seen hitching with it, but it hasn't turned up. An oversight, if someone's still got it. Though it would be easy enough to dispose of after the killing, I suppose. There's always the sea. Here, these are some of the clothes she was wearing. Some of the slashes went right through, as you can see from the bloodstains, and some didn't. It was a long narrow blade. That's a puncture wound, there, and another two here. This is a piece of her knickers, the top edge. There aren't any semen stains that we've found yet, which is a pity, because if there were we could send that away for a DNA profile. Gets his kicks this way but can't manage the other is a possible guess. All the bloodstains so far match with hers, so that's not going to help you either. The finger-marks on her throat suggest leather gloves, we think. Oh, here's a bit of rope she was bound with – the blood on that's hers too.'

He had spread out the tattered remnants for them to see, his voice perfectly factual as he delivered his chilling list. Perhaps that was the only way of handling the job. Jane pushed away the memory of what she had seen downstairs, but found herself swallowing hard before she spoke.

'She was still tied up when she was found, wasn't she? Was the other one, Catherine Jones? Sorry, we've had the report but just at this minute I can't remember.'

'Um, let me think. No. No, we didn't have any rope from that one. They said she had been tied, but there wasn't anything still there. That's the one we thought had been done more slowly – stains in her clothing from different times, that kind of thing.' His voice was still unemotional. 'This death looks to have been much quicker. So, is there anything else you want to ask? I think I've given you everything we've got, bar the full test results which I'm afraid I can't—'

'No, that's fine, thank you.' Jane glanced briefly at Steve, who made a motion of agreement. 'Thanks for your time. It was nice of you to let us come and bother you.'

'No problem – glad if I've been of help. What we usually get is phone calls saying "Where the hell is that report, what on earth have you been doing, we needed it yesterday", so it's a nice change to have someone actually come in and see what we've got to contend with!' The forensic officer gave Jane a pleasant, crooked grin. 'See you again, maybe!'

It wasn't the best thing he could have said, with its echo of a future, similar occasion. Nevertheless, Jane managed a smile, and to thank him again with an added, 'I'll remember in future about the phone calls!' She and Steve went down the stairs and out into the fresh air, and she was gulping an unusually large amount of it into her lungs when she felt him seize her elbow.

'Come on, we're going for a drink! There must be somewhere due to open . . .' She saw him glance at his watch and then remember. 'Blow me, I still get caught by the change in the licensing laws! All right, then, there's bound to be somewhere near here that's open all day!'

'Should be. You drink, I'll drive, if you like—'

'No, you have a large one, and I'll have a coffee, if you insist on being picky. Or we'll both have one and then something to soak it up. No one's desperate for us to get back, and by now we're basically off duty!'

He was looking grim-faced, so Jane didn't argue. He drove through the town until he found somewhere large and noisy. A loud celebration party at one end of the public bar was just beginning; there was also a juke box blaring out a steady stream of old Elvis hits, with two games machines adding a whining and bleeping background. Glancing at Steve as he downed a whisky – a single, rather surprisingly if he was feeling the way she was – Jane wondered whether, if he had been on his own familiar ground, he would have gone in search of a strip club and spent the rest of the evening whooping it up in the broadest possible company. At least the noise of the pub made rational conversation impossible.

She thought she had pulled herself together by the time she had downed the large brandy he had planted in front of her without asking. And a second smaller one while he had a beer. She even began, as they finally came out of the pub, 'They might find that luggage . . .'

'Not now, OK? There must be a McDonald's in this town, so let's go and look for it. I quite fancy a large bun. And some junk-food chips, of course.'

Neither of them referred further to any aspect of the case, while he dragged her all round the centre of the town in search of the familiar logo; not then, and not when they were seated at a small round plastic table with polystyrene cartons in front of them. It was quite a lot later by the time they finally started back, the summer light dusking down. Leaning back in the passenger seat, Jane reminded herself that as Steve had said, no one was desperate for them to get back. So the road from Dover was just as good as any other place to be. Work tomorrow, more routine. Morland to be avoided perhaps – definitely – and the next section of the fraud file to be fitted in, and those burglaries . . . No, those were solved, of course they were: Darren Smith. Well, the shop break-ins, then. And there was something else she had planned to do, only it had vanished from her mind at this moment. Steve was a good driver, as lazily accomplished at that as he was at everything else . . .

Abruptly he pulled over into a lay-by and killed the engine. She turned to look at him in surprise, with a flatly steady question.

'Why are we stopping?'

Chapter 11

'Because you've been getting whiter and more detached for the past hour! Yes, I know I jumped on you earlier for mentioning the case at all, but I was wrong, OK? Let it out, we both need to!'

'Or I need to? Being a woman and the frailer sex?'

'Oh, climb off that bloody wagon just for once, can't you?' His voice was rough but he reached over to pick up her hand, wrapping his tightly round it. 'Stop being a professional all the time. There's such a thing as trying too hard! And I need a hand to hold, if you want to know. Who wouldn't who was even barely human, after—'

'*You* managed to stuff your face with food, God knows how!' she retorted, in a sudden scathing burst of anger. '"Let's go and find a McDonald's, I fancy a bun" – Jesus Christ!'

'So I turn to junk food; is that a crime? Yes, I did see you pushing your chips round on your plate in a ladylike fashion. D'you think mine weren't choking me? But I'm driving, aren't I, so fat chance of just going out and getting pissed out of my mind!'

'Which is the answer to everything, I suppose!'

'Go on, yell at me. At least that's better than – You won't cure anything by going on like the Frost Queen with a splinter of ice in her heart, or whatever that story was! She ended up frozen right through, as I remember it.' That he of all people should come up with a poetic image out of a fairy-tale caught her with a faint surprise, but he was already going on, with a jeer. 'No mere male is supposed to tell you how to behave, and you've got to prove you're tougher than the lot of us?'

'Is that how I seemed?' Suddenly her anger was receding, and the warmth of his hand in hers was setting off all the other reactions she had been so rigidly denying. 'I wouldn't mind going out and getting pissed out of my mind myself, if you want to know! It isn't – I can't . . .'

'It's the worst case I've ever had to look at too. Jesus. I've seen some of the things that people do, but those two bodies could make you wonder what kind of animal—'

'Yeah.' Jane swallowed hard. 'Oh Christ, Steve. The – the faces most of all . . . and then the Ducherain girl's clothes . . .'

He made no answer in words, but took his hand away from hers and leaned over to flick open the clip of her seat-belt, then pulled her close against him with his arms wrapping right round her. She could sense that he needed the comfort as much as she did. She held him just as tightly, sliding her arms round his waist under his jacket, fitting herself against him. Letting his warmth and closeness blot out thought. There was a deep shiver inside her which had little to do with sexuality, more an urgent need to be close to another human being and feel herself alive.

If they had been somewhere else than in a car, in a lay-by, beside a main road, that kind of desperate longing and hunger for forgetfulness might have led them anywhere. She knew it when he turned his head after several moments and began to kiss her. Hard, mouths finding each other instinctively, hands moving . . . It was he who pulled away first, breathing heavily, and with a ruffled frustration; but also with an entirely practical gleam of regretful amusement in his eyes.

'Not the moment . . .'

Relaxation of tension sent her into a shaky laugh. 'No, we'd look a pair of right nanas if a patrol car came by and stopped to see who we were! What shall I say . . . "Feeling better?"'

'*Better*?' His snort said a great many things, and so did his uncomfortable shift in the seat, but there was humour as well as acknowledgement in his face. 'Let's just say you pack as much punch as I thought you would . . . Mutual? No, don't answer that, since this really *isn't* the moment! Just get back to your own side of the car and put your seat-belt back on!'

She did, with a chuckle, but sobering as he turned the key to start the engine and glanced in the wing-mirror to check for an empty road. He was right: this wasn't the time or the place. But at least the shared closeness had cured that shut-off feeling, and she could allow herself to think again.

They travelled on in a silence only broken by his switching on the radio for background music, and were coming into the outskirts of the city when she turned her head to look at him.

'If you drive round by the hospital, you could drop me there. I'm too bushed to get my car tonight, so I'll leave it at the station and walk to work in the morning. Why the startled look?'

'You're bushed enough to want to go to a hospital?'

'No! Sorry, I suppose you didn't know – my flat's right beside it. I'm not falling to pieces. Sorry if I made you think so!' She added, 'Take a right at the next lights and we can go up the back way. It's a short cut.'

He followed her directions, and then pulled up outside the block she pointed out. She hesitated very briefly, covering her pause by gathering her things together. Then she asked, 'D'you want to come in? I could find you a coffee—'

'I'd like that. But not tonight, unfortunately. I've just remembered I'm on a promise for a card-game – the sergeants' pool, you know?'

She knew about the weekly card-game which went on into the small hours – and also that 'sergeants' in this case ignored anyone of that rank who happened to be female. She didn't bother to make an acid comment. He was offering her a regretful shrug, his hands spread wide.

'OK, no problem, it was just a thought!'

She was already swinging her legs out of the car. And heard

161

him say behind her, 'Raincheck for a better time, OK?'

'Sure,' Jane agreed lightly, coming to her feet. 'See you tomorrow, then. Enjoy your game!'

She was inside the apartment block's entrance before her sense of humour began to re-surface, with an exasperated but acknowledging thought: *He's right, it's no time to start a relationship when every bloody uniform sergeant is going to make assumptions if he doesn't turn up at the card-game when he was last seen with me!* All that, and Morland waiting to pounce? With that bunch of gossips at the station all too ready to speculate? It would be the ultimate in bad timing!

She stumped up the stairs, knowing that it was even more annoying to be aware that she had checked from the car windows and seen that none of the flat's lights were burning. So had known Matty must conveniently be out . . .

She took herself to bed in the empty flat, tossed for a while, then slept. Unexpectedly without dreams of gaping wounds. Sometime during the night she surfaced to hear Matty coming in, the bleeper sounding, Matty going out again. At the moment they were having a spell of seeing nothing of each other, both intensely busy and never somehow coinciding. Waking finally to morning, Jane found Deirdre rising immediately into her conscious thoughts. And with her, a stubborn but oddly definite feeling which said, *No, that one's different. There may be things about it which look the same, but the Deirdre case is different!*

Like but unlike. Maybe, in spite of everything, too unlike? That was something no one else seemed even to be considering now. So thinking that way wasn't likely to get her very far.

Except that it gave her the urge to go on following up her own investigations, quietly, in her own time if necessary, just to prove to herself that she had covered every possibility.

She left Matty a note saying, *Will see you when I see you???
We're out of eggs, I'll buy some!* Maybe milk too, since what was in the fridge seemed to be well past its sell-by date. Then

162

she walked down to the nick, feeling the freshness of a blowy morning which had brought various seagulls this far inland to toss themselves on the high breezes, or perch on roof-ridges looking, with their fierce curved beaks, somehow sinisterly displaced.

There were facts to be given to the Incident Room so that they could be entered under Elise Ducherain. Jane had already been working there for half an hour by the time Steve put in an appearance, looking heavy-eyed and frowsty.

'Morning, but don't say it too loud . . .'

'I wouldn't dream of being so unkind.'

'I won, anyway. John Clay still owes me a fiver, just in case he comes in search of me! You look as if you got a lot more sleep than I did,' he added, managing to make it sound part-grouch, but adding a look of appreciation.

He looked over her shoulder at the notepad where she had been scribbling various comments and a lot of question marks, so she shared her thinking.

'I was wondering if Elise Ducherain could have picked someone up on the Hovercraft over from France. We could be looking for someone who comes from further afield, if he travels quite often . . . But then that doesn't fit in with her hitching, does it? Unless . . . supposing it was a ferry worker? She might have accepted a lift from him because she'd already talked to him on board, so thought he seemed safe?'

'Could be, and certainly worth passing back in case they haven't had the same idea. If she was standing there with her thumb out, though, why do you think she wouldn't have accepted a lift from just anyone?'

'My Police Judiciaire contact described her as a "respectable girl", that's all. So you'd think she'd be a bit careful about choosing a respectable lift? Maybe not. I just thought, Dover, and someone last seen on the road to Ramsgate from Dover . . . None of that fits with Deirdre, though.'

'Unless it's a ferry worker who lives on our patch?'

'Yes, that's an idea! I expect there are some who do. They needn't necessarily live right beside the job! Will you put that to the guv? Oh, I've told him that it'll be you who'll give him a written report of yesterday, OK? Since I'm getting all the facts entered in here!'

She well knew how much he hated paperwork. But was feeling in no mind to take the job over from him, when she had already given Dan Crowe a verbal summing-up while *some* people were still dragging themselves in late and hung-over. Luckily no Morland planning meeting had been scheduled for this morning, since he only insisted on them once a week. There had been no summons from upstairs, either; in fact, Dan Crowe was behaving as if life was in its usual state of normality. The storm about Jane's status had perhaps passed over, or was dying out in a frustrated rumble upstairs . . . Steve shot her a faintly martyred look for her brisk efficiency, winced as if moving his eyes was unwise, and took himself off in the direction of the CID room.

Dan Crowe looked in a little later to say that a ferry worker living locally sounded like the first bright idea anyone had had, and added that he'd been on to the ferry companies for a list of their employees. All the companies, not just the one which ran the Hovercraft Elise had taken. 'You're the one who can jabber away in French, so get on to our opposite numbers in Boulogne and Calais to see if they've by any chance had any similar cases,' he said, and added with an approving growl 'Good thinking!'

'Thanks, Guv, but should I check with Dover first, to see if they've already done all that?'

'They haven't, from what I've heard. And if a few personnel managers can get off their arses and send us those lists, we might have something constructive to be doing!'

There certainly seemed little else for the Deirdre Incident Room to get on with. A depressing lack of information had already meant a winding-down to minimum manning – before the Elise Ducherain case had woken things up again. Jane made her phone calls, but found neither Boulogne nor Calais had anything to offer her. They seemed grateful to be alerted. She exchanged pleasantries with her opposite numbers across lines as clear as if they were next door and then rang off. Nothing else to try, as the guv had said, until those lists came in . . .

Except maybe an opportunity for a follow-up of her own, to tie up some loose ends while things were quiet.

Other CID work offered Jane the chance to go out for a while. She took that option mid-morning and, an hour later, came back by a route which would bring her past the Crayshaw estate agency.

She was counting on the idea that Anthony Crayshaw would normally go out to lunch. He did, emerging to walk away briskly in the opposite direction just as Jane was approaching on foot. That was highly convenient of him. There would definitely be repercussions if word got back to Morland that Jane had been 'bothering' the Crayshaws again. She had decided to pump the agency's office manager instead.

The girl was there in the showroom, behind a desk with 'Tracy Pargeter' written in neat capitals on a sign in front of her. There were no customers in at the moment and she looked up with a bright smile at Jane's arrival, plainly not recognising her immediately.

'Good afternoon, can I help you?'

'Not with a property, I'm afraid,' Jane said, smiling at her. 'It's Detective-Sergeant Perry again – remember?'

'Oh yes. I'm afraid none of the staff has thought of anything more they can tell you. I did say to everyone that they were to get in touch with you if they did!'

'I really only popped in to warn you that the tabloids may start bothering you,' Jane said, giving the girl a smile. It was a fair enough warning, after all: there was no hope that the national press would fail to make the tie-up between the three cases and start to rehash everything in gory detail. The Deal case had made the local TV news with a fairly brief, 'girl's body found . . .' but the Kent weeklies had it this morning, bringing the fading Dover story back into prominence along with it. Any minute now some sharp-eyed reporter would come up with Deirdre's name and the three cases would be publicly linked, making anyone who had known any of the three girls fair game for a 'personal comment'.

'Oh, oh, I see.' Tracy was round-eyed. She came to her feet in a sudden hurry. 'Jill, will you take over here for the moment? I just want a private word with the sergeant.'

She ushered Jane into the rear area. Into Mr Crayshaw's private office, in fact. She shut the door firmly behind them and turned to look at Jane, appealing to her in a hushed voice and with horrified anxiety, the words tumbling out of her. 'They won't start writing about poor David, will they? That would be awful! Mr Crayshaw would be so upset if—'

'We certainly shan't give out anything with David's name in it,' Jane said reassuringly, knowing it to be true. It was interesting that Tracy knew about David and Deirdre . . . She was given the reason a second later.

'Mr Crayshaw confided in me,' Tracy said, looking slightly pink. 'He's very fond of his boys, and – Oh, you don't really think the papers are going to start writing about it again, do you? Or, have you caught the murderer, is that it? I suppose if you've got him, that's a relief, anyway! Who was it? Or aren't you allowed to say?'

'Sorry, I'm not allowed to give out any information at this stage. I just wanted to warn you that you might get bothered by reporters.' Jane gave a sympathetic smile. Then she added, as if suddenly remembering, 'Oh, there is a small detail you might be able to help me with, to save me coming back and bothering Mr Crayshaw. It's not about Deirdre. Just a bit of paperwork I need to clear up! About his stolen car. I know when he reported it, and I know when it was found. I just don't seem to have a note of when he actually missed it. Would you know?'

'Yes, I do! It was taken during the night of May the twenty-ninth – Friday. It had gone by Saturday morning. I remember because Tony said on the Saturday that it was annoying, since he only really likes driving his own car, but at least David's was sitting there in the garage for him to use.' Producing the information with helpful triumph, Tracy didn't seem to notice that she had used her employer's Christian name. Or perhaps she did, since the pink in her cheeks suddenly deepened. When she spoke again it was with a sudden air of defiance. 'All right, I told you last time that I didn't work on Saturdays, so now you're wondering why – Well, Tony comes to see me on Saturday nights. We're in love. And if it wasn't for his bloody wife . . . She just uses the fact that the money's hers to keep him under her thumb, that's all! If he tried for a divorce she'd demand her money back out of the business, and then it would go under! And besides that, he's so fond of the boys . . .'

Her face was crumpling, the careful make-up threatening to smudge with overflowing tears.

'Look, why don't you sit down?' Jane said quickly. 'It's all right, I'm not going to shout a private conversation around the town!'

'I wouldn't care if you did!' Tracy dabbed at her eyes with a tissue, her voice miserable. And bitter. She added at once, 'No, I don't mean that. It'd only hurt Tony . . . He's such a wonderful man! Really kind and thoughtful. He never forgets when it's someone's birthday, and he brings his home-grown vegetables in for all the staff! And he's really sweet with Jeremy. *He* doesn't try to hide the fact that he's got a Downs Syndrome son, not like that bitch! It was her who insisted Jeremy had to be sent away to live in a home. *She* wasn't going to spend the extra time and attention he needs, was she! Or let people see him – she'd rather pretend he didn't exist! Not like Tony. Look—' She dived round the desk to pull open a drawer and

167

produced a photograph out of it, holding it out for Jane to see. A small posed portrait of a smiling-faced boy with an over-wide grin, small round eyes set on a slant, a wide head. 'You see? He keeps this beside him – and he goes to visit Jeremy regularly! That cow doesn't. She goes off and plays golf instead! Tony doesn't deserve a wife like that!'

'So he comes to see you, and gets what happiness he can out of that.' It was an inadequate comment, but Jane tried to make it sound comfortingly sympathetic. 'At least you have your Saturday nights. All of them, I hope . . .'

'It's been bloody difficult lately. I think she's got him on a string again,' Tracy said bitterly – but at least picking up Jane's lead. 'That Saturday, the thirtieth, was the last time he managed to get away! And even then I had the curse . . . And besides, he was – Oh, it doesn't matter, and I know I shouldn't be talking about him – particularly not to you.'

'Why particularly not to me? Detectives are discreet. Anyway, let's say I'm on my lunch-hour, and off duty. It dawns on me,' Jane said, mildly thoughtful, 'that it must have been really uncomfortable for him when I turned up asking for details about a Saturday evening, and what time he locked up and who was there and all that.'

'The last time that girl Deirdre was here, you mean? He was with me that night, if that's what you're asking!' Tracy said with a sudden sharpness. 'I can tell you exactly when, too! He came at eight and left at two the next morning!'

'I wasn't asking,' Jane said, smiling pacifically to defuse the other girl's abrupt (and perfectly justified) suspicion, but noting the times in her head.

'Sorry . . . I know Tony was really upset about that girl going missing, and worried that you'd think he might be involved, just because he employed her. Particularly after you found her body,' Tracy added with a shiver.

'Difficult for him to provide an alibi when he had to keep you a secret,' Jane agreed, adding, 'I shouldn't worry about it, because if he was with you until two in the morning he certainly has got an alibi, hasn't he? If he'd needed one! Forgive my asking, but – well, in view of what I've seen of his wife, how does he manage to arrive home so late without questions being asked?'

'He tells her he's been playing poker. She doesn't like the people he'd be doing that with, so she wouldn't be likely to ask them. His friends wouldn't tell on him even if she did,' Tracy said promptly, with a curl of scorn. She added, 'They have separate bedrooms anyway, he told me so. It's only a marriage in name! He wouldn't stay with her at all if she couldn't blackmail him with her bloody money – and because of David, until he's through school . . .'

'It's a tough old life, isn't it?' Jane said, aiming to bring things to a close, since she had got what she wanted. And more. A confirmation of Steve's guess about Anthony Crayshaw and his office manager: trust a male copper to catch the scent of sex in the air! 'I'm glad we've talked,' she told Tracy, 'and thanks for helping me about the car: I didn't really want to bother Mr Crayshaw again when it was only a routine question, and now you've cleared that up I can—'

The sudden opening of the door made Tracy jump, and Jane look round. She saw something she could have done without right now – Anthony Crayshaw himself, returning with a plastic-wrapped sandwich in his hand. He stopped dead, turning remarkably white at the sight of her.

Tracy provided a diversion. She swept towards him, pulled him inside the room, half shut the door again behind him, hissed, 'Tony, I've told her!' and then fled, shutting the door with a thump behind her. He stood there helplessly staring at Jane, and then found his voice, with some apparent difficulty.

'Sergeant—?'

When in doubt, brazen it out. 'Sorry to be lurking in your office in your absence,' Jane said pleasantly, 'and I've only looked in as I was passing, to have a word with your office manager. Another girl's body has been found, and since we're now assuming all three to be linked, you may find yourselves being pestered by reporters.'

'How nice of you to warn us!' He had regained control of himself, and if his pallor had been that of rage, her explanation sent him back into friendly heartiness. *Almost* real. 'Another girl? How dreadful. Oh, that one in this morning's paper? That is quite appalling. I'm not surprised Miss Pargeter seemed upset.'

'It means we're likely to start getting national coverage, I'm afraid, so . . . I'm here in an unofficial capacity, actually.'

'Yes I see, and that's very kind of you. Very kind.' He was looking so inordinately grateful that she might have felt guilty: he was thinking of David, she guessed abruptly. It was a surprise when he went on quickly, 'I think I know what Miss Pargeter – Tracy – told you. That she and I – that she's my mistress? I'm sure you understand how difficult it would be if my wife found out.'

'She won't find out from me. Thank you for being so frank. Miss Pargeter gave me the information unsolicited,' Jane added, being deliberately formal, and with the clear knowledge that she was aiming to cover her rear. The man wasn't a suspect now, after all . . . It was only an outside chance that had ever made him one, and she could put him thoroughly in the clear after today. He had an alibi from Tracy for the Saturday night, and then from his wife and son all through Sunday.

'It was really very awkward having to answer questions in front of Virginia.' He seemed eager to explain. 'I hope I didn't seem evasive, but I was continually afraid you'd ask for my movements! I spent the whole evening that poor girl disappeared with Tracy – Miss Pargeter – and didn't leave her to drive home until the early hours, so it would have been extraordinarily awkward if I'd had to—'

'Give us quite different names to check up with?' Jane said

drily. She remembered immediately that it behoved her to be particularly polite; the spectre of an outraged Morland hovered. 'Thank you, Mr Crayshaw, I do understand. And I certainly don't need to take up any more of your time now.'

'If Virginia found out about my little affair it would be quite disastrous. Her feelings . . . and our boys . . . It's difficult enough that Virginia's a light sleeper and always wakes up when I get into bed, she's grumbled about that more than once! You must think it stupid of me to take the risk of damaging my family. My only excuse is that Miss Pargeter's an extremely attractive girl and—'

'I'm not a judge, Mr Crayshaw. Just a member of your local CID quietly getting on with her job. Which I must get back to now.' She had to stop him somehow, since he appeared pathetically eager to give her all the details of his private life. And to make her see things from his point of view. It was noticeably different from Tracy's. 'I'll show myself out,' Jane finished, 'please don't let me take up any more of your time!'

He insisted on escorting her just the same, shaking her fulsomely by the hand on the doorstep. Definitely a man with a bad conscience . . . Not a conscience for murder, though, merely for adultery.

Also a man who looked on the edge of falling apart. Perhaps that was natural with both his very private life, and his son, involved.

Was it the thought of David which was bothering him? From suspicion (or even knowledge) rather than just concern for the boy's obvious misery? No, that wouldn't work . . . The very outside chance that David had killed Deirdre by mistake, then used his father's car not his own to take the body somewhere to hide, had to be discounted. Mr Crayshaw had by all accounts been using his own car that weekend. And for his own very private purposes. With every minute of his time accounted for, too; he had gone from his mistress's bed to his

171

wife's . . . *Not* separate bedrooms, clearly, whatever he had told Tracy!

Jane had a few more small facts to put in her own personal, unofficial file on Deirdre, but that was it. Just a few more details, to make sure to her own satisfaction that she had covered them. Other than that, she was suddenly aware that she'd had too much of other people's private lives. Two people had chosen to confide in her, one with encouragement, one not. She had a marginal sympathy for Tracy (who, to put it bluntly, was a mug) but no mind at all to play kindly Agony Auntie to Mr Anthony Crayshaw for his 'little affair' on Saturday nights when he was supposed to be playing poker.

She went back to the station and to routine matters. Later in the afternoon she caught up with Steve who was looking healthier by now, almost back to his usual self. He glanced up with a welcoming grin when she walked in to find him at his desk in the CID room.

'Just the person I'd like to see, and for more reasons than one!' he said cheerfully. 'First things first . . . What would you recommend I do about this tip-off we've had on a landlord possibly running a Social Services fraud? It seems to have landed up in my in-tray.'

'That one? It was an anonymous call and could be spite. Even if it's genuine it doesn't sound like much, does it? Just one family house with two spare rooms? Social Security has its own investigators anyway: I'd say either file it, or pass it over to them with our compliments!'

'OK. That was more or less what I thought. I just wanted to know if you had a usual drill round here!'

'That's usually shoving it on to someone else's desk while they're not looking. Then when it's been round a few times . . . No, we do pass them on – when we get a minute, and if they haven't got lost in transit!' She grinned at him. 'No thanks, I don't want it on mine. Try Kenny's!'

'Done. What a nice efficient system. Now, next – oh, before I get to that, how about tonight for the meal you owe me? You remember – that agreement we had in your favourite Thai restaurant, that it was your turn next?'

'Oh dear, it'll have to be another raincheck, I'm all tied up with friends tonight! Remind me some other time, and one day I'll stand you a lunch.'

His expression indicated he knew perfectly well she was back in her strong-minded mode, and granting no quarter. But also showed an amused but definite intention to find his way round it. 'Pity,' he said. 'Particularly when I was going to suggest that I wouldn't hold you to its being your turn to pay, because we could spend my winnings instead! Oh well, I might as well just hand you your latest telephone message, then – a further communication from the dashing Major Dalkeith!'

'Dennis? What did he say this time? If it's just "Hi" again—'

'No, this time he's left a phone number for you to call him back,' Steve said amiably, and handed her the torn-off corner of a piece of much-used scrap paper. 'Here you are – along with your tattered reputation, since it landed up with me via about three different people!'

Jane cast her eyes up to heaven, but had no time for a tart answer, since Dan Crowe emerged from his office at that moment. He was in search of someone to go and look something up in Records, whose internal line was engaged too long for his patience. He elected Steve for the job, so Jane was left to her own devices.

She wondered what Dennis wanted of her. Probably nothing at all urgent, but she would ring him when she got home tonight, and find out.

Chapter 12

Dennis didn't seem to want anything vital, just a family chat.
'I forgot to get your private number off you when I was down,'
he said when she got him at her second try, 'and your place
won't give out that kind of information over the phone, even to
the likes of me. Fair enough, I suppose, how could they know
you'd want them to? And them's the rules! Got time for a
natter?'

'All evening if you like.'

Her evening yawned emptily, with nothing more promising
in view than the telly or a book. So did tomorrow, the start of a
non-duty weekend unless something vital in the murder
investigations occurred to call her back in. 'If you were hoping
to speak to Matty as well,' she told Dennis, 'you won't get the
chance, I'm afraid – I haven't seen her myself for days! We just
communicate by notes. I leave her one, she leaves me one.
Hers starts, "Don't buy eggs, I did, look in cupboard!" So that
means we've now got twice as many as necessary, since I'd
already been to the shops . . . Still, at least it solves my menu
for the next couple of days, and one thing I can cook is
omelettes!' Dennis's chuckle sounded in her ear, and she went
on, 'The trouble is I can't read the other half of what she's put.
Honestly, I thought it was only GPs who took special lessons
in writing illegibly!'

'Try it on me in case I can guess.'

'OK, let's see. I've got it right here. It looks like, "Have you –
something something – the dragon." And then another word
which could be . . . "question"? Or "guesting"? As a message it

175

does leave rather a lot to be desired, doesn't it?'

'Have you fed the dragon, question mark? Have you fed the dragon in question? Have you got a dragon?' Dennis asked, as if the enquiry was a perfectly serious one.

'Idiot, where would I keep it? In the fridge? It's no good, I'll just have to wait for a translation until Matty actually comes in! I reckon she must have been doing a lot of long sessions in the operating theatre, because her writing never used to be that bad. And I hope she's actually getting some sleep when I'm not here,' Jane added, 'she certainly doesn't seem to be spending much time in her own bed at night!'

'And you don't feel that could be for other and more interesting reasons?'

'You know Matty, and she's still just the same – eyes down on work and no more than a sweet, kind, but evasive smile for the legion of admirers! But do tell me something," Jane added on a dulcet enquiry. 'Why do you take it for granted that "other reasons" would be more interesting than her career? Is your sex life more interesting to you than *your* career?'

'I refuse to be drawn into one of your fights,' Dennis said comfortably. He went on, 'All the same, I shall definitely come down some time to take you both out and remind you there's more to life than work! Don't think I'd missed the fact that all you're doing with a free evening is talking to me!'

'And relaxing. Give us a chance! I've got my feet up as I talk!' Jane said truthfully, stretching them out to regard them critically and wondering absently whether to paint her toenails. If she could be bothered. 'Some of us,' she went on with the receiver cradled against her ear, 'do quite a lot of work, you know! Rather than swanning around being nice to VIPs! Seriously, it would be great if you paid us a visit. Always supposing you can spare time from the likes of Arabella!'

'*Anna*bella,' he corrected. 'And I was on duty then. I was supposed to be looking after her. Her Daddy's a South American millionaire, and there'd been kidnap threats. Not just an idle swan, see? Anyway, tell me how you've been occupying yourself in the last couple of weeks? Any interesting cases to keep you busy?'

She wasn't going to talk about the murders: let there be at least one evening when they weren't on her mind. 'Just the general morass of police work,' she said instead. 'The odd burglar burgling, a few old ladies trampled to death in the sales, you know the kind of thing! And just to show you how mundane my life can be, this afternoon I acted as interpreter when a student came in wanting something and didn't seem to know any English. Or, at least, just enough to say very slowly, "Someone – speak – German?" when he arrived at the desk! So they rang round to discover if there *was* anyone who spoke German, and landed up with me. Then the lad insisted on seeing my warrant-card before he'd talk to me – I think his parents must have told him never to talk to strangers, even in a cop-shop! – and all it turned out to be was that he'd found a twenty-pound note lying in the street, and wanted to hand it in like an honest citizen.'

'A very honest citizen!'

'Yeah. He seemed like a nice lad – earnest type, with thick glasses. He went away happy, and the twenty will probably land up in the charity box. Since I can't imagine anyone will come in with proof of ownership!' Jane chuckled. 'Oh, by the way, about your escort trip – two weeks tomorrow, right?'

'Yes?'

'Just thought I'd warn you. Don't bring your royal down by the M2-A2 route, because we've just had word that they're starting emergency roadworks around then; so it'll be all cones and chicanes!'

'It's all right, we were going to helicopter him in from London with an official car waiting at your end, but they've changed all that now anyway. They're going to send him in by a military plane and land at Manston – the other side of you. It was decided at that end that they'd rather keep him out of

177

main airports in case some Basque Separatist had smuggled himself in as a baggage handler. That lot have been stirring recently.'

'They don't seriously think ETA's going to try something here?' Jane asked.

'No. I don't think so. It's just that the Spanish king made some fairly tactless remarks against Basque separatism not long ago, so any relation of his is being given an extra guard. I can't think they'll try anything off their own turf – and anyway ETA's such a bunch of known faces, and they're all being watched like hawks.' He sounded comfortably certain – though, being Dennis, he went on jokingly. 'Worried that you're going to find small dark men with heavy moustaches, thick accents, and bombs in their pockets turning up on your territory for the princeling's visit? It's all right, nobody like that will be allowed near your patch!'

'Be serious. It's me you're talking to!'

'So it is. And I meant what I said, it's all right, we aren't anticipating any trouble! A minor royal on the briefest possible visit? No way!'

That was reassuring – particularly since he himself would be the first in line if someone did throw a bomb. Jane opened her mouth to tell him with cousinly affection that she was glad to hear it, for his sake, but he had already switched to another subject.

'Tell me, how are you getting on with my friend Steve Ryan?'

'He's an easy guy to work with,' Jane said lightly. 'A good colleague—'

'And a bit of a lad. Popular with the women, is rather the impression I got in London. Mind you, I'll never understand women's tastes!'

'Fishing, Dennis dear? I said, he's a colleague. Just one of the guys! So if you had it in your head to think I needed a warning—'

'Goodness no. What me, try to run interference on your life?' His voice was extremely innocent. Then he spoiled it with a laughing addition. 'I've never understood your preferences anyway, have I? *Henry*! I'm not sure I wouldn't rather see you with an East End copper with a roving eye than a stuffed shirt—'

'Shut that! You can lay off *all* comments on my private life, Dalkeith, got it?'

'Yes, ma'am. Shall we talk about something else, then?'

He was always aware when his teasing went over the edge, and they conversed quite happily on other subjects until they both ran out of steam. They parted on his renewed promise to come down on a purely social visit some time after his escort-duty trip; and with his usual brotherly, 'Take care!'

'I will, I do. You as well! If I'm around somewhere when you pass by with the prince, I'll give you a surreptitious wave!' It was unlikely she would be; uniform would be in charge of seeing that the prince arrived at the right place in the university in the morning, then clearing his way down to the cathedral for the two o'clock wedding. Jane would probably be somewhere else doing CID work; business as usual. She gave a grin as she left the phone and went to switch on the television. Talking to Dennis always cheered her up.

She had missed the late news and there was nothing much on bar the continuation of a highly unlikely mini-series, so she took a book to bed with her, keeping an ear open for Matty. But had heard nothing before she dropped into sleep. In the morning, though, she found a heap of clothes on the bathroom floor as if someone had flopped out of them in a state of exhaustion, and a damp towel which hadn't been there last night.

Matty's bedroom door was shut. Jane scratched on it very lightly, then eased it open to peep in. Well, she was here, anyway, if dead to the world . . . All Jane could actually see was the top of a black frizz sticking out above the bedclothes, and the outline of long limbs. Sleeping the sleep of the just, and definitely not to be disturbed!

She picked up the mysterious note again as she went back towards the kitchen. *Have you fed the dragon?* No, the dragon can feed itself. *Have you,* something something, *the dragon* something . . .

Suddenly she could see what it meant. Damn and damn, no, she hadn't, she'd forgotten all about it!

Have you thought yet about the drugs question? Matty's patient, the student with head injuries!

Was it too late? No, it couldn't be, or she wouldn't still be asking. Jane knew she had forgotten it when David Crayshaw turned up; and then Matty's problem had gone out of her head completely when Elise Ducherain's body had been found . . . and ever since. Christ, eleven days!

But still just in time – as long as the student wasn't threatening to discharge himself.

She'd thought of asking Steve's advice. OK, she'd go in this morning and catch him: he was CID Sergeant on duty this weekend, so he'd be there. She could surely get him alone for a minute or two. She showered, then dressed quickly, glancing at her bedside clock. She'd slept in, but in a way that meant a better chance of catching him in an idle moment . . .

As she drove in to the back of the station she saw a television camera set up outside the front entrance with a young woman talking animatedly into its lens. The press had jumped in, then. Just as well she'd fitted in her Crayshaw visit yesterday . . . She found Steve in the Incident Room gazing thoughtfully at the information on the walls, and he looked round at her with a raised eyebrow.

'You're a glutton for punishment. You're supposed to be off! Or did you decide to come in so that you can see exactly what the press statement's going to be?'

'I saw the cameras outside. There's going to be a release from here, then?'

'Yes, now it's hit the national news. You didn't see the bulletin this morning?'

No, she hadn't. 'Who's doing the statement from here,' Jane asked, 'the press liaison officer?'

'The Super will, I think. And let's hope he asks them politely not to get under the police's feet . . . It's going to be bad enough when they find out how little we've got to go on!'

Like most working coppers he thought of press intrusion as mainly a nuisance – bar a grudging admission that publicity sometimes brought in information. It was only the upper echelons who seemed to like the chance to appear on camera and get their names and faces known. Jane gave him a wry look to betoken her agreement, then glanced round at the couple of PCs who were working in here before she looked back at Steve.

'Any chance of a private word? In the canteen over a cup of coffee, maybe? If you're in the middle of something I can wait.'

'Now's as good a time as any.' He paused to tell the others where he could be found, then led the way. The canteen held only a few people at this time in the morning and Jane picked a table in one corner, remote enough to be undisturbed by any arrivals. When they were sitting down Steve looked at her questioningly, obviously alerted by her desire for privacy and wondering where it was leading.

'It isn't another Humpty-Dumpty problem, is it?'

'No, he seems to be lying doggo at the moment, though I expect he's rushing around in small circles over the press release,' Jane added with a chuckle, at the vision of the DCI trying to make sure that only the right things were said to – and about – the right people.

'So – what's bugging you?'

'I want some advice. I suppose it *is* Humpty-Dumpty-related, come to that, given that his attitude makes it harder for me to put a foot out of line.' She ran through the information for him quickly – the student brought to hospital with head injuries,

Matty's certainty that the boy had been on drugs, his plainly frightened refusal to say what had caused his injuries. 'He won't talk, and ethically she can't make him. He was pretty badly hurt. She asked me if I could try to get something out of him unofficially. You see the problem? If I get information, and then I can't pass it on?'

'Mm. If you can't persuade him – then your doctor friend's in schtuck for breaking confidentiality?'

'Right! It's going to look bad enough if anyone finds out afterwards that I knew something and didn't say, isn't it? I did pass "a rumour" to John Clay about drugs in the university, as a floater . . . If the police had been called in at the start, when the boy was found semi-conscious, it wouldn't be a problem, but he was just loaded into a car by his friends and dumped in Casualty, I gathered. And the friends took off without giving any names. Casualty was busy; it was an emergency; we weren't informed because that isn't the hospital's job . . . All this was ten days or so ago,' Jane added, with a distinct twinge of guilt, 'but we've had so much else on—'

'He's still in the hospital, though?'

'Yes. Yes, I'm sure he is.'

'So he can be visited. Purely unofficially. Would you like me to give it a go?'

'I didn't mean I wanted to push it off on to you. I just wanted some advice!'

'Easier for me. I'm temporary here, no one's putting me in the firing line, I can cut corners and look blank about it afterwards.' He sounded practical. 'Let's see. This weekend? Yes, why not? You said he was convalescent by now and that you'd got to decide quickly before he was discharged. Seriously, I'll handle it, if you want!'

'Are you sure?'

'Yes, why not? All I can do is try. And, like I said,' he added with easy cynicism, '*I* don't have anything to lose! Can you get your doctor friend to take me in and point me in the right direction, so that I can be – oh, a hospital visitor, or something? I'm not sure about today, tomorrow would be easier.'

'Tomorrow might be better anyway. I've got to talk to Matty and she was asleep when I left. She works heavy hours.'

They left it that she would talk to Matty and phone through with Sunday's hospital visiting times. Steve's reaction to the problem still gave Jane doubts because she was landing him in it instead of herself, but he said it was no sweat. She decided not to wait to hear what the press release was going to be, after that – just in case Matty was called from her bed and vanished again – and took herself back home and found Matty still asleep. She woke at noon to emerge from her room like a somnambulist, taking several minutes to get her eyes properly open.

'Oh, hi, stranger . . .' She blinked at Jane and yawned. 'Yes, it is you, not a blur! Bless you if you've been keeping quiet for my sake, though I'm not sure I'd have heard!'

'Heavy night?'

'Just six hours in theatre. No one should ever give a sixteen-year-old a motor bike.' There was a bitter note in her voice for a second, but she visibly shook off its cause, and managed a smile. 'Haven't seen you practically for ever. You been busy too? Oh – I left you a note.'

'Yeah, and I'm sorry I never got back to you on that one, but it's in hand now! Are you awake enough to hear?'

'Give me a minute and some strong coffee and I will be!' Matty yawned again as she made for the kitchen, and asked over her shoulder, 'How's your murder? Have you cracked it?'

'My murder's now three murders and about to be all over the press. Let's not talk about it, though, OK? You have too much on your own plate to need to hear what's been on mine!' Jane followed her into the kitchen. 'I'll tell you something cheerful while you're waking up. Oh, you're not going to get bleeped and have to rush away, are you?'

'No, I am definitely off duty, and from now until tomorrow!

'Touch wood and all being well—' Despairing of finding any wood in their plastic-laminated kitchen to go with her heartfelt plea, Matty compromised with a rapid tap on her own forehead.

'Right, then. Dennis is on a promise to come down and take us both out – you'd better be free then, come hell and high water! Probably in about three weeks' time. He says he feels our lives need lightening.'

'Oh, lovely! Bless the man. Do we have any bread? I do fancy real toast instead of canteen leather . . . Angel, is that proper ground coffee you're getting out of the cupboard?'

Once she was settled over an extremely dark cup of Douwe Egberts, Jane put it to Matty about her student patient. 'Steve's offered to try and pump him. I won't go into the ins and outs, but he suggested doing it and I said yes. So, is tomorrow OK? And is there a time when the boy won't be likely to have any other visitors?'

'He doesn't have any, so that's easy. His parents come from up north, I think – and he wouldn't have them contacted, anyway.'

'He's still just as scared then?'

'Still frightened to death and trying not to show it. And it's to do with leaving hospital, too. When my consultant started talking about discharge dates the other day, he practically shrank into his pillows. Thanks, Jane—'

'I'm sorry it's taken so long. Anyway, you'll have to thank Steve, not me. He said, can you take him in under the guise of a hospital visitor, or something?'

'Can do, if we can fix a time. So I'm going to meet your Steve!' Matty added on a grin, looking up at Jane with a quizzical expression. 'That I shall find interesting . . .'

'Don't start! You're merely going to meet one Steven Ryan, rank not to be mentioned. You stop grinning, girl, and keep your trap shut, or I'll take that coffee away from you!' Matty cradled her hands in instant protection around her mug and folded her lips tightly shut – though not without a muffled

184

laugh coming through them. Jane spared her another mock-threatening look, and then turned to the more serious matter of fixing a time when Matty could introduce Steve to her patient.

When Jane rang through to tell him, later, she made it sound casual in case switchboard was listening in. 'Main hospital, Devlin Ward. Three o'clock Sunday if you can make it, and ask for Dr Ingle, OK?'

'Will do. Do you want to know what's happening here?'

'Something interesting about the press release?'

'Better than that. Two things at once, and quite a break. They think they've found the house where Elise Ducherain was killed – an empty furnished one, up for rent, and not far from the building site. They're matching up bloodstains now. Some repairs were going on there and it looks as if that's where the blue plastic sheeting came from.'

'Great! When will we hear more?'

'Soon as they have anything, but you haven't heard the second one yet. There's a definite report from a lorry driver that he saw Elise getting into a dark-coloured car on the road to Ramsgate. One male driver, he thinks, but from the high cab he couldn't be sure. And he didn't get the number, either, says he was too far away. Still, it's better than anything we've had on either of the others, isn't it? And don't rush in,' he added, 'stick with your time off, we may get more tomorrow!'

'I'll come in tomorrow lunch-time, anyway.'

They had agreed on that this morning, at her suggestion: her presence would make it simpler for him to get away. She rang off, thinking triumphantly, *a break*! Someone had seen Elise Ducherain.

Things might be starting to move.

Arne had done his job, and done it intelligently so that it was confirmed without mistake. The Widow knew what she had to contend with now.

185

The young woman she had seen had been the Rees-Perry girl. Jane. Calling herself merely Perry now, but the names were too similar for error. And the guess the Widow had made, after considering how familiarly the Rees-Perry girl had spoken to the police – a suspicion which had made her give Arne that as a place to start – was confirmed too: she was a policewoman herself nowadays. A Detective Sergeant, and stationed right there . . . Arne had seen her warrant card, so the identification was complete.

It threw everything out. Only Simeon, now, could take up residence in the house in the city. His 'wife' could only arrive at the last minute. It was fortunate that the Widow had already walked the chosen ground, since she wanted no one else to take this coup and the credit for it. It had to be hers. But the Rees-Perry girl was standing like a block across her way—

The block would have to be disposed of.

But with care, and the right timing.

Could it even be turned to advantage?

There might be a way of doing that; a method which would kill two birds with one stone.

She had already told Arne to continue watching. The identity he had adopted would carry no suspicion, and he could provide all the necessary information.

A few almost forgotten old scores moved gently in the Widow's consciousness. They could be added to the present problem – and its solution.

She bit down on her anger, and almost smiled as she began to set her mind carefully to the best method to be used.

Yes . . .

Chapter 13

When Steve came back into the Incident Room late on Sunday afternoon he was wearing a very blank expression — maybe because he had been warned Morland was in the room. The DCI was making a point of finding out how things were going, and doing it while ignoring Jane's presence entirely. Not so with Steve, she saw, when Morland turned round to greet the sergeant heartily with a deliberate, 'Ah, Sergeant Ryan, you can show me what we've been doing!' He then proceeded to talk exclusively to Steve with a discussion on how the press was being handled, and the need that everyone should be reminded that all press enquiries must be referred upstairs. And that was said as pointedly as if he thought Jane might rush out in search of limelight . . . What did he think she might do, she thought sarcastically? Put on a spangled tutu and do a little dance for the nearest camera?

If the man wanted to be childish . . .

When he'd gone she raised a questioning eyebrow at Steve, and got a brief gesture of one hand held out palm-down with a balancing movement. Maybe; could be getting Matty's student's confidence, but not sure yet. They still weren't alone so he didn't offer more. It was done without his usual smile, though; in fact he seemed abstracted. And when he came over to where Jane was sitting a moment or two later he didn't make any amused comment under his breath on Morland's behaviour, either. Jane raised the subject softly herself.

'At least you're not in the doghouse, I'm glad to see . . .'

'Mm? Oh, yeah. Got anything else in on the bloodstains in that house?'

'Not so far.'

'You may as well go home, then. No point in your knocking yourself out on your free weekend. Go away and relax, no one's going to pay you any extra for being here.' He sounded remarkably like Dan Crowe for a minute. 'Go on, then, shoo!' He did smile at her this time, with a gleam of his usual humour.

The following day he should have been off duty, and should have missed Morland's interminable morning planning meeting, moved now to Mondays from Thursdays. However, when Jane arrived in carefully dutiful time for it, she saw Steve was there, having apparently chosen to change his duty. Or perhaps had been asked to do so. The meeting was shorter than usual, because the lists from the ferry companies had arrived at last, and Dan Crowe wanted to use as many of his staff as possible to start checking through them before anything else came up.

'All right, everyone take a page and mark down anyone who's on our patch,' the DI said when they were back downstairs. He added, 'They're doing the same thing at Dover, having taken the idea on board, with a particular look at anyone who's local to Deal. When we've found out who we've got, they'll all have to be called on and interviewed. Strictly in pairs, and if we use some of the woodentops to help, no two women together, got it?'

'Yes, Guv.'

It was a reasonable precaution in the circumstances, and not one to raise Jane's hackles. She bent over her page, but found just one local name – and a female at that – which made her lift her head. 'Are we looking at men only, or both sexes?' she asked. 'Oh, and . . . will they have included new employees, the casuals they take on for the summer?'

'I asked for the lot. And we'll talk to both sexes, but in the case of the women just show them all the victims' photos and ask if they've seen them. They might have, with chummy, or have noticed someone who makes a habit of picking up young female passengers, and be able to point the finger. You never know.'

The final list was a short one. Four men with addresses in the city itself: one cook, one purser, two stewards. It appeared the car-handlers and crewmen didn't choose to live this far inland. There was a first officer living in Herne Bay and a catering assistant in Sturry with 'bar staff' in brackets after his name. Three women's names turned up but they were all down as very recent employees – students, probably, taking on summer jobs stewardessing the minute their exams were over, to earn money to keep themselves during the long vacation. There was no one at all on the local list who would have been working on the Hovercraft on which Elise Ducherain had travelled.

'We'll talk to them all, anyway,' Dan Crowe decreed. 'When you can find them. Nobody thought to include a list of their working shifts. If any one of them was coming off duty at a time which fits with the Ducherain girl's arrival, I want him invited in for an interview to help with our enquiries. Oh, and if you get trailed by any reporters, dodge! I don't want anybody jumping any guns, it's bad enough having them on our necks with all that "Seaside Maniac", and "Police Baffled", garbage!'

'Who's got the barman?' Jane asked, and Steve put up a hand. 'I was just thinking . . . that matchbook? I suppose it isn't all that relevant, but—'

'I'll bear it in mind.'

'The headlines weren't as bad as I was expecting,' Kenny commented, when he and Jane started off. She had given him the nod to join her, since Steve was paired up with Gary. 'At least they haven't started weighing in with "Is no one safe?" or "Where were the police?"'

'Maybe they're saving that for the later editions. Anyway,

where would they expect us to be? This lot wasn't exactly predictable!'

'It's a pity they're right about us being baffled. We haven't had a sniff about our girl, have we?' Kenny gave a sigh. 'Looked a lot simpler when we just had to find her, didn't it? And when everything pointed at Michael MacArthy. I still think there was a lot there to finger him – like why he lied when we wanted to know where she was! We seem to have lost sight of that now it's all tied together.'

'Yes, the same thought's occurred to me once or twice.' She wondered if he, as well as she, had that undefined feeling that Deirdre's case was different, that if they didn't treat her as such they might miss something. 'I still wouldn't mind finding out the reason for that one . . . and the reason why Deirdre vanished between work and home! Off a public street with people around. She wouldn't have accepted a lift from just anyone, would she, when she was only going home and there was a perfectly good bus route? We know she left the office as usual at six. So, why—?'

'A stranger asking the way, and she said, OK, I'll show you?'

'She's never sounded as if she was that foolish. A bit naive, maybe, and not what you'd call street-wise – but not up to getting into a stranger's car! I can't see that. It would have to be someone she knew.' They were coming to the first of the addresses on their list, so had to concentrate on work in hand, not alternative theories.

Now wasn't the time for the owner of the first address either: he was out. A knowledgeable neighbour said if they wanted George he was due back around six this evening, but if they wanted his wife she'd be home at lunch-time after she'd picked up the kids from nursery school. Their second call netted a steward who was sleeping off his last shift, lived at home with his mum, and had been to-and-fro-ing on one of the large car ferries at the time Elise Ducherain arrived in England in fact it was clear that he would have been mid-channel at

190

the time she was seen getting into an anonymous dark-coloured car. There didn't seem to be any reason at all for him to have known Deirdre, either.

'At least if they're on the boats they can tell you exactly where they were,' Kenny commented.

'And we can check it and see whether it tallies, too. Though I rather think it will, with that one. OK, next?'

Two of the recently employed stewardesses shared the same address, and one of them was at home. As Jane had thought, they were students working for the summer. This one was a very pretty Finn who was doing an exchange degree at the university.

'No, I don't know any of these girls,' she said with apology in her only faintly accented English. 'Except I saw that one's picture in the paper? And that one – wasn't there a notice up about her in town, a few weeks ago?' She had pointed out Catherine Jones and Deirdre MacArthy. 'I'm sorry I can't help, but I've only worked for the company a week! My friend, too. When she comes off, shall I ask her if there's anything she remembers?'

'Thanks, that would be a help. But she needn't get in touch with us unless she remembers anything definite.' It would be highly unlikely, given the dates; Elise had died more than a week ago. 'Anything at all that could be helpful,' Jane added, giving a brief outline of what that might be. 'And while I'm here, can I advise you to take care about how you travel home, and who you're with—'

'Oh yes, I already know to be extremely cautious!' The girl spoke grimly, and with a firmness which showed she meant it. 'The one which was in the paper – that would make all of us be careful!'

'As long as they stick to it,' Kenny said glumly as they came away. He cheered up to add, 'I should think that one will, though, she looked like a bright girl!'

'Yes, but while I don't want to start a panic, it seems worth giving a warning . . .' Against a possible next time. Though, please God, they would solve it without there being a next time. 'Where next – the third stewardess, isn't it?'

It was, but she was away working a shift too, and according to her boyfriend who shared the same address, had also only worked on the ferries for ten days. That pinpointed her first day of employment as the day after Elise had been murdered. The boyfriend was on crutches with one leg in plaster, which ruled out any tenuous possibility that he might have been driving a car near Dover on the relevant day.

Jane and Kenny left him with the same message: to get in touch if anything at all occurred to the girl which might be helpful to the police. It had to be phrased carefully so as not to look as if they were starting a witch-hunt against ferry employees. The press would really love that.

Jane drew another line across their list. 'OK, that's all for now. We can't get hold of George the cook until this evening.' She turned to Kenny. 'How are the holiday plans? Did you manage to get hold of that extra tent you were trying to borrow?'

'Yes, I did, and that's going to give us a bit more space. And a few less fights, too, about who's got their feet on top of whose head!' Kenny said with paternal thankfulness. 'The boys can have one tent to themselves now and the girls another, and Val and I can have a bit of peace! Friday week – I can't wait!'

'Well, send us all a postcard of Durdle Dor or whatever the place is called!'

'Oh I'll do better than that, I'll bring you back a stick of rock, shall I, Sarge?' he said cheerfully.

If the murder investigations here produced as many blanks as they had so far, he certainly wouldn't be likely to get his leave cancelled. Jane hoped not, since Kenny deserved his break. Things would be focused much more on the Dover and Deal end. She let her mind drift back on to the total lack of progress they always seemed to meet over Deirdre, the absence of any connection . . . Unless one of the other CID teams had come up with something which would offer a link.

When the others came back, their results were much the same as hers and Kenny's: one or two of the local names uncontacted yet, the others found and crossed off the list. The barman in Sturry had, like Jane and Kenny's steward, been in mid-channel when Elise would have been arriving at Dover. The first officer who lived in Herne Bay had been on a shift-break today. Found pottering in his garden, he was in his fifties and coming up to retirement, was concerned to be helpful if he could, but could show that he had definitely been on a turn-around at Ostend at the relevant time. The second steward hadn't been tracked down yet but was likely to be at his home tomorrow. And the purser didn't live at the given city address any more; his house was being rented by an American architect who had just moved into it.

'Pleasant bloke called Waldstein, but he'd never met the owner so he referred us back to the agent he's renting from,' Steve explained. 'It appears our purser and his wife have moved to France. They couldn't sell the house on the present market so they decided to rent it out. They went two months ago.' He added, 'I rang the ferry company to query it.'

'And did they explain why they couldn't pull their fingers out to give us the right information in the first place?' Dan Crowe asked on a growl.

'Computer error – they claim. They've given me the man's French address now, if that's any use to us. Though if he's been living over there for the last couple of months . . .'

'Don't cross him off, give the French address to Jane and she can do one of her links with the other side to get him checked. All right?'

'Yes, Guv,' Jane agreed, as he glanced her way.

'Nobody's found anyone else so far who looks worth checking?' Heads were shaken all round. 'All right, fit in the return calls for the ones you've missed when you can – and remember what I said, two of you; no solo visits! Meantime, Kenny, I want you and Gary over at the Jet Service Station at Fordwich. Life goes on, murders or no murders, and they had an attempted hold-up last night with a sawn-off. The night attendant had the sense to stay behind his bullet-proof window and press the panic button, but they think they'll have got the guy on video. So go and see!'

There was a return call to be made on George the cook in the evening. Jane took Kenny with her again: it put them both over hours but this was their baby. They found a big, gentle-looking man with a jolly manner; another one who could be given a clean bill, too. Once again, he could prove he had been at sea, 'doing my fry-ups for the lorry drivers'.

'They're all going to be blanks, I guess,' Jane said dispiritedly, when they left awash with the cups of strong tea which had been pressed on them.

'Cheer up, Sarge, the ferry idea was a good one and worth trying, anyway. And it could still be someone off the boats who isn't on our patch!' Kenny seemed to feel she needed consoling. George's small children had been rapidly banished to play next door so that he and his wife could savour the full gravity of a visit from the police, and it was obvious that their enquiries would be thoroughly gossiped over by the entire street. Kenny added now, 'People don't half like to chat about the case now it's made all the papers, don't they? Still, once people start talking, you never know if we might get word that someone's spotted something, somewhere!'

'And at least we're being seen to be doing our job and leaving no stones unturned.' Jane smiled at him. 'Thanks for the optimistic pep-talk! Let's get off home, shall we, so your wife doesn't have to complain too much about how late you are for your tea! I think George would have offered us one of his fry-ups at the drop of a hat!'

As they paused to cross the flow of traffic and get back into the police station yard, Jane caught sight of a half-familiar face. Oh dear, *not* that German student again . . . What could he want now? More lost money to be handed in by Honest Johann? Thank goodness, it appeared he was only there by chance, since he suddenly began to move away.

Kenny went off home, but Jane decided to look in and file a rapid confirmation that one more ferry worker had been seen and could be crossed off. She had expected the Incident Room to be dark, since it officially closed for the night when the evening shift came on, so she was surprised to find everything still lit and Steve leaning over the collators' table talking to one of the WPCs who sometimes worked there. And WPC Laidlaw was thoroughly enjoying his proximity, Jane noted drily, seeing the way the girl was gazing up at him. When Jane spoke, she looked round guiltily, as if she had been far too absorbed to hear the door open.

'Something new and interesting to keep you late?'

'No, just the eliminations from today's interviews. Melanie was kind enough to offer to come through and log it all in,' Steve said, giving the WPC a smile. He glanced at his watch. 'Hm, I've got to be off. There's a friend I want to visit in hospital tonight. Thanks again for dealing with that for me, Melanie!'

'That's all right, Sergeant.' The WPC cast him another adoring look and gave a little wriggle of her shoulders. Steve gave her an amiable grin and went away. WPC Laidlaw's eye-fluttering might have prompted Jane to warn the WPC not to make an idiot of herself while on duty, but she resisted the temptation, particularly since the behaviour of uniformed constables wasn't part of her remit. She took a quick glance at the information which was being logged in instead, added her own to it, and decided to head for home.

Or would have done if an impulse hadn't changed her mind just as she was getting into her car. The local paper lying on the back seat reminded her there was a film she had vaguely thought she might like to see. Its late show would be starting shortly, so she left her car where it was and walked to the cinema. It was only two streets away. If she had to go on her own, so be it; a light comedy would at least offer relief from thinking about work all the time. Matty would probably be out again, so she might just as well go to a movie as a distraction.

The German student she had nicknamed Honest Johann had apparently fancied the same film, because she bumped into him in the foyer afterwards, and he offered her a grave smile and a shy, '*Guten Abend!*'

Goodness knows what he would have made of a comedy which was all quick-fire dialogue, and no subtitles. She didn't stop to ask him, but gave him a brief friendly smile in return and walked quickly away.

Chapter 14

'Another two days of blank nothing from our end,' Jane said, resting her chin on her hands at the kitchen table and answering Matty's tentative query as to what was getting her down. 'I had what seemed to be a good idea, but it obviously wasn't.'

Deal had come up with some hopeful clues about their murder, but Deirdre's still floated undefined. If there was nothing new by the end of the week, Jane decided suddenly, she would go to the guv and ask if they could back-track. She looked at Matty across a breakfast they were sharing, rare recently, and made herself smile. 'Take no notice of me. I'm just feeling frustrated by life, that's all! How about you? You're looking pensive. How's your druggie patient?'

'Steve hasn't told you?'

'I haven't had a chance to ask. I've been belting around on some mugging cases, and chasing identification of an attempted blagger who tried to hold up a filling station. Steve's made a breakthrough with your boy, then?'

'I expect he's being ultra discreet,' Matty said. 'Yes, he got the boy to talk. About all sorts of stuff in the end. He's very . . . patient, isn't he? And good at getting someone's confidence, too.'

'He seems to have managed it remarkably quickly, as well. But he's sorted it? I'm glad!'

'It isn't quite fixed yet. He's still got to do a deal, he said. But I expect he'll manage it.'

'So,' Jane gave Matty a look across the marmalade, 'what

did you think of him, then? Steve? You did say you were curious!'

'He seems like a very nice guy.' Matty got up as she spoke, apparently in search of the milk since she fetched it and put it down on the table.

'And did you see what I meant about him being fanciable? Not,' Jane added drily, 'that I've seen much of him for the last few days to find him anything!'

'As I said, I think your Steve seems like a very nice guy. So go for it, give him a bit more encouragement. Listen, do you want me to do a big shop at the supermarket?'

'You're actually off duty? Wonders will never cease!'

'I've got three whole days. Hard to believe, isn't it? And by the time I go back, my consultant will have discharged that boy as fit to go home, so all that will be over.' Matty moved absently round the kitchen and paused to stare out of the window. 'I was wondering actually whether to go away for a couple of days, make it a complete break. Go and sit beside the sea or something.'

'Not London and the bright lights?'

'I don't feel much like that. You sound as if you think the seaside's a bad idea? Oh – your murderer. Is that what you were thinking?'

'It hadn't entered my head, but now you say it, I suppose I'd advise you to be extra careful anywhere round here.' The newspapers were keeping the story whipped up by raising a flap about all seaside resorts, warning tourists about strangers.

'Your job can get even nastier than mine. At least I get to save a few.' Matty sounded unusually depressed for a moment, then made an obvious attempt to shake herself back into lightness. 'You know, I think you're right. I *will* go to London for a couple of days! There are various people I can look up, and it'll make a change, won't it?'

'Make sure you add Dennis to your list of people to look up. I'll give you his number.' It obviously would do Matty some good to get right away, from the way she was looking, let alone the hours she had worked lately. 'If you're not here when I get back tonight I'll know you've done a flit, then,' Jane said cheerfully, getting to her feet.

Taking herself off down to work after passing on Dennis's phone number, Jane wondered why Steve hadn't even tried to slip a word to her about his success with the boy in hospital. True, they hadn't seen each other for more than a few moments at a time in the last few days. Matty was probably right, and he was taking extra care that there shouldn't be any suspicion of a trail leading back to Jane. And in that he was probably wise, all things considered, with Morland endlessly in search of reasons to find fault with her. Any deal would be off if Morland thought she had anything to do with the case.

She went into the CID room to find Steve already closeted with Dan Crowe in the guv's small office, visible through the door's glass panel and talking earnestly. Mike was at his desk and she asked with deliberate casualness, and a flick of her head towards the inner office, 'Any idea what's going down?'

'Dunno, Sarge. By the way, someone's come forward to give us the name of that sawn-off perp. Uniform's out collecting him now. His brother-in-law fingered him.'

'Such family feeling!'

'Yeah, no love lost. Lucky we know the perp got rid of the gun. Could've been nasty if picking him up had turned into a siege situation!'

'Yes, that's all we need, with the press on our heels already!' Luckily the nationals had mainly moved off now from this less interesting case, and were keeping their stringers at Deal.

There were at least things to photograph there, such as a house with bloodstains in it. The rope Elise had been tied with turned out to have come from there; a piece of washing-line. They had even found the weapon, a kitchen knife with a tiny trace of blood still on it, obviously only cursorily washed before it was returned to the drawer in which it usually lived.

And there had been a partial fingerprint on the knife handle: that was the biggest breakthrough.

It seemed the murderer had taken what he could find, rather than carrying his deadly necessities with him. Or had been aware that he would find exactly what he needed in that house? Either that, or he had taken Elise there on some excuse and then improvised. He must have known the house was empty, so had been sure it would be a safe place to go after he had picked Elise up in the late afternoon. Why hadn't he simply left her there, as he had left the Dover girl? That was probably a clue someone was following up, too.

Dan Crowe's office door opened and he and Steve came out together. 'I'll have to see if we can go along with that,' Dan Crowe was saying, 'but it sounds like the kind of deal we might cut, if he gives us enough names! I'll go upstairs now and see if I can clear it. You're absolutely sure he isn't going to do a runner?'

'Too scared. He's convinced they're only waiting for him to come out. And I gave it him fairly, that I might not be able to swing it. Also that we'd still have the robbery to charge him with – even if he didn't give us the names.'

'But names are what we want off him, so let's hope everyone agrees. Well done. I won't ask you where you got your tip-off. Nothing like getting two things cleared up at once, though!'

Dan Crowe went off out of the room, looking pleased and giving Jane and Mike an acknowledging nod as he passed. Jane raised a querying eyebrow at Steve.

'Two things cleared up?'

'That Herne Bay smash-and-grab. The one which happened the day I arrived? Somehow I seem to have managed to run into our mysterious perp for that, who as far as we could see had never tried to get rid of the stuff but had just vanished into the ground . . .'

'Where did you find him?' Mike asked – with interest, since he had been one of the people trailing round possible fences n search of the stolen jewellery.

'In a hospital bed, would you believe? It was an amateur job
by a kid desperate for money. Well, not exactly kid, he's
twenty. I'd better not give you the rest until the guv's cleared
things. Let's just say it has connections with that rumour
about a drug scene at the university. The boy wants to make a
deal, so the guv's going higher up on it.'

'Sounds like a double success for you, then. Great!' That
Matty's patient might also have been involved in the Herne
Bay robbery hadn't occurred to Jane, even in her wildest
dreams. A student in despair for money to pay his drug debts,
and not even knowing how to get rid of the stuff – well, it
made sense. He must have landed in hospital before he could
do more than begin to try to sell what he'd taken. And no
doubt his supplier wouldn't touch hot goods offered instead of
cash.

'We'd better give you everything out of the dead-end file,
Sarge, at this rate,' Mike said cheerfully, grinning at Steve.
'Let's see, there's—'

'No thanks! I'm probably all out of lucky chances, anyway!'

He was summoned upstairs shortly afterwards, and when
he came down again, Jane heard that a deal was being
processed: the name of the main drug supplier and his heavies
in exchange for a recommendation for probation for the smash-
and-grab, and a place in a drug rehabilitation unit. Far from
picking on Steve's unconventional method of doing things, the
DCI was making a point of showing how pleased he was with
the result – as Jane could see for herself when he came down
later to visit the Incident Room.

'I'm glad to see we're getting results on something at last,'
he commented pointedly, 'instead of following up time-wasting
ideas!' It was more than clear that he was referring to the
check on the local ferry workers. He frowned pointedly in
Jane's direction, trying to look as if he had only just noticed
her. 'Sergeant Perry, there's been a complaint call which is an

201

obvious one for a woman officer to handle. The nurses' hostel? Shouldn't you be handling it?'

'I sent DC Lockley to look into it, sir. I thought they might feel more reassured by a male officer.'

'Oh dear, please *don't* try to think. Reassuring these nervous nurses is quite obviously something for a woman's touch! I suggest you go along there now, and take one of the WPCs with you.'

'If that's what you'd like me to do, sir,' Jane said with proper deference, and making sure it didn't come out between clenched teeth.

Jane left the room, seething gently. If Morland couldn't officially demote her, he was obviously going back to his technique of sidelining her into cases he classed as requiring a 'woman's touch' . . . and that didn't include murder, even the murder of young women.

She requested, without expression, a WPC to accompany her on the DCI's say-so, and was rather glad to find she'd got Rachel Welsh. The girl had been proving herself as highly intelligent when she worked in the Incident Room, showing a shy helpfulness as well as a capacity to think – and a capacity to ignore admiring glances in the direction of her bust from the males around the station, too.

'We're going to look into a report of a Peeping Tom,' she told Rachel as they set off. 'I suppose you could call it all part of a detective's day!'

Rachel Welsh grinned shyly at Jane's dry comment. 'I'd like to get into CID. I know it's too early, when I'm only just out of basic training, but it *is* what I'd like to do in the end!'

'Is it? I'll have to be honest with you, you can go further quicker in uniform!'

'As a woman. I know, that's what my Dad says, and he's in the force – at Rainham. But you chose CID just the same, didn't you, Sergeant?'

'Yes, I did. It was always what I wanted to do.' She cast the girl a sidelong smile. 'Though it's "for my sins", I sometimes think! No, it's still the most interesting part of police work – to me. Is your father in CID?'

'No, he's always preferred uniform.'

'Well, you stick with your ambitions, if you know that's what you want! Now, this Peeping Tom: let's hope it's just understandable nerves, but we obviously can't ignore it in case it leads on to something nastier. I sent DC Lockley up to give some male reassurance. Rachel, was that a snort I just heard?'

'Sorry, Sergeant.'

'Well, yes, but I suggest we don't go into DC Lockley's liking for the girls, because he is a good detective as well, you know!'

The nurses' hostel was at the far end of the same road as the hospital, and a moment later Jane was pulling up outside. It was a large and once-elegant Edwardian town house set behind a thick hedge of high laurel bushes. Mike Lockley's car was parked outside. And when Jane rang for admittance she found him talking to a slender, attractive girl in the hallway, with every evidence that he was enjoying the conversation.

'The complaint was from a new nurse who sleeps on the first floor, Sarge,' he told Jane. 'She thought she saw someone hiding in the bushes at the front just by the ground-floor windows. I've done a check for footprints or any other signs, but there aren't any. Oh, this is Jenny – Nurse Makepeace.'

'It was just Lydia panicking,' Nurse Jenny Makepeace said, giving Jane an apologetic smile. 'Anyway, if there had been anyone there, a whole group of us would have gone out and given the guy what for!'

'A bit rash,' Jane said reprovingly, but the girl shook her head with a grin.

'Not really. We've all got good muscles from lifting! By the time you've moved a few heavy orthopaedic patients around ... He'd have learned not to try and spy on nurses undressing, I can tell you!'

'Not very advisable. It's always better to call us than to try rough justice. Seriously.' Jane smiled at the girl but made her words forceful; then she turned back to Mike. 'DC Lockley, have you got all the details, and talked to the girl in question, and everything?' He nodded meekly, though Lydia, whoever she was, had apparently retreated back to her upstairs room. And he had been completing matters by chatting up the prettiest nurse he could find, Jane guessed.

'It's all right, I'm not checking up on you,' she told him when they were outside, 'it was just that the DCI wanted me to – put in an appearance for public relations. So Constable Welsh and I will just make a point of looking at the bushes, and the garden round the back as well, OK? I expect you did that?'

'Yes, Sarge, I did a good tour round. Oh, and I checked that they've got good locks on all those downstairs windows, too.'

'Good. OK, then, you can go and write up the complaint and what came of it while we finish up here.' And he'd have made a note of Jenny Makepeace's phone number if she knew Mike.

The hostel garden inspected again and a visible presence shown, Jane could return to the station. As she re-entered it with Rachel beside her, she felt something in the air again – that buzz, that sense that *something had happened*. Last time, it had been the discovery of another body . . . Please God, not that! Jane sped to the Incident Room without waiting for anyone to tell her. She flung open the door – and saw bright faces turning towards her, grins, the whole place on a high.

'They've got him, Sarge!' Kenny called to her across the room.

'Where? And who?' Jane asked urgently.

Steve was grinning broadly as he answered her. 'I've only just got in myself and heard. Deal – a local man – small builder and repairman. He was doing some work on the house the day before, that's how he knew it was empty! The guv's gone straight down there to sit in on the interrogation, but the man's fingerprint matches with the partial on the knife, so they've got him! That's *it*!'

Relief was sweeping round the whole room. Now to tie him in with the other killings . . . but it had to be so, didn't it? Deal had found the man they were all looking for, incontrovertibly. It was over.

Chapter 15

'Look, about the boy in hospital – I'm getting all the credit, which seems unfair. I'd share it with you, but—'

'No, for heaven's sake keep shtum or you'll wreck the whole thing! Humpty-Dumpty's up on his wall again and you'd be just asking him to find a snag!'

They were in one corner of the Incident Room, emptied now of everyone else. Jane looked at Steve and raised her eyebrows expressively; he gave her a half-hearted grin in return, but he had no need to feel guilty, she thought. He was the one who had got the student to talk, after all. 'Don't give it another thought!' she assured him.

'Well, OK, I won't, since the whole thing's going to take a while and we don't want anyone running interference. Oh – when I went back to see the boy at the hospital and give him the news, I was told Dr Ingle's away on leave . . .'

'Don't worry, I'll pass it on when she comes back. When I saw her this morning she'd decided to shoot off up to London for a couple of days, but she'll be back on Saturday. Steve, this Deal guy they've got for Elise's murder – will they be able to connect him with Deirdre? I still think—'

'Like you said, we'll see. Builders move around. We may find he's done repair jobs over this way – even on the Ribden Road estate, maybe! Or Crayshaws could have used him for a cheap repair on a house they were selling. Anyway, when the guv gets back, we'll hear a bit more about it!'

Steve got up and moved away. He didn't say – as Jane had thought he might – 'Let's go out for that dinner tonight and celebrate!' In fact he wandered off towards the door, looking back only to say, 'Don't hang around too long, it's going home time!' And gave her a brief, friendly, but abstracted smile before leaving the room.

It was a bit like seeing the same guy but with an inner light switched off. The identifiable light of sexual interest, Jane thought drily. And just when . . . No, she would refrain from thinking it was inconvenient of him not to be in the mood, just when Matty was away, the flat was empty, and there was a result on the murders to celebrate. Oh, damn, and just when she'd felt a strong inclination – rash as it was – to take a chance for once . . .

Anyway for all she knew he had probably given up on the difficult and opted for the easy instead – WPC Melanie Laidlaw, for instance. Well, if that was his taste . . . Jane flicked the carousel in front of her round with an irritable finger, forced herself into rueful humour, and thought firmly, *Just as well!* Stay switched off, Steve Ryan, and find your amusements elsewhere!

The murder cases were solved at last. That was a positive thought to take home with her, to the empty flat which showed by its untidiness that Matty had packed up and left in a hurry. It was the first time Matty had stirred from base since Jane had lived here, and it felt quite strange to have the flat entirely to herself with the knowledge that the door wouldn't open, and a bleeper wouldn't make its shrill presence felt in the middle of the night. It was even – ridiculously – slightly creepy. Reaction, Jane decided, deliberately resisting an urge to draw all the curtains. That was all it was, a too-abrupt descent from having the murders as a constant nag in the back of her mind, to the flat calm of knowing it was over. She stopped pottering restlessly and took herself off to have a long hot bath.

They probably *would* find the Deal builder had done some work on the Ribden Road estate or for Crayshaws – to make

Deirdre know him by sight and innocently accept a lift from him on her way home from work. The MO for the killing was only different because – oh, because of any number of reasons . . .

The next morning papers had 'DEMON SLASHER FOUND!' (the *Sun*) and a more cautious, 'Man Helping Police with Enquiries' (the *Independent*), both of them carrying the almost obligatory picture of someone with a blanket over his head being hustled into or out of a car by police. It wasn't until the afternoon that the satisfaction around the station started to be replaced by murmurs, raised eyebrows, looks of disbelief. By that time Dan Crowe was back, looking weary and grim-faced; he appeared in the CID room doorway half an hour later with a snapped instruction.

'Sergeant Perry, Sergeant Ryan, all DCs – where's DC Lockley?'

'Out, Guv. He's on a—'

'Never mind. He can hear it later. Incident Room, all of you!'

'Christ, don't say it's not a true bill after all?' Kenny muttered behind Jane as he followed her. 'It has to be, doesn't it? With that partial on the knife . . .?'

'It looks as if they've got the wrong man,' Dan Crowe said grimly to the assembled company. 'It seemed clear enough: well, it wasn't. They're letting him go.'

'What about the knife?'

'And the print? They said for definite it was his.'

'Shut up and listen!' Dan Crowe commanded above the immediate buzz. 'It'll sound like a farrago to you, it did to me when I first heard it, but this is how it goes. This Ron Taylor admits he was at the house the day before. Claims he used a knife out of the drawer to cut the crusts off his lunch-time sandwich because he had toothache – shut up, I said! – and nicked his finger while he was cutting. Rinsed the knife but maybe didn't do it very well. Packed up mid-afternoon and went home, didn't go near the place again because he'd finished the job. But he did leave a piece of blue plastic sheeting behind . . . He gave the key back to the agent – that's confirmed. Mind you, the front door lock's the sort anyone could open with a credit-card. The point is, the next afternoon he spent in a dentist's chair having an abscess drained, his eldest son took him there because he was in too much pain to drive, waited for him, took him home again, and he was *at home from then on,* with all his relatives to prove it!'

'But what about—?'

'I haven't finished! If we hadn't got all that, forensic says: first, that's not the knife which was used on the Ducherain girl. Doesn't match the wounds. Neither does any other knife found in the house. Second: the trace of blood on the knife at the house *is* Ron Taylor's, and isn't the same group as the Ducherain girl's. Oh, and Ron Taylor drives a white van, his wife's got a red Skoda, and nobody around him has a dark-coloured car to fit the description we've got. Any other questions about why they've let him go?'

'We're back to square one, then,' somebody said flatly.

'Right back.' Dan Crowe said it disgustedly.

'There isn't a hope that—?'

'No, there isn't. Not one bloody fucking hope! Just one frightened little man who cut his crusts off because he had the toothache, and was shitting bricks when he found out what he was being accused of! Oh, and another thing: he didn't come forward when he read about the bloodstained house in the paper because "he didn't want to be involved"! He won't ever make that mistake again with information the police might want,' Dan Crowe said grimly, and added, 'All right, you all know now: we're back where we were and starting again! Sergeant Perry?'

'Yes, Guv,' Jane said, coming to his side as he beckoned her over.

'Keep the department ticking over, I'm going home to bed! We were up all night grilling that—' He broke off without finding the word he was looking for, his weary and disgusted shrug saying it all.

'OK, Guv.'

'And just when we thought we'd got him . . .' He sighed, beetled his brows at her, and left, shouldering his way through the disappointed figures drifting out of the room.

'Back to square one,' Steve echoed quietly beside Jane. 'Shit!'

'Yeah.'

'So, what now? We've done everything we can from our end, haven't we?' Steve glanced round the Incident Room. 'Hope for the next break, I suppose . . . Oh, Kenny, did you and Gary manage to have a quiet word with the African student who bought a gold chain off my boy? And tell him there wouldn't be any charges but we wanted it back?'

He moved away. Other things to be done – there were always other things. And still no answers for the Deirdre case.

Dan Crowe was back on Friday morning, growly, but no more so than usual. Jane gauged his mood, then decided now was as good a time as any. She tapped on his open door.

'Could I have a word, Guv?'

'Feel free.' He watched her as she came in and shut the door. 'All right, what?'

'Deirdre MacArthy. I know we've been lining her up with the other victims, but I'm still not sure. Could we go back on it? Look at her case individually again?'

'What do you want to do that we haven't done?'

That wasn't a *no*, anyway. 'Target Michael MacArthy again,' Jane said. 'Go back to the fact that he lied in the beginning! We all felt he was hiding something. Maybe he's cleverer than we've all given him credit for? If he did have something to do with Deirdre's death,' she went on quickly, 'he'll be feeling safe right now – sure he's got away with it because all the papers are making the tie-up between all three murders – so now's

211

the time we might get something. He won't be looking over his shoulder.'

'How do you want to handle it?'

'Follow him around? See if there's anywhere at all he goes. A lock-up we don't know about? An empty house he's got the key to, a barn, anything? If he killed Deirdre, he has to have somewhere he could have left the body. Before the heat came on and made him go out and dump it. Kenny said something at the beginning: "Maybe he found out about the posh boyfriend and lost his temper and hit the girl too hard." And I thought then – we all did – that he might have been at the girl sexually. Maybe she found the courage to say she wouldn't play any more, threatened to tell, and he killed her for that? If he turned up to meet her after work in his car, that would explain why no one saw her after she left Crayshaw's.'

'All right, you've made your point. And it's worth trying. Who can we put on to follow him that he hasn't seen?'

'Gary? Or Mike, but Gary's less noticeable.'

'Gary it is. And Mike can spell him; let's do it properly! We'll give it a try and see if anything comes out of it. Is Gary out there now? Send him in, then, and we'll clear him from everything else, for the moment!'

Once he'd decided to go for it, he set it up quickly: Michael MacArthy to be shadowed unobtrusively until further notice. Jane knew they were unlikely to keep it up for long if nothing came of it . . . but it was a start! And at least the guv hadn't shrugged off her ideas. Time was passing, and if there was anything to find it had better be found soon. Before any further evidence might be disposed of.

Time was approaching too for Dennis's escort duty with his Spanish royal, she remembered absently – a week tomorrow. Well, she wasn't likely to be anywhere near his itinerary that day, though she had heard some chat amongst uniform about who was going to draw point duty at the university and who in the cathedral precincts. Some of the WPCs were hoping for the cathedral so that they could see the society bride in all her finery and watch the elegantly-clad guests going in.

Jane was on doubled-up duties so as to leave Gary and Mike with clear schedules; something she didn't mind at all if it meant Michael MacArthy was being tailed. She thought Steve might comment on her idea, but he was abstracted – he *had* found someone else to play with, she decided drily – though Kenny was approving. 'Good idea, Sarge,' he offered, 'better than sticking with everyone else's dead-ends, and we know for a fact he's a violent bastard, don't we? No, I don't mind going out to talk to that pub landlord instead of Mike. Give it here!'

Nothing new was coming in from Dover or Deal: after their frustrating near miss they were back on the ground too, plodding for more clues . . .

'Hi, friend!' Jane greeted Matty, knowing she'd been home since last night, because there'd been a bag and scarf flung down on the sofa, but it had been so late that Jane had crawled directly into bed. 'Can't stop to ask you properly how you enjoyed yourself. Hope you had a good time, though?'

'It was OK. I came back yesterday morning. You're looking bright.'

'Not really, I'm just suffering from natural optimism!'

Matty herself was looking less than bright, Jane thought: slightly less tired than she'd been before she went away, but unusually moody, for her. If she still had the blues for some reason it was a pity there wasn't time to stop and talk.

Jane braked sharply from her rather too rapid exit from the parking-space behind the flats to avoid a cyclist who had stopped to inspect his tyres. Somehow it just had to be Honest Johann again, her German student. He must have digs near here, since she had seen him several times when she was leaving in the mornings. She'd glimpsed him once or twice in the evenings, too. His repeated presence made it seem almost as if he was haunting her . . . She gave a shrug and forgot him.

213

Who was on today? Not Steve: it was his off-day – and he'd gone pretty smartish last night, too. Which indicated something or other. Like she'd missed her chance? Well, she was too occupied with other things to remember – much – that life was duller without his easy sparring. Just her and Kenny in CID today, then, ready to take on anything which might come up. And the guv, if he decided to come in.

Mid-morning, it happened. Jane had nipped down to the canteen for a cup of better coffee than the machine offered, and was only halfway back through the CID room door when Kenny was giving her a thumbs-up.

'The guv's looking for you. Bingo! Michael MacArthy took his wife and all the children down to Mass, but then he didn't stay. Gary picked up on him when he slipped out again, and he's just phoned through. There *is* a lock-up! Tucked away round the back of Wincheap, and our man let himself in with a key!'

'Jane! Come on!' The guv was there, and in a hurry. 'Kenny, you stay here and mind the store, we're taking a couple of uniforms with us. Let's go and nail that bastard at his secret address he didn't tell us about, and see how he explains that.'

They picked up Gary and approached quietly: two cars, though it only needed one to block the cul-de-sac. 'He's still in there,' the young DC said. 'It's quite a size, goes back a bit. No rear exit, though, I've checked. Looks as if it might have been one of those old chapels or something. Not much sign of use, but it had a stout padlock on those double-doors, and there's a second lock as well. He's parked his car well away round the corner.'

'Is he in there on his own?' Dan Crowe asked as he studied the shabby-looking building. Nobody actually lived down here: there was a small warehouse plainly used for storage, a padlocked metal gate leading nowhere with an old notice tacked on to it saying 'DC Automotive Parts', and a new-looking office block which took up most of the other side of the cul-de-sac.

'I didn't see anyone else, and the doors were padlocked from the outside when he let himself in,' Gary answered.

'Right, let's go in and get him, then.'

The padlock had been removed, but the second lock had plainly been clicked in again after entry. Dan Crowe pointed silently to where he wanted the uniforms to stand, then banged on the wood of the doors, sending a few flakes of old paint scattering.

Nothing, only stillness from within.

The DI banged again. 'Mr MacArthy? It's the police. We want a word!' His voice must have carried clearly, but there was still nothing. 'We know you're in there, Mr MacArthy,' Dan Crowe said patiently at the lack of response. 'Are you going to open this door?'

An innocent man would have, surely, with some of his ready Irish excuses tripping off his tongue. Jane could almost feel the man standing the other side of the door, with that wary, bull-necked stance. A pause, then Dan Crowe muttered, 'All right, we've got grounds!' and raised his voice again. 'If you won't open this door, Mr MacArthy, we will!' and he signed to the constable who was standing ready, equipped with a heavy sledgehammer.

The wood round the lock splintered on the second smash. As the other constable's shoulder pushed the doors rapidly inwards there was the harsh brilliance of strip lighting, the shape of a pale-coloured car up on blocks with its bonnet open, a surprising workshop tidiness. Then in an abrupt flurry of movement Michael MacArthy came charging out in a rush, a large spanner gripped and swinging in one hand.

His attempt to break through did him no good at all. He went down on the ground hard, tripped by a swung foot, and was rapidly disarmed.

'Doesn't look as if he wants to talk to us!' Dan Crowe was

saying within a few very short moments, breathlessly but with satisfaction. He regarded the figure which was being sat on heavily. 'Resisting with intent . . . Well, we can hold him on that for a start. And let's have a quick shufty at what we've got here, because it looks like a right interesting little set-up to me!'

'You can't have me for working on a car for a friend—' a muffled voice began from the ground, angry, but with a belated attempt at innocence. The protest ended in a grunt as someone sat on him harder, and Michael MacArthy let out a painful-sounding cough against the dusty tarmac under his face.

'Can't we, though? Gary, what does this look like to you?' The DI and Gary exchanged a very interested look as they both regarded what was clearly a working repair shop. And an extraordinarily secretive one. Dan Crowe obviously remembered Jane just then, because he turned to give her a look of approval. 'You were right. We'll shut this place up and get a proper SOCO team to go over it before we touch anything. Let's see what else they can find! All right, take him in, he's got a lot of questions to answer!'

Not least, about the body of a girl which might have been hidden here, in a place to which Michael MacArthy had very private access.

Chapter 16

After a total going-over by a SOCO team, there was frustratingly nothing to show that Deirdre's body had ever been in Michael MacArthy's secret workshop. No traces of her hair. No sacks which could be matched to the threads on her clothes. No corner with straw and grains of chemical fertiliser dust in it. In fact the place was clean altogether, well swept, the far end of it a remarkably tidy array of workbenches and tools. Machine-oil, and metal filings . . . if forensic had found those on Deirdre's body it would be an open-and-shut case. But they hadn't.

It didn't necessarily mean she hadn't been there. There had been time enough for all traces to have been removed. If Michael MacArthy had been clever enough. And he certainly wasn't as stupid as he had once seemed.

They had plenty of other reasons to hold him. The car he'd been working on was stolen; no question. He had been in the middle of filing off its engine and chassis numbers. Its original number plates were tucked away under a workbench, along with a variety of others. There was also equipment for respraying, a selection of wing-mirrors, various other items for giving a car a different trim. The question was answered now as to where he'd been getting his extra income – by altering stolen cars.

'And we'll hope to get some other names off him!' Dan Crowe said with satisfaction. 'He's not in this alone, that I *will* bet. Who stood him the equipment for that workshop, for a start? There were some good tools in there! Who brings the cars in, and who takes them off him again when he's done his bit? It all sounds very like that ring we had a sniff of before – the one Vern heard a whisper of from his snout! I've had Gary on the listen since, though we haven't had enough to go on to follow up until now . . .'

'How about Deirdre, Guv?'

'Yes, it's all right, I haven't forgotten that side of it. That comment of his, about her being "hot for it like all bitches"? He *had* been at her or after her, I reckon. And particularly with that rage he showed about what he called her "fancy boyfriend"!'

That part of the interview with Michael MacArthy could have been sick-making if it hadn't been part of Jane's professional job: the leering and plainly sexual fury he'd shown – with little attempt to put on his earlier pretence of grief – over his fourteen-year-old stepdaughter.

He had bitten down on his fit of anger sharply, though, with a sudden dip of his head, his eyes veiled, a whine coming into his voice as he claimed it was 'only that the girl had brought the polis's attention down on him, God rest her poor little soul', which was more sick-making than ever.

At least they could keep him banged up, and work on him – almost indefinitely, with the other things he had already been charged with. No duty solicitor had a hope of getting him bail.

Ruth MacArthy had to be approached again, to see if they could budge her on all those alibis as to where her husband had been, and when. And there was a distinct slide of her eyes – even with a sharp denial – at the open suggestion that Michael MacArthy might have been sexually interested in Deirdre. Known but unadmitted, maybe . . . The circumstantial evidence was mounting up against him.

'Line it up like this,' Jane tried out on Kenny, when she came back from another session with Michael MacArthy on Monday afternoon. 'He picks the girl up after work – never mind for the moment if Ruth MacArthy insists he was at home – and takes her to that lock-up. Maybe he has before . . . She resists him because she's in love with David. Maybe she even tells him so. Yes, why not, if he was on at her to say where she was when she came in late on Friday night? He'd already belted her for that, hadn't he? So this time he takes a spanner to her. That wound on her head, the one that killed her? They said it was probably caused by something metal. Or maybe he just goes for her with a fist and she falls . . . There's enough metal things in that workshop she could have fallen against!'

'And he cleans the place up after, which is why the SOCOs didn't find any traces.'

'The guv thinks he wasn't the only one using that workshop – though he hasn't got any names out of him yet – so where did he put her?'

'In the boot of one of the stolen cars?'

'No good, if someone else is working on them too. But at least we know he would have had the use of another car when it came to dumping the body!' Jane added. 'So it doesn't matter that we got a negative when we took his machine to pieces.'

'Alternative scenario for you, Sarge. Same as what you said at the beginning, he picks her up and takes her to the workshop. Tries it on, but this time she says no – and that if he doesn't leave her alone from now on she'll tell about the lock-up and what goes on there. Gives him an even better motive for doing her in, doesn't it?'

'Yes! He needn't have killed her by accident; it could have been by design. Good one! But *where did he put her afterwards?*'

'We'll get it sweated out of him,' Kenny said comfortingly. 'Or you and the guv will, between you! Good thing you stuck to your guns about him. Everyone round the station knows it was down to you!'

It seemed she had quite a faction of backers against the Morland technique. She should be careful of that, though, grateful as she was; a station taking overt sides wasn't the best way to keep things running smoothly. 'Thanks,' she said lightly, and added deliberately, 'I think the DCI's pleased with what we're doing, too. Oh, has there been anything more from Chief Inspector Rivers at Dover to say if they've got anything else on their two girls?'

There hadn't been any new leads. They were perhaps even beginning to despair of finding any, with time going by and no results to show.

No new revelations came from Michael MacArthy either, as the rest of Monday wound through to its close. Nothing on Tuesday either, though he made a brief appearance in court on the charge of handling stolen property (and attacking police in pursuit of their duty) to keep within the statutory thirty-six hours. He was duly remanded in custody.

'We'll get him!' Dan Crowe said grimly. 'And I'd have had him in court on the murder, too, if what we'd got wasn't all circumstantial! Go out and see that wife of his again. See if you can't shift her thinking! Tell her he'll be going inside anyway. Maybe that'll crack her, if she's just scared of what he might do to her!'

Coming back from that unproductive visit – Ruth MacArthy was obviously troubled, but wouldn't be budged – Jane drove into the station yard to find Steve had drawn in just ahead of her. He walked over as she got out of her car and gave her a brief smile. He leaned a hand on the roof of her Renault, apparently wanting to chat.

'Sounds as if you were right all along about Michael MacArthy. And this does seem to be a month for solving two things at once, doesn't it?'

'Not for sure, he's still wriggling on the murder. How's the one with the boy? All lined up and no snags?'

'Seems so. Rainham have got the big supplier, he came from their patch. Jane . . .'

'Yes?'

'I wouldn't normally ask.' He pulled a wry face. 'No way. But I've heard on the grapevine that I may be posted back to

London pretty soon. So . . . how many favours do you owe me?'

'Quite a few, I reckon. You want to call them in? OK, what can I do?'

'Yeah. Well.' He stopped, ran his hand across his hair, looked thoroughly confused. 'Christ, this is difficult! It's not the sort of thing I'd normally ask *anyone* . . .'

'So you said, so stop being mysterious and spit it out! After all, what are friends for?'

'Quite. Listen, it's Matty. Matty Ingle.' He said that as if Jane might not know who Matty was without the surname. 'I've – well, you're going to say, don't be stupid, you've only known her ten days . . . Light's dawning, eh? All right. I've fallen for her pretty hard. I wouldn't usually ask for help, and I'm feeling a right idiot as I speak, because—'

'Because you don't usually have any difficulty getting attention when you want it? Sorry. But I can't help you with Matty, I'm afraid,' Jane said, swallowing surprise. 'First, I'm not her keeper, and second, I hate to break it to you, but she's notoriously fireproof. I mean people keep falling for her all the time, they have ever since I've known her!'

'I can see why they would,' Steve said – and without any kind of gleam of humour in his face. Oh dear, oh dear. 'But this – Oh Christ, could you stop looking at me as if I was some kind of errant schoolboy? It's bad enough to feel like one, for the first time since I was about fourteen!'

'Sorry. I guess I'm just suffering from surprise. Maybe I would have said you were fireproof too,' Jane added lightly. She bit back other comments. 'I don't honestly see what I can do, and that's not to say I wouldn't if I could!'

'The thing is, I could have sworn . : . It's *not* conceit, but you know how you can *feel* if a spark goes both ways?' All at once he had the grace to give her a rueful grin. 'That was different, though, wasn't it? You gave me a pretty clear warning as to where I stood, and I just took up the challenge – for fun, both of us? This thing with Matty . . . She just knocked me out. And I'd have sworn there was something there for her too!'

'Then she'd have told you. She's a very direct person and she knows her own mind.' That was what had happened before, on the rare occasions when Matty had let someone sweep into her life . . . But would she have told him? This time?

Possibly not. Out of a misguided idea—

'I could have played it slowly if it wasn't for this business of getting posted back to London,' Steve was saying, explaining, putting himself on the line in a way Jane was sure was totally uncharacteristic of him. As too the look of bewilderment – and the appeal for help. 'But as things stand – she won't even see me any more, and God knows I've tried! It's like – oh, I don't know, as if there's something getting in the way!'

'Maybe her career,' Jane said drily. 'Had you thought of that?' And better he should think of that, rather than whatever else might be going on in Matty's head. 'She's pretty keen on it! A fact which, if you've noticed anything at all about her besides her face, you presumably know!'

'I do, and what did you think I was aiming to do? Try and chain her to a sink? I'm not that stupid, so don't you be!' He caught himself up on that, tried the wryest of grins. 'Sorry. You can sound pretty acid! Particularly when it comes to that bandwagon of yours . . . All right, don't tell me, it's Matty's too! She's just rather – gentler about it. We did talk a lot over coffee, each time after I'd seen her student . . . Anyway, you can't help, right? I suppose I just had this mad idea that you were close to her, so you could maybe find out . . .'

'As I said, I'm not her keeper. What's between you can only be between *you*. I can say, keep trying – but that's about it, I'm afraid! Um – sorry, but do you mind if I go in now? I've got some more Michael MacArthy stuff to process.'

'Sorry. I shouldn't have started this at all, should I? And, well, thanks for not raking me down further than I am already.'

Steve, consulting her as an Agony Auntie? Anthony Crayshaw and his Tracy had been bad enough! Jane took herself rapidly into the station before the sheer unlikeliness of life could seize her entirely. And tried not to think that she and Matty had never been in competition before. Well, they weren't now. Plainly, no contest. But it would also do Steve Ryan no harm at all to come up against one of life's real impossibilities – as Matty had always so gently and quietly been towards those she didn't want!

But what if she did want Steve, and was simply being unbearably scrupulous? Because of those conversations on the subject she and Jane had had. What if that was the reason for her moodiness over the last ten days?

There was absolutely no possibility that Jane could think about all that just now; she had far too much else to do. She'd have to think about it later . . .

She did, but only to conclude that she couldn't leave Matty a note saying, 'I don't want Steve, he's yours if *you* do!' as if he was some kind of trinket they'd been fighting over. Besides, she might have her facts all wrong. Maybe when she wasn't crawling in late after another session with Michael MacArthy . . . He was on the edge of cracking about the motor thefts, but he was still all whines, tears and angry protestations about Deirdre. False as hell, he had *definitely* had his eye – if not his hands – on the girl. And probably worse. The guv was certainly going for that. If they only had just one more thing to pin on him; one piece of concrete proof.

Wednesday. Thursday morning . . . They would let him stew today, Dan Crowe decreed; ignore him totally. He had broken at last about the car-theft ring and given them names: his associates were being picked up, when and where they could be found. There had been a London villain running the operation and word had been passed on. But about Deirdre, Michael MacArthy was still wriggling, twisting and turning like an eel. So let him have a day to himself to wonder what else the police might have found out.

Jane felt it was a bit like being able to draw a breath of clean air to be simply moving ordinarily between CID and the rest of the station again, even for one day. It actually felt no hardship to attend Morland's obligatory morning planning meeting, switched back again to Thursday this week. He was quite subdued, and didn't even try to send Jane off on any lowly chores. And she was around to be offered an amiable comment by Inspector Grainger that 'Major Dalkeith will be passing through this Saturday!' Dennis, goodness yes, that was this week too; in fact the day after tomorrow. With all this going on, Jane had forgotten about it completely.

Today she could occupy herself with ordinary CID calls. One came in during the late afternoon which took her out to Harbledown, a village so close to the edge of the city that it was almost part of it, but still retained its own small, decorative, village main street. The caller had asked for her particularly, and it turned out to be a nervous elderly lady who wanted advice on security. A uniformed sergeant could have done the job just as well, but the old lady obviously preferred to let another woman look round her home. Jane took her time over it, gave the standard advice on window-locks and door chains, and accepted a companionable cup of tea. It wasn't what could be called an urgent call, but it was pleasant to be out in the villagey atmosphere, and to be shown a small and pretty garden with flowers and runner-beans, in the summer afternoon.

As Jane drove away she felt a vague prickling along the back of her neck. An atavistic sensation of being watched . . . It was nothing; a glance round showed only parked cars along the village street and someone consulting a bus timetable pinned to a lamppost. She must be getting imaginative. All that intensive questioning of Michael MacArthy might well set anyone's nerves on edge.

If they could just find where he had kept Deirdre's body . . .

Jane was driving between the two roundabouts which carried the main road to the city proper when something caught the corner of her eye and made her slow and look again. She had passed this way many times without noticing, but now she found her attention caught by the rows of green plots, each with its little shed. Allotments for keen gardeners. People who wanted to grow their own runner-beans like the little lady she had just been to visit, but hadn't the space at home . . . Allotments? The gardens at the Ribden Road estate were meagre, and who would be more likely to want to grow vegetables than a man with a lot of mouths to feed? They hadn't – no, of course they hadn't; there were far too many of them! – looked at every allotment shed when they had been searching for somewhere which might have held Deirdre's body. Jane swung quickly to the side of the road to get out of the way of the traffic which had slowed behind her, then pulled out again and drove on to the next roundabout. She swung round it and turned back along the other side of the dual track. There must be a way in to those allotments along here, surely?

An opening wide enough for a car led down from the side of the road, and ended at a gate. The gate had a chain loosely bound it, but apparently only for show. Parking in the entry way, Jane pushed the gate open and walked down to the burgeoning field. Various people were scattered about, each to his or her own plot. And every shed which was near enough to see – of varying sizes and types, some stout, some tumbledown – had a padlock on it. Jane approached the man nearest to her, who was concentratedly stripping what looked like withered pea pods off a vine.

He was hardly the jolly gardener type, in fact he was thin and lugubrious-looking and viewed her arrival sidelong with a great deal of doubt.

'Evening!' she said pleasantly. 'I wonder if you'd mind telling me, do you each own your own allotment? I mean, do people buy them? I hadn't really noticed they were here before, but was wondering . . .'

'Council,' he said briefly, stripping another line of dea peas.

'Sorry?'

'Council owns them. We rent them. There's a waiting list though, if you want one.'

The look he gave her suggested he didn't think she wa the gardening type. Which was actually true. Jane tried t look crestfallen. 'Oh dear, is there? And are these the onl ones?'

'There's another lot behind Abernathy Road, between tha and the farm. You won't get one of those, either; take you good five years! Well, unless you know someone who's givin one up and they let you fiddle it. That's done! If you know th right people in the rents department to get yourself jumped u on the list,' he said, his expression showing a distinct lack faith in council honesty. Then he added sourly, 'There used t be more, but they've sold off the land for housing, haven they? Just the two left now, this one and Abernathy Roa Mind you, for all the care some people take with theirs . . . stil you won't get one!'

'Yes, I see. But the council has a list of tenants, you said And I could at least ask.'

'Ask all you want. Putting the rent up's all they're good for he told her with a sniff. 'That all? 'Cause I want to get on.'

'Sorry, don't let me stop you! It looks as if everyone work very hard,' Jane said pleasantly, letting her eyes drift roun the field. 'And most people have a shed, I see, and all we locked up!'

'Have to, don't you? Some people'll nick anything. Seed griddlers, anything they can get their hands on. And it's wh I said, some work hard, some don't! Like a few courgettes?' h asked unexpectedly, and with a glare which dared her refuse.

'Well – thank you. That's very nice of you. Are you sure?'

'I've got more than I need. They've grown well this year, spite of the dry. Not like this lot – blight, this is!' He left the plant which had been occupying him and moved crabwise to swoop down on some unidentifiable growth, coming up with a handful of plump, shiny courgettes which he held out to her. Here, then.'

'Can I buy them off you?'

'You'll have them as a gift or nothing!'

'All right, then, thank you very much indeed. And thanks for telling me that it's the council I should ask about an allotment – even if I won't get one!'

He made a noise which sounded very like 'humph!' as she walked away, possessed of her unexpected gift of vegetables. Cross-grained he might be, but he was also generous – and informative. Jane's mind was racing. If Michael MacArthy was on the council list as having an allotment . . . Damn, it was too late today to ask. The council offices would be shut by now. First thing tomorrow morning, though, she would make it a priority to find out.

There was that prickle, briefly, on the back of her neck again as she backed her car carefully out of the small turning, a car having stopped politely to make way for her. She waved her thanks at the shadowy outline of the driver within, and swung back on to the road, to head back the way she had come, then negotiate the first roundabout again to get herself into the right direction. The dark grey car which had stopped for her, and was now just behind her, luckily seemed to want to do the same manoeuvre.

Tomorrow morning she could find out if her sudden and illuminating idea was a good one. It was an outside chance – but why not? Michael MacArthy might be relying on its being such an ordinary thing that it would escape notice. Was he cunning enough for that? Yes. Yes, *maybe* . . . A pity she couldn't check it tonight. She could go and ask Ruth MacArthy, of course. But better not! Ruth MacArthy might be uncertain but she was also hostile.

If Jane couldn't get on to the council tonight, she might just as well go straight home: the guv had told her to do that after her call, anyway. Frustrating it might be not to be able to follow up her sudden idea at once, but there was nothing more she could do tonight.

She stowed her car in the parking area round the back and ran lightly up the two flights of stairs to the flat. Theirs was the only one on the top floor this side. She let herself in juggling courgettes and key. It was nice of the man, but how did you cook the things, anyway? She was hopeless in the kitchen . . . She probably ought to be more interested but for her food was simply *food*.

It was a pity he hadn't pressed a lettuce on her instead. She could have coped with that rather more easily. Imagining the reaction she'd have got if she'd asked for a swap made her chuckle. Oh dear, no way . . . but he had given her the information she wanted!

And she couldn't follow it up until morning. Stop thinking about it, then. Have a shower, change into jeans, do some ironing even, to stop the restless feeling that there was some thought nudging in the recesses of her memory . . .

It was beginning to get dark outside by the time Matt came in. She paused at the sight of Jane curled up on the sofa with a book on her knee, but then gave a smile and came forward to look down over her shoulder.

'That's one of mine, isn't it? I thought I recognised the cover. You, poring over a cookery book, and a vegetarian one at that. How the world changes!'

'It's the only one I can find with an entry for courgettes since I've got some and I haven't a clue what to do with them.'

'Slice them, dip them in seasoned flour, and fry them in butter. They're nicer if you leave them to marinade in lemon juice first.'

228

'Don't give me words like marinade, I'm lost! I'll just leave it
you, with your odd areas of expertise! And how you ever
ave the time, when half of these say "preparation time one
our, cooking time two hours"!' Jane snapped the book shut
d cast a grin upwards. The smile she got in return seemed
echanical, and Matty was turning away. 'Hey, Matty? Since
e're both here at the same time for once and not rushing in
fferent directions, are you going to tell me why you've had
e blues for the last ten days? I know I haven't been in much,
t I can still spot when you're trying to hide something!'

'Oh, it's nothing – only work stuff, you know.'

'Is it? Because,' Jane said lightly, 'I've had a lovelorn swain
yours drooping all over me. Nothing new in that, but – Yes,
at is it, isn't it? From that look on your face? Now tell me
raight, is he being a nuisance, or are you just being bloody
rupulous? And quite unnecessarily, too!'

'Jane . . .'

'You're an idiot!' Jane came to her feet, since somehow it
emed easier to press her point if she could move around.
anding there looking bloody guilty! Steve, right? Just because
said I fancied him? Well I did, momentarily. He's fun. Simple,
nserious fun!' Not entirely true; she might have fancied him
ther more seriously if other things had been equal. But she
ad to convince Matty otherwise. 'Maybe I even blew it up a
t because it was impossible!' she said cheerfully, pulling a
liberately wicked face. 'Oh, you know what I mean.
mething you don't really want, but because it's there in
ont of you and quite out of the question, it's amusing to
angle? But to think I might mind because he's gone and
ipped over his toes about *you*—'

'You don't? I thought—'

'No way. He and I were having a nice little flirtation, like
ips that pass in the night. I have to tell you he's gone down
ard over *you*. You've thrown him right off balance! And that's
ne – if you happen to want him. Even if you don't, and you're

229

just doing the guilty bit because he made a pass at you an you thought he was mine!'

'Yes, I did. I mean . . .'

'You want him, or you don't? Go on, put it in the clea Because if he's just being a pest, I might even give him talking-to!'

'No, don't do that! I do . . .' Matty gave a tremulous grin. 'It crazy, isn't it? I mean, he's not even someone I'd say was n type! The wrong colour, for a start! But somehow this time–

'You fell for what Dennis called "an East End copper with roving eye"?'

Matty gave a husky chuckle. Her face was so much bright than it had been a few moments ago that it was transformation. 'A roving eye? Well, that's no revelation. Ste said that himself. Anyway I've roved myself when I felt like and so have you! Do you realise – Jane, why are you lookir out of the window?'

'Sorry, I just keep getting bugged by a feeling down th back of my neck. Maybe there's a draught.' Jane reached up pull the top window shut against the darkness outside, an turned round to lean against the windowsill. No, she wou not move, and give way to the creepy feeling that there w. someone out there. 'You started to say, "Do you realise What? That Steve's a nice enough guy to send you into a tiz. for once? Yeah, he's OK – quite a good bloke, and I've lik working with him. He told me he may be going back to Lond soon, so—'

'Yes, I know. But London's not far!' Matty said with dancing grin. 'No, what I was going to say was: Do you realis I actually thought you were reading a recipe book because y were getting domestic ideas?'

'Good God. The incredible conclusions you can draw ju because I'm landed with some home-grown vegetables– Jane broke off abruptly, frozen into her position by the windo her face very still. Her thoughts were suddenly flying. 'Oh n